THE FURY UNLEASHED

The Belandria Tarot Book 5

By Alex McGilvery

The Fury Unleashed

978-1-989092-44-6
ISBN

Beta Reading

Emily Gilson

Sarah Hamill

Proofreading

Tammy Hadawa

CHAPTER 1

THE COLD ROAD

Prenny's leg hurt enough to distract her from the memory of the blade cutting Thom's throat. She hadn't even tried to rescue him.

"He was dead the instant he left the carriage, my lady." Yennet handed her a chunk of bread. "But it doesn't make surviving any easier. You must find your own way to give it meaning."

"Am I terrible for valuing my life over his?" Prenny stared at the bread. The thought of eating it made her queasy.

"He thought you worth dying for."

"Then I must make my life worth his sacrifice." Prenny tore a piece from the bread, chewing until she could swallow safely. She methodically ate the entire chunk, then washed it down with water. "I will rest. Yennet, make sure Garr'son gets a chance to warm up."

The howl of the wind woke her.

"Blizzard, my lady." Garr'son handed her a cup of tea. "We'll wait it out. Too easy to lose the road in this."

"Thanks." Prenny forced her hand away from the bandage on her leg. "While we are waiting, tell me everything you know about the Rau'ch."

"They are exiles from the northmen, descended from people who refused the rule of the thanes. Their only rule is strength. The old chieftain must have died for them to be attacking like this, but it doesn't help that the coast has been neglected for so long. We're isolated and weak."

"We have to hope the Rau'ch are content with sacking the villages and not going after our people."

"We can only hope, but the blizzard will hide any tracks. The hunting camp they will retreat to will be uncomfortable but keep them alive."

"My lady, what are your plans?" Yennet sat, feet curled under her on the seat across from Prenny.

"We need to check what is happening in Hildastown, then find the De'e'tcha. I have to give our messengers time to get to the king. It will be hard to bring an army up through the winter, and I'm guessing that sailing would be no easier."

"You are right about that." Garr'son poured a tea and wedged himself between the seats. "Even the northmen don't sail in winter. Something must have made the Rau'ch desperate enough to gamble on an attack from the sea."

"From the lessons at the palace, wars are started over resources. Land, food, wealth." Prenny tugged her cloak about her tighter. "They aren't going to get much wealth from the villages, so land or food. The invaders didn't look starved."

"You think they are expanding their territory?" Yennet tilted her head thoughtfully."

"They've been here for generations, long enough for there to be more people than they can easily support. That's bad news for us. There will be more of them to fight."

Garr'son clambered out of the carriage to check on the horses.

"They're in the lee of the carriage, and I've got heavy blankets on them. I'll take them more heated water later. As long as the storm doesn't last too long, they'll be all right."

The morning brought eerie calm. Prenny put her winter gear on and went out with Garr'son. The horses stood placidly between the carriage and a huge drift of snow.

"I don't think we'll get any further by carriage, even with the runners. Snow's too deep for the horses to break trail and pull."

"Can we load what we can on them and walk?" Prenny turned full circle. Only a few sparse trees broke the white of the landscape.

"Walking could get us into trouble."

"We're already in trouble, Garr'son."

"It will be worse trouble if they capture you."

"I understand that." Prenny shuddered. "But I don't think our people can survive the winter hiding out."

"I haven't done much winter training." Yennet sorted through the gear in the coach, frowning.

"We want to wear layers, the more the better. Nothing too heavy. Anything essential, we carry on our backs. The horses can take the rest." Garr'son packed a couple of pots. "We'll need fire, for warmth and to melt snow for water."

They strapped snowshoes to their feet and loaded the horses who weren't happy about pushing into the snow. After a hundred feet, fortunately, the drifts dropped to Prenny's knees and they made better time.

She could hardly see for exhaustion when Garr'son led them off the road. He dug into a drift making a cave large enough for the three of them to crawl in. A tiny fire heated snow for them and the horses.

The next day was worse, but Prenny refused to give up. Garr'son held her arm and muttered curses about headstrong girls. Yennet ranged ahead as if she'd been born on snowshoes, coming back periodically to report.

"The next hill gives a view of the village." Yennet drew in the snow. "If we crest the hill, we'll be spotted. There are at least six wolf boats in the harbour, but they look to be pulled up on shore. A handful of houses, but ten longhouses with smoke coming from all of them."

"That sounds like a settlement." Prenny rubbed her hands together under her cloak. "Did you see any women or children?"

"There wasn't much movement at all except for a few carrying wood and such."

"The slaves." Garr'son clenched his fist. "When I came through years ago, the place was deserted."

"When we didn't respond to their taking the village, it told them we were weak." Prenny closed her eyes in thought. "I don't need to see the village. Yennet's observations are enough. We'll head west to the forest now."

"Can't take the horses to the forest." Garr'son patted one of them.

"We set them loose, leave anything we can't carry on them. The Rau'ch may backtrack to the coach and assume we froze to death. Garr'son, can we hide our trail going west?"

"I can try, depends on how good trackers they are."

"Let's go." She put on her mitts and gave the horses a rub. "Goodbye, I hope they treat you nicely."

Yennet took the lead. Prenny worked to match her track exactly to hers, and Garr'son came behind dragging blankets to make their trail a little less obvious. Her heart sunk. No one would miss it.

They came to a ridge where the snow lay only a hand's breadth deep and they moved quickly. The blanket looked to make more of a difference. The ridge took them north and west. The smell of woodsmoke carried to them.

"Don't run," Garr'son said from behind her. "Save it for if we are spotted." Prenny's skin crawled, even more so when they could see rooftops less than a quarter mile away. A well-used track crossed in front of them heading into the forest.

"Do we follow it?" Prenny pointed along the trail.

"We meet someone, things will get messy." Garr'son shrugged, "But it will get us out of sight of the village more quickly."

"We will follow it. Yennet, be ready for trouble."

"I'm always ready." Yennet stepped onto the track and moved ahead. Prenny followed, the gloom of the forest making it hard to see.

Only a few minutes after entering the forest, Yennet whistled softly.

"That's a warning, not a stop or run," Prenny hissed to Garr'son. He nodded, and they moved ahead slowly.

In a small clearing, Yennet stood with her knives out facing two men who knelt, shaking, in the snow. Prenny couldn't understand how they hadn't frozen in their light clothes. Leather collars circled their necks.

"Garr'son, tell them they can join us or die." Yennet didn't turn away from the men.

He spoke in a harsh language. Prenny recognized the word for surrender. One of the men rushed at Yennet but died with a knife in the throat before he'd gone three steps. The other didn't move, his head down. He said something to Garr'son.

"He said he's a coward and doesn't deserve death."

"How long before they're missed?" Prenny's gut twisted. What kind of person saw death as a privilege?

"Not long. Their lord is cold."

"Let's move." Prenny waved them ahead. "Garr'son, take lead and watch him. Yennet will bring up the rear."

They followed another track to a second clearing. No other trail left this one.

Garr'son pushed the man under the trees, and they had to slog through deep snow.

The man said something and Garr'son called back to Prenny. "He said we've entered ghost country and none of us will leave the forest alive."

"Cheerful." Prenny forced away the jangle of nerves.

The dim forest grew darker until Garr'son called a halt.

"We will camp here." The snow was too soft to dig a snow cave, so they crawled beneath a tree with branches almost reaching the ground.

"Yennet will take first watch." Prenny flopped to the ground and huddled in her cloak. "Wake me for the second."

CHAPTER 2

THE HOT ROAD

Leandra wiped the sweat from her face.

"They're getting farther ahead of us."

"Looks to be a group of five or ten warriors." Hojiam fingered broken plants. "They either don't know we're here or they don't care."

"It doesn't matter." Leandra squeezed Raphael's hand. "The evil is with them. We follow the best we can."

"As you wish, Shi'iposu." Hojiam picked a fruit and tossed it to Raphael, then another to Leandra. "We'll eat on the trail."

Raphael followed the Nekkest, his face determined. He was the one who set their pace. Leandra refused to shame him by complaining or worrying. She followed her son.

Other than the jaguar eyes, Raphael hadn't changed. He never mentioned dying but talked about Nekhaise as if they were best friends.

"The big cat is sad about his people." Raphael dropped back and took Leandra's hand. "Will the bad thing hurt them more?"

"It is what bad things do." Leandra walked for a while in silence.

"Sometimes we do bad things because we're afraid. Sometimes because we don't understand. The bad thing will feed on our fear and ignorance."

"Norance?"

"It means not knowing or choosing not to know."

"Oh."

Hojiam waited for them by a tiny waterfall.

"The water is good here, so we'll stop. We won't catch them before they get to the Confederacy. I think we should visit the tribal land."

"I don't want to take longer than necessary."

"The Confederacy wants to start a war. The Nekkest are still recovering from the last one. It took the best and wisest from us. The elders may see fit to argue against the war."

"It's a long shot." Leandra frowned.

"K'nekket has the eyes of Nekhaize. They will listen."

"I see." Leandra looked down. The imp's existence weighed on her soul. She wanted to find it and destroy it. The feeling was so strong, she didn't trust it.

"Raphael, what do you want to do? Should we follow the bad thing or talk to Hojiam's people?"

Raphael sat on the ground, his head in his hands. Leandra left him to think, fighting tears as she pulled vegetation down to make beds on the jungle floor. *Why did I ask him? Am I that afraid?* She looked over at him and fell to her knees. *I was almost Lichou.*

"Visit Hojiam's people," Raphael announced, then crawled over to her. "You tell me not to pick at my scabs." He curled up and put his head on her lap.

Leandra played with his hair. It was long enough to tie back. She picked a thread from her clothes and used it to put his hair into a ponytail. It would be cooler on his neck.

"He is wise." Hojiam handed her a fruit. "I will gather more food for our meal." They vanished into the jungle.

Leandra practiced her meditation, looking within herself with the same ruthlessness she'd once practiced on Rodrigo. Fear hid in her heart; fear of failing, of making another bad decision, of losing Raphael to the strangeness of Nekhaize.

How did Rodrigo find his balance? The Champion of the Rehego, a position not known since the exile – how did he do it? As if he spoke beside her, she heard his question. *What happens after?* Wasn't that his guide? She'd thought him a wastrel, someone unwilling to carry the responsibility of rule.

She hadn't truly become the White Queen of the Rehego until he'd walked into her camp and upset everything she thought she knew.

I never thanked him.

A jaguar dropped out of a tree overhanging the waterfall. It bent to lap at the water, then turned to stare at her. Leandra froze, her pulse racing through her ears, but the huge cat jumped back into the tree and vanished.

Hojiam returned to make a fire and put bundles wrapped in large leaves into it. They filled a waterskin at the fall, pausing for a long moment where the jaguar had stood.

"Nekhaize is watching over us."

"It would be nice if his watching didn't almost make my heart stop."

Hojiam laughed. "What would he be if we didn't fear his power?"

"True, we Rehego aren't used to gods and such. The Balance is more a source of wisdom than of power."

"Strange."

Hojiam sat watching the fire until they dragged the leaf bundles out with a stick.

"Raphael, supper is ready."

The boy sat up and rubbed his eyes. "Are we eating bugs again?"

"When have we not eaten bugs?" Hojiam's eyes twinkled.

***

Leandra followed Hojiam up to a fence in the jungle. It had no vines on it, and the tops of the logs forming it were sharpened to wicked points.

"Who comes?" a voice called from above them in Nekkest,

though oddly accented.

"One seeking wisdom, one seeking peace," Hojiam replied.

"And the boy?"

"He has Nekhaize's eyes."

"I don't know you. Wait."

They waited, Hojiam like a tree, Leandra trying not to fidget. Raphael crouched down and poked at a large beetle on the ground. He stood up and took Leandra's hand. Then a section of the fence lifted, and two Nekkest stepped out holding spears with leaf-shaped blades. An old woman walked between them straight to Raphael.

"Has Nekhaize sent you here?" She lifted his chin with a finger and her eyes widened slightly.

"He didn't say not to." Raphael shrugged. "We aren't going to hurt you."

"Very well." The woman let go of him and returned through the gate. Raphael tugged Leandra after her, and Hojiam followed.

The village inside the wall could have been the Oasis built of wood. Brightly coloured birds flitted about, and monkeys chattered at them from above. People stopped to look at the three of them, then went back to whatever they'd been doing.

At a huge hall, more guards opened the doors for the woman, so she didn't have to change her pace the slightest amount. Unlike the hall in the Oasis, there was a raised dais at one end. Six of the seven chairs were filled. The woman sat in the last one.

"What does one of the lost ones want of us?" A man at the end, the youngest of the seven, spoke at Hojiam, making no effort to disguise his contempt.

"I know where I live." Hojiam met the man's gaze evenly. He flushed red and sat back in his chair.

"You come here seeking peace?" An old man near the other end of the line rubbed his chin.

"Is there no peace here?" Hojiam tilted their head. The old man nodded as if they'd said what he'd expected.

"Stranger, you stink of thakgoki." That was another old woman who leaned on a stick.

"I do." Leandra sighed. "I carry a burden given by Nekhaize. Perhaps you can teach me to live with it."

"It is easy to say the name of Nekhaize, harder to prove he has touched you."

Raphael dropped her hand and walked toward the old woman. A guard lowered his spear to block his way, and Raphael stared at him until he moved out of the way.

The old woman pushed back in her seat as Raphael stood in front of her.

"Nekhaize," she whispered, and Raphael returned to Leandra.

"Show them to rooms. They are guests." The woman who'd come to meet them waved at one of the guards. He saluted her and waved at them to follow him. Leandra and Raphael followed, Hojiam behind them. A flurry of conversation started up behind them.

The rooms were in a long wing running out the back of the hall. They walked nearly to the end of the hall.

"The baths are next door." The guard pointed at a door. "Someone will be by to see to your needs." He turned and left. Leandra shrugged as sudden exhaustion dragged at her. She opened the door and entered the room. Two beds occupied left and right walls, sheer fabric forming tents over them. A breeze blew in through the open window at the far end. Birds fluttered in the rafters over their heads. Raphael ran to the window and peered out it.

"Wow!"

Leandra joined him at the window. They looked out over a gorge. Far below, a river threaded through fields. In the distance, a waterfall thundered down the cliff.

"We are in the Gate," Hojiam leaned on the windowsill. "Down below is the true home of the Nekkest. The only path down starts not far from here. My ancestors tried to recreate home at the Oasis. They left but didn't leave their love of home behind."

"I understand that." Leandra sighed and went to drop into a chair. "I spent half my life trying to end our exile."

"Why did you stop?" Hojiam sat in another chair.

"I learned there are worse things than exile." She leaned back and stared at the birds in the rafters. "In the end, it wasn't my action, but watching an Empire consume itself taught me much."

"I see." Hojiam stood up. "I'm going to the baths. Everything looks easier after a good soak."

"Raphael, want to have a bath?"

"Do I have to?" He didn't turn away from the window.

"No."

"You might enjoy it," Hojiam went to whisper something in his ear.

"Really?" Raphael spun around and ran to Leandra. "Let's go."

***

After an hour of running naked between the different pools and under small waterfalls, Raphael was tired enough that Hojiam carried him back to the room wrapped in a soft towel. Leandra had one around her, feeling clean for the first time in weeks.

"The zuthi didn't come into being until after the split. At the Oasis we have our own bath." Hojiam dried her hair, the white shift they'd worn in the bath almost dry.

"You are who you say you are." Leandra sat, still in the towel.

"It is as you say."

Leandra started nodding off in her chair, so she crawled into bed beside Raphael and let herself drift into sleep.

***

The elders were split between those who wanted the Nekkest to earn honour in combat and those who remembered the losses of the last war with the north. They argued constantly on their dais while the population came and went, ignoring the dialogue. After the first morning when they'd grilled Leandra and Hojiam on the situation, the elders had refused to speak to them.

Leandra walked through the streets to the house of the man who was training her. Raphael spent his days with Hojiam in the bath or watching out the window. None of the children would talk to him.

"The first law of magic is to not begin what you can't control." Hanvo waved his pipe at her. "It matters not what your intent is if you lose control."

Leandra had to agree, but none of the rules told her how to rid the world of the imp she'd called.

"You are impatient with the laws." Hanvo glowered and leaned back.

"They seem wise enough to me." Leandra rubbed her temples. "But they are not helping me know what to do next."

"You began what you couldn't control." The pipe jabbed at her. "You broke the first law. All your trouble stems from that failure. Learn to obey the laws and you will know what to do."

"According to your law, if Lichou had finished his ritual and been able to control Nekhaize, he wouldn't have broken any law."

Hanvo huffed at her. "If you want morality, speak to the priests. Using magic is about control, not intent. Do not begin what you can't control. Do not falter in your purpose. Understand the consequences of failure. Need I recite them all again for you?"

"No." Leandra looked down. "I will meditate on this."

"Make the laws so much a part of you that breaking them is unthinkable. Then you can worry about intent." Hanvo shook his head and put his pipe on the table beside him. "Do not think I care nothing about good and evil, but that is a question which should not arise until you have mastery of your power."

"So how do I know if I can control something if I've never tried it before?"

"Ah, now you ask a good question." Hanvo picked up the pipe. "If you cannot imagine every stage of your magic down to the slightest detail, you can't control it. But once you start, you must continue. If you don't think about consequences until you start, it is too late."

Leandra thought of the runes. They forced her to think about the entirety of what she planned. Having the power of a thakgoki had made her lazy and she'd acted without thinking. She had to go back to the runes for her answers.

"I begin to understand." Leandra stood and bowed to Hanvo. He waved her away, and she walked back to the Hall.

The guard at the door let her in.

"The elders will see you."

Leandra wound her way through the tables to the elders.

"We have decided." The old woman with the stick rapped it on the floor. "We will not support the war, but we cannot forbid it. Only those who desire to fight will go."

"Thank you." Leandra bowed, her gut churning.

"You don't wish to argue?" The younger man sneered at her.

"It isn't my place to argue. These are your people, not mine." Leandra closed her eyes briefly and breathed in deeply. "You are wise not to give an order you can't enforce."

"Have you found wisdom then?" the old woman with the stick asked.

"I have learned it exists." Leandra's frustration leaked into her words, but the old woman laughed.

"You will leave tomorrow. Be ready."

Leandra bowed again, then walked away trying to decide if this side trip had accomplished anything useful at all.

At least Raphael had enjoyed the baths.

CHAPTER 3

THE PRISON

Even the bird's eggs tasted of fish. Lydia frowned but didn't stop eating the food on the wooden plank functioning as a plate.

"So you just let your cousin send you off without a fight?" Vakate pointed her carved spoon at Shu, the supposed King of the World. He scowled at her and kept eating.

"Quiet, woman." Wen lifted his hand.

"Strike her and I'll cut off your hand." Shu didn't look up, but Wen paled and sat back.

The other men ate methodically, none of them paying Lydia or Vakate any attention. The women might as well have been ghosts.

"Was I to split my people for my own pride?" Shu set his plank aside. "I have no desire to rule. Let Bhotta ride the king's horse."

"And will he be good for your people? Vundr wants to be chief of my tribe, and there couldn't be a worse man for the job."

"What does a woman from the forest tribes know of rule?"

"We didn't always live in the forest. My people rode the plains until your people came and drove my grandfather's father into the forest. Even then we traded with the plains people until they started taking us as slaves."

"My father was always greedy for more." Shu shrugged and stood to stretch. "It is a good thing for both our peoples that he is dead."

"Why did the spirits send me to talk to a man like you? Vakate yelled at him.

"Ask your spirits, not me." Shu walked away to where he'd sit on the edge of the cliff and stare at the river.

"Vakate, let's walk." Lydia clambered to her feet. Her balance was off these days, and she had to be careful. "The wind is too chill to sit on the rocks."

"He is the most frustrating man I've ever met, Hoárr."

"Does it matter what he did or didn't do as long as we are on this island?" Lydia sighed. This was an old path, but she had nothing else to do but walk it again. "You are demanding he act like he has power. Why do you think he sits on that rock all day? Not because the river is so interesting. He is regretting what brought him here."

"So why can't he say that?"

"Do you like talking about your mistakes?" Lydia stumbled and clutched Vakate's arm.

"He's frustrating."

"He stopped Wen from hurting you. By his word, we are as safe in this place as we can be."

"Shu is wasted here; he could be so much more." Vakate sat in the lee of a rock.

"I agree, but as long as we are here, it matters not." Lydia dropped to the ground, half falling on Vakate.

"You are so clumsy, if it was anyone else, I'd think you carrying a child." Vakate wrapped her cloak around them both, but Lydia didn't notice. Could it be? Would God allow it? She put her hand on her stomach and tried to count the days.

"Hoárr?" Vakate shook her. "You're scaring me."

"I will not bear a child in this place," Lydia vowed. *You hear that?*

"You *are* expecting?" Vakate didn't sound like she believed Lydia.

"It is possible." Lydia's face heated and she ducked down. "They took me a week past my wedding night. God said I wasn't completely bereft of my husband."

"We must tell Shu." Vakate started to get up, but Lydia pulled her down.

"We will not. It is possible, just that."

"But he needs to know. It is important."

"How will it change anything?" Lydia gripped Vakate's arm. "We will still be trapped by the raging current and the hunfish. Will a child create a bridge across the river?"

Vakate sighed. "Very well, since you command it."

The argument at supper changed from the past weeks of arguing about Shu's abdication of his position.

"Have you thought of how to escape this place?"

"We could fly, if only we had wings." Wen rolled his eyes. "It has been close to a year that we've been trapped on this bit of Hel. Do you think we'd be here if escape was possible?"

"Does Shu want to escape?" Vakate waved her spoon like a sword. "It would mean he had to do something about his cousin."

"Why?" Shu rumbled, more emotion in that single word than Lydia had heard from him since they were abandoned on the island.

"Wouldn't you want to check how your people are doing under your cousin's rule?"

"No." But Shu looked away. Vakate let a smile cross her face before she finished her meal.

***

Lydia woke and scrambled out of her cloak to be sick on the rocks. Vakate's eyes glinted in the morning light, but she didn't say anything.

"The other shore is so close you could throw a rope across."

"If we had a rope." Wen waved at the island. "You going to weave a rope from rock and feathers? Even the wood we burn comes from the river."

"Bhotta expected you to starve here."

"Likely," Shu grunted.

"Why stay alive if there is no hope?"

"Not all of us chose life." Shu stared into the tiny fire. "There were more of us in the beginning."

"They were cowards," Wen growled.

"Or perhaps we are." Shu walked away from the group. Lydia followed him. "Stay back from the edge." Shu didn't look at her. "I'll not have a woman with child fall to the hunfish."

"You know?"

"I have a dozen wives, more children than I can count."

"And Bhotta will keep them safe?"

"It is the law."

"Did he follow the law when he challenged you?" Lydia sat on a rock away from the drop-off.

"He didn't challenge. His men surrounded me. He'd have murdered me if it wouldn't have cursed him."

"That is a different story than what you've told before."

"I agreed to abdicate to save my family and my men. If I return, their lives are forfeit."

"I see." Lydia watched the river. The water endlessly changed and yet remained eternally the same.

"Why do you speak Imperial?" She asked finally.

"Our tribes have so many languages, choosing one for everyone to speak would have caused endless feuds, so we speak a tongue we all hate."

***

As Vakate pointed out, the far shore was a stone's throw away. Wen said the men had entertained themselves by throwing rocks across the river until they'd gotten bored.

The current would sweep a swimmer away in an instant. The men who'd rowed them to the island had to fight hard to make it to the shore. Wen pointed to the rock which sheltered the boat from the worst of the water's turbulence.

"If it was only the current, it would be possible," he'd said. "But the hunfish are our jailors."

The fish thronged in the river, eating anything which fell into the waters. A bird tossed into the river caused them to froth white and bloody until only bones sank to the bottom. To get off the island, they'd have to get past the voracious fish. It wasn't possible.

Her morning sickness continued, but at the same time, Lydia recovered her coordination. No longer afraid of falling, she stood on the edge of the cliff and stared at the far shore.

"What are you thinking?" Vakate asked her one night.

"I will not bring a child to this place." Lydia shivered as a cold finger ran down her back. Tears flooded her eyes and her heart raced. It was as if God was daring her. *Fine then. If you want me alive, you will preserve me.*

The morning had mist hanging over the rock.

"The winter is breaking. Soon the river will be halfway to the top of this rock. We will be hungry until it drops." Shu stirred the coals. "Even the hunfish fear the river's rage in the spring"

Lydia finished her sparse meal and took her place on the cliff. *I will not wait.* Her hands shook as she dropped her cloak, then peeled off layer after layer of clothing. She folded it carefully on a rock, then backed away from the edge. The wind cut through her thin shift as if it weren't there.

Shu shouted at her and ran from his perch, but he wouldn't get to her in time.

"All right, show me if you really want me." Lydia screamed the challenge into the wind, then sprinted toward the edge. Vakate screamed and the other men yelled, but Lydia's foot pushed off from the rock and the wind whistled in her ears as she dropped toward the water.

CHAPTER 4

A BARGAIN WITH DEATH

The knife cut a burning line on Rodrigo's chest and Amunia's grin widened. She lifted the knife to taste his blood.

They'd bound Rodrigo to the table so he couldn't move. Given time, perhaps he'd have been able to work his way free. There was no time. He couldn't even take a last look at his family.

"The plague is the despair of the Empire made real." Rodrigo spoke to Striphona, ignoring the pain of the cut. "Whatever you do to increase that despair will only make it worse. It isn't just Lusia. People across the land are dying."

"Only my enemies will die." Amunia cut another line. "I will rule."

"You want to be the Empress of Death?"

"It is my right. You stole it from me. I barely escaped with my

19

life." She made another cut, blood tickled as it dripped down his ribs.

"Get on with it." Striphona ground out the words, then coughed.

"You're already dying." Rodrigo closed his eyes. "You will all die. The Lusia will be a city of ghosts before the cure reaches you."

"Cure?" Striphona pushed Amunia aside and leaned over Rodrigo. "You know a cure?"

"What is the cure for despair?" Rodrigo met the emperor's eyes. "I have the cure."

"You won't rob me again!" Amunia stabbed Striphona in the back. He spun, his own blade in hand and ran it through her heart.

"Your Majesty." One of the guards ran over to him.

"Leave it. Like everything else she did, she did it poorly." Striphona shook Rodrigo, hands slipping on blood. "Cure me."

"Untie my daughter. Do what she says."

"The cure."

"Untie her and obey her orders," Rodrigo sighed. "Or ignore me and die; it is all the same to me."

As if in rebuke, something tugged at him. There was something he needed to do to the northeast. He'd deal with that if he survived.

"Let the girl loose!" Striphona shouted, then coughed hard enough to bring him to his knees. The guards cut her loose and removed her gag.

"Bring everyone in the house here." Aimee's voice shook. Guards ran out of the room. Striphona's cough grew worse, and he struggled to breathe. People poured into the room until it filled with fear. It made Rodrigo's skin crawl.

He felt more than saw the glow from his daughter. The people murmured as Aimee spoke to them of hope and love. People wept as she talked, then went silent. When no sound disturbed the silence of the room, Rodrigo started talking to Aimee.

"Remember the first time you went swimming? You saved my life. Then spent the voyage plotting to make me look like a pirate..." He told the stories of his family's love for each other until Aimee came to stand beside him. Tears ran down her cheeks. She pulled the small blade from his hook hand and cut the ropes holding him down. A guard handed her a cloak that she wrapped around him.

"I liked that outfit," Rodrigo muttered. The cuts didn't hurt anymore. "How about you let your mother go, and we'll talk about what to do next."

"You can't leave." Striphona stood and glowered at Rodrigo. The people in the room muttered, and the emperor glared at them.

"Do you think you can keep this secret?" Rodrigo walked to where his gear was scattered about the floor and dressed in his last set of clothes. He packed up the rest including the hand with the spring grip.

"I need to go to the cathedral." Aimee stood in front of Striphona. "If I don't, you will rule over corpses."

"Eat and rest." Striphona slumped his shoulders. "My people will take you there in the morning."

The meal was far from the lavish feast Rodrigo would have expected from an emperor's table.

"So how did you end up as emperor?" Rodrigo swirled his cup of wine. It was tolerable but not as good as Belandria's vintage.

"After that riot, the first legion tore itself apart. I kept my people out of it until the legionnaires who were left begged me to take the throne and restore order. I bargained with Amunia to bring her people to my side. Most of them had deserted her anyway. She only got worse over time, sure that she should have had the throne."

"With Veng, she might have sat on the throne, but she'd never have ruled."

"The story is that anyone who used the Imperial sword went mad." Striphona breathed deeply, as if still not sure of his cure.

"If anything, the stories understate the effect of the sword. It was corrupted beyond belief. It would have been worse than the plague."

"It is lost with Veng wherever he went."

"To hell." Rodrigo lifted his cup. "And the sword is not far from there."

"The plague is only the worst of the problems besetting the Empire." Striphona stared into his wine, then set the goblet aside. "The legions in the north are running wild, battling each other and trying to claim their own slice of the Empire. Trade has dropped to nothing. I've even heard rumours of raiding on our eastern borders."

"The Empire has fallen. All you can do is build on the ashes,"

Milene said from the other side of the table. "Draw a line around what you can hold and let the rest go."

Striphona puffed up but when he opened his mouth to argue, no words came out. Then his shoulders slumped. "I'm not even sure I can hold Lusia."

"Then begin here." Milene put her arm around Aimee's shoulders. "Hope can spread as fast as despair. It is all in what you choose."

***

The emperor and his guard walked with Rodrigo and his family through the city. When they reached the cathedral, he ordered the archbishop to ring the bells.

Inside the building, people sat listlessly. Even the priest celebrating the Eucharist at the altar sounded despondent. The bells brought more people until the crowd overflowed into the courtyard. The whisper that the emperor himself was present went through the people like lightning.

"What is this about, Your Majesty?" The archbishop frowned at Striphona. "We have things to be about without…"he flipped his hand at the crowd, "a mob of common people." He glared at Rodrigo. "Or waggoneer's."

"Common or not, they are my people." Striphona lifted a hand to silence the archbishop. "As you are, unless you have had word from the Holy City?"

"It remains sealed." The archbishop frowned. "But God's word is still our guide."

"And what has God been telling you?"

The man humphed and turned away.

At that moment, the bells stopped ringing.

In the space between the last ring and silence, Aimee started singing. The words were in a language ancient before the formation of the Empire, but it didn't matter. Her voice was as if gold and crystal had been given a voice, as if the light itself joined the song.

The priest at the front of the church carried on, oblivious to the song or perhaps he was deaf.

As Aimee's voice filled the huge sanctuary, her light grew. As the crowd knelt silently, a circle of stillness spread. Rodrigo's eyes watered as he watched his daughter. She more than glowed with golden light; she became light.

"God gives you hope and love. Live..." Her words echoed but cut off as radiance burst from her, spreading past the people and the walls and out into the city. The bell at the altar rang as the priest lifted the bread high.

Rodrigo jumped forward just in time to catch Aimee as she fell. He could see his arms through her body, and it weighed nothing.

"The Cup is broken. Love poured out." Aimee's whisper barely reached Rodrigo's ears as she vanished.

"But I need you, Aimee, not the Cup, not the magic, however wonderful, but you." His voice broke as Milene's arms wrapped around him and Aimee. He dropped to his knees from the pain in his heart.

Would you trade the Empire for your daughter? The question rang in his head.

"She isn't mine to trade." Rodrigo slumped to the floor. "Aimee was never mine, I just loved her with all my heart."

Love never fails. Something brushed his soul then left him alone.

Milene gasped and Rodrigo lifted his head to see. A bar of light stood in front of him. It took shape, feet, legs, his gaze travelled up until his eyes met Aimee's.

"Looks like you're stuck with me." She put her hand on his shoulder. He threw his arms around her, still not believing what he saw.

She hugged him and the warmth of her arms convinced him she was real.

"How?"

"I have no idea." Aimee looked down at the white shift she wore. "Oh great."

The emperor wrapped his cloak around her shoulders.

"Thank you." He knelt in front of her. "I will try to rule so as not to waste what you've given us."

"You'd better." Aimee grinned as the emperor face snapped up to stare at her.

"The Cup is gone." She pulled the cloak tighter. "It is like that part of me is out there." A wave of her hand took in the still silent people. "The rest is up to you."

"You heard her." Striphona spoke to the crowd. "The plague was our despair eating us. Do not allow yourself to fall back into it. We can't rebuild the Empire, so we'll build something new. Spread the word."

All the way back to the palace, it was as if they walked through a festival. Striphona took time to be seen by as many of the citizens as possible.

At his palace, he sent messengers out to invite in merchants and nobles.

"We have to get trade going. I'll send people out to the farms around Lusia as well, but the harvest wasn't good this year. There are reserves, but they won't last forever." Striphona strode about like a new man organizing the rejuvenation of the city.

Rodrigo left him to it, retreating to their rooms to spend time with his family.

"Do you think we can get some food?" Aimee held her stomach. "I'm starving."

CHAPTER 5

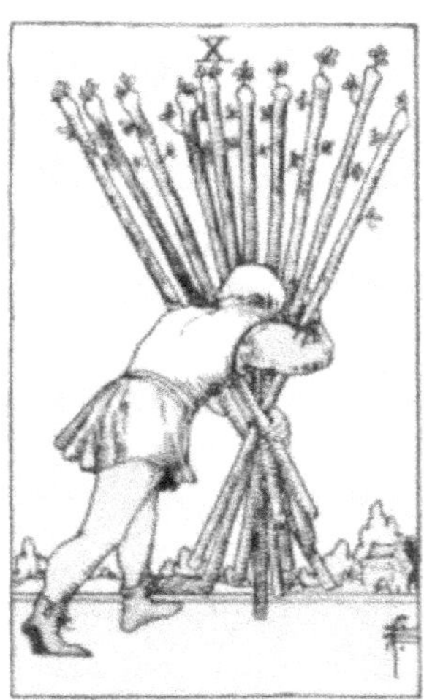

THE ENDLESS FOREST

Prenny slogged through the wet snow. The snowshoes were disintegrating from the damp, and finding wood to burn became all but impossible.

"Don't be thinking the winter is broken, my lady." Garr'son leaned against a tree to catch his breath. "We'll see more cold yet, and the storms will be worse."

"I'd rather not think about that right now." Prenny shivered. Her wool clothing kept her warm enough for survival but not for comfort. The slave they'd brought with them wore her cloak. "I'm freezing, and I'm dressed for the weather. How is he not dead from the cold?" She pointed at the slave.

"I don't remember feeling the cold until after I got rid of my collar. It must be some Rau'ch magic." Garr'son looked away from the man. "Sorry, my lady, I don't like reminders of my origin."

"How did you escape?" Prenny stretched as Yennet returned. "Sorry, Yennet, just taking a short break."

The maid nodded.

"No sign of any trails. My lady, the forest stretches the breadth of Belandria from the ocean to the western mountains. Expecting to happen across the De'e'tcha is unreasonable."

"We have no choice but to continue." Prenny stretched again. "I'll break trail for a while. I need to warm up."

"We've been wandering for a week. It isn't like we could find our way back." Garr'son passed his long staff to Prenny.

She prodded the ground ahead of her, then pushed through the thigh-deep snow. After she'd fallen into a deep hole, Garr'son had cut the staff. The experience of being buried in snow wasn't one she wanted to repeat.

Garr'son dug to the forest floor, finding nuts and roots for them to eat. Prenny had shot rabbits with her bow until the last of the arrows broke. Hunger cramped her stomach. Two days since she'd eaten enough to satisfy her body. Prod, step, prod, step. Prenny journeyed through the endless forest.

"Listen." Yennet held up her hand.

Off in the distance, a faint rumble tickled Prenny's ears.

"River, a big one." Garr'son pointed off to their right. "More likely to find people near water."

It didn't sound any closer by the end of the day. The light lasted longer, but night still ruled. Yennet found a cleft between two boulders with a dry floor. Wood stacked against one stone wall made lighting a fire easier.

Garr'son pulled out his find from the day. A pitifully small amount for the four of them.

"I'm going to find wood." Prenny picked up the staff. "I don't want to leave without replacing the supply. It doesn't feel right."

"I'll come with you." Yennet stood smoothly. The woman was tireless. They stepped out into the dusk.

"Light won't last long." Prenny headed for a tree with branches hanging under the weight of the snow. Its trunk had been picked clean.

The next one had a few dry branches low enough for her to climb up and break them off. When her arms were full, Yennet carried the staff, and they followed their trail back to the camp.

"Hold." Yennet froze in place. Prenny stood shivering, trying not to lose her grip on the wood. In one smooth movement, Yennet threw the staff like a spear.

"Blast, I missed." She fetched the stick, then one leg dropped down and Yennet winced. "Stupid." After standing back up the maid felt her way to the staff and returned to Prenny.

"You're hurt."

"Back to camp. Can't do anything here."

Yennet limped back to the boulders, leaning heavily on the staff.

"My apologies, my lady. My foolishness may cost us dearly."

"We need to live with what is." Prenny pushed away the panic gnawing at her gut. "Suze used to say that a lot."

Back at the camp, the fire welcomed them. Garr'son set the slave to breaking up the wood and stacking it neatly. Prenny looked at Yennet's leg. The ankle was already swelling and turning purple. A ragged scrape ran down her shin. A few prods produced grunts from Yennet, but the foot moved normally.

Prenny pulled a shirt off and wrapped it around the ankle. She fit two sticks on either side of Yennet's leg, then bound it with rope.

"You'll be slow, but I don't think anything is broken. We'll get another stick for you to lean on."

"I will slow you down."

Prenny laughed, then wiped her face. "It isn't like we're in a rush to get somewhere. We're lucky it isn't any worse."

The heat from the fire warmed the rocks and allowed them to peel off layers of damp wool to let it dry. Prenny slept without shivering for the first time since leaving the coach.

The wind came up in the night, and by morning they couldn't see anything but white outside of their camp. The storm lasted three days. All of them had growling stomachs by the end of the first day.

"At least we had enough wood." Prenny stepped outside and surveyed the snow-covered forest. The temperature dropped. She had on every layer she owned and wished for more.

We'll be able to use the snowshoes again." Garr'son held them up. "They don't look great but should help."

Prenny discovered she could walk on the thick crust of snow, so she made the slave wear them.

"Are you sure he doesn't have a name?" Prenny moved cautiously through the trees. The slightest slope held the risk of sliding out of control.

"Not that he can tell me." Garr'son walked with knees bent. Even with the snowshoes, he frequently fell through the crust.

"Maybe I should give him one."

"It is up to you."

"You don't sound like you approve."

"Names are personal things, my lady."

At one of their breaks, Prenny waved the man over along with Garr'son.

"Please tell him that I would like to call him Ash. It is a strong wood but often overlooked. When he finds a better name, he can tell me."

Garr'son translated, and Prenny was sure Ash's eyes held a new gleam.

That afternoon, Yennet struggled to walk, her face drawn and bleak. Ash stepped up beside her and put his arm around her waist and helped her. They struggled on like a three-legged creature.

The roar of the river was definitely closer that night. Prenny checked Yennet's leg. The bruising was worse, but there was nothing to be done about it.

Late in the afternoon the next day they arrived at the river. It roared and frothed past them. The spray from the river froze in icicles on the trees and rocks making footing even more treacherous. A small bay eddied at the end of a rope lying across the rocks.

"Probably a fishtrap." Garr'son rubbed his hands together. "We'll eat well tonight."

"I don't know." Prenny stared at the rope. "I don't think stealing from them is a good way to start a relationship."

"We won't last much longer in this cold without food." Garr'son frowned at her.

"Take just enough for one meal, no more." Prenny sighed and rubbed her stomach. "I'll find a way to make it up to them."

"Nobody is here. Who will know?"

"I will." Prenny crossed her arms. "I remember days in the forest with the bandits when we didn't have enough. One or two fish could make the difference between life and death. It is winter for the De'e'tcha too. I'll not harm their chances by being greedy."

Garr'son bowed, then crawled along the rope to the fishtrap. He picked out one large fish and dragged it back with him.

"The trap is full. Someone will be along soon to collect their catch."

Prenny laid a fire and prepared the tinder. She struck a spark, taking several tries before a tiny flame appeared to be stuffed under the stack of wood.

Yennet cut sticks to cook the fish. Ash wandered close by and collected more wood.

The smell of the cooking fish made her stomach hurt. When Garr'son declared it ready, he put equal portions on their plates, then put a pot on to melt snow for water.

As Prenny licked the last bit of fish from her fingers she saw the man standing in the shade of the forest watching them. His face gave her no clue to what he felt about the theft of his fish. Her face burned.

"Garr'son, please invite our watcher to join us." She pointed with her chin. "And apologize for our taking some of his catch."

Garr'son called out, and for a moment she thought the man would vanish into the trees, but he walked over to them and squatted by the fire. He pulled out a bag with leaves and, after a brief conversation with Garr'son, dropped some into the pot of water. He walked surefooted over to the trap and pulled out two more fish and carried them back to the fire. One he handed to Garr'son, the other he cleaned with a knife which was hardly a sliver of steel. When the task was completed, he carefully cleaned the blade and returned it to the bag on his back.

While they waited for the new fish to cook, the man spoke to Garr'son. Garr'son replied and pointed to Prenny. The man nodded and spoke more to Garr'son.

"He asked why we only took one fish." Garr'son translated after the visitor's face grew completely confused. "I explained you didn't want to steal his fish. He said that the fish were there to be eaten. I'm not sure he knows what I mean by steal. There isn't really a word for it. I said something like, taking without asking the clan."

"Try this." Prenny put her hand to her forehead to think. "I knew the fish were to feed his clan. I didn't want to make his clan hungry to fill my own belly."

Garr'son spoke again, and a long dialogue followed. Finally the man peered at Prenny, then nodded.

"Whew." Garr'son wiped his forehead. "Who knew talking was so much work?" He turned the fish over. "He understands your desire not to make his clan hungry but says they are good hunters and would have welcomed us and fed us. I said you were sure they were good hunters and would share but didn't want to take away their opportunity to invite us by assuming they'd share. He understands the need to preserve the honour of host and guest and thanks you for your care."

"Thank you." Prenny relaxed slightly and felt less guilty about looking forward to eating more of the delicious fish.

The visitor spoke again, pointing upriver.

"Their village is half a day to the west. If we have no other destination, we are welcome to visit them and see for ourselves their prowess."

"We would be delighted." She smiled in relief.

***

The village had no wall. They walked out of the forest into a clearing with long humps spreading out like spokes in a wheel. Their guide took the bag of fish to the centre of the village where people came out of the ground by the humps to claim fish until they were all gone. Some looked curiously at Prenny and her friends, but no one approached them.

They were led down into a long low hut. A fire burned at the far end, but no smoke clouded the air. It was stuffy but smelt more of earth than anything. Halfway down the room, an old person sat on a fur. Prenny couldn't tell if they were male or female. The person waved them over and pointed to the ground in front of them.

"Why do you break the treaty?" The old person's words were

formed strangely, but Prenny could follow the meaning.

"My apologies, I didn't know of a treaty."

"How not?" The person said. "We tell the story of the treaty from father to daughter, mother to son."

"It may be written of in the archives, but we don't have the same history."

"So it is as if we never shared the feast to make the treaty." The person's voice shook.

"I will find the treaty and tell the story. We will honour it."

"Yet you have broken it."

Prenny bowed low, her voice breaking. "Elder, will you tell me the story of the treaty? Let me reclaim the honour of my people."

"Many grandmothers before, we roamed this land between mountain and sea. We hunted what we needed, planted seeds in the ground, traded with the cat people far to the south. Then people came on ships. They landed and built towns. Our grandmothers and grandfathers went to these people and said they were welcome on the land. We lived in peace, but more ships came and more people. They built more towns, and the peace was disturbed.

"The elders gathered. We could not drive these people away since we'd welcomed them, yet they lived in the world differently than us. They sent three of our elders to speak to the elders of the ship people. They stood before the one who sat on a stone chair and explained these things.

"The one in the chair understood and asked the elders where the ship people would not be welcome. After much talk, the elders said the forest in the north joining mountain and sea. The one on the stone chair held a feast and swore to the elders that the ship people would never trespass in the forest. Each elder was given a token to show the stone chair's honour."

"I have trespassed, unknowingly, but nonetheless. Whatever punishment is due I will accept." Yennet and Garr'son both started to protest, then stopped at Prenny's raised hand."

"The elders must decide." The person tilted their head and peered at Prenny like a bird. "But for now, tell me your story."

"I am Prenny. I was set to watch over the people who live by the sea to fish. When they are troubled, I am to work to ease their trouble.

If they are hungry, I share their hunger." Tears ran down her cheeks. "Men came from the north to attack. They brought death and fire, and I could not stop them. Many of my people died. The others live in hunger and fear."

"We have heard of these people. They have no treaty. Some of our people were taken and made to serve in their villages." The elder pointed at Ash. "He is such a one. Others like him have been welcomed."

"I came to seek the De'e'tcha for their wisdom and help." Prenny bowed low again. "Please do not punish all my people for my trespass."

"You must speak to the elders." The elder put a hand on Prenny's shoulder. "You are young, and your elders didn't teach you the stories. Yet you desire to learn."

A man came into the longhut and sat in front of the elder. He looked familiar.

"Kel'aaka," Prenny asked, "How is your sister's son?"

The elder translated her question, then his response.

"He remembers your kindness. You welcomed them though they had the fever and honoured his sister's daughter and his mother. He would go to the elders and speak for you."

Kel'aaka spoke again, longer this time.

"Your people are sick and hungry on the edges of the forest. In memory of your kindness, Kel'aaka's family have hunted for your people and built longhuts for them to live inside away from the cold."

Prenny tried to thank him, but sobs shook her. At least some of her people were alive.

The elder waited until she regained control. "You are young, yet you carry a heavy burden for your people. Kel'aaka is right to aid them. It is not against the treaty to do so. I will ask other hunters to help."

"I have another favour to ask, elder one." Prenny sat up straight. "My king, the many grandsons of the man in the stone chair, needs to know of the treaty so he can tell the story to our people. I can write the story for him and send a token to show it is a true story."

The elder sat in silence while Prenny's heart raced painfully.

"Kel'aaka will carry your story." The elder patted his knee.

"Garr'son shares his language and can help the king hear your words."

Kel'aaka said something in his language, and the elder nodded.

"Garr'son is a man of honour and comes from the slave-keepers. He is not bound by the treaty. Prepare your message."

CHAPTER 6

A CHANGE OF JAILORS

Nikay rubbed at his wrist. The chain had scraped his skin raw, but the pain was the price for them sitting in the wagon instead of crammed into the narrow space below the floorboards. Fury sat beside him, also chained to the wagon.

The fields passed in monotonous emptiness. The snow had mostly melted here in the south, but it was too early for anyone to work the land. Their captors didn't speak to them other than to give them orders.

"We could escape," Fury whispered in his ear. "I can handle that pair."

"I believe you," Nikay murmured back. "Yet somehow we need to go where they are taking us."

"Mother and Father will be worried. They will send people looking for us."

"I hope so." Nikay dropped his head. "Have you thought about why they grabbed you?"

"I am the king's daughter."

"If someone goes to the king and says, 'We have your daughter.' What will happen?"

"Father would throw them in prison."

"Perhaps. He wouldn't want to do anything to hurt you."

"I am a princess. I would die for Belandria."

"I know that, even your father knows that. But remember the stories of your birth. He gave an estate to that woman who helped when you were born. I'm thinking that anyone who holds you, holds your father's heart."

"You're saying the person who wants me knows that story."

"It isn't a secret. All kinds of people know it. The question is who would think they could profit from it."

"They must be taking us to a ship." Fury breathed slowly. "There is no one in Belandria who would dare try to use me."

"Remember your favourite part of history?" Nikay raised an eyebrow.

"The war on the southern border." Fury shook her head. "We beat them and told them never to come back. They wouldn't dare."

"You see, until we know more about who is behind this, we have to play along. We'll try to get a message to your father to let him know we're all right."

"How will we do that? They are hardly going to allow us to write a letter."

"I dropped my ring on the road last time we crawled out of the hole. Someone will find it. If they try to sell it, word will get back to my father. He has estates in the south."

"I hope you're right."

The man driving pointed ahead at a column of smoke in the distance.

"Back in the hole. Any noise, you know what will happen."

The woman undid the chain and watched as they squirmed into the hiding space.

***

They hadn't seen a town for days, and the landscape had grown dry and dusty. Nikay had tied a cloth ripped from Fury's nightgown over each of their mouths and noses to keep the dust out of their lungs.

"We'll find the caravan track soon and wait for one to join." The man looked around with jerky movements.

"Are you sure?" The woman sounded more nervous than the man.

"We can't cross the desert alone. It will be all right."

They kept rolling south. The days were warm, and the nights cold enough for Nikay and Fury to huddle together in a corner of the wagon.

"Too late to make a break for it now," Fury said. "I hope you're right."

"Me too." Nikay leaned his head back to stare up into the blue sky. "I haven't had any of those dreams since I joined you."

"Maybe that's a good thing."

"I don't know."

Fury put her hand on his.

As night approached, the man's scanning of the area grew more frantic.

"If something happens, don't fight," Nikay whispered to Fury. "The other people won't know who we are. I know you're the best, but even you can die of an arrow."

"You're so comforting." Fury bared her teeth at him but squeezed his hand.

"Quiet back there." The woman turned around to glare at them, so she never saw the arrow that killed her. It poked out of her chest as she looked puzzled for a moment before falling over. Nikay almost felt sorry for her.

"It's scary when you're right." Fury leaned against him. "Get down."

They lay on the floor of the wagon as the man drove across the ground, Nikay could hear his panicked breathing. Then a wheel caught a stone and broke, tilting the wagon. Fury held Nikay with an iron grip as they tumbled across the dirt, coming to rest lying on the ground beside the broken wagon.

"Blast, I wanted that wagon." A rough voice approached out of the dark.

"We can fix it," another voice wheedled, immediately making Nikay dislike the speaker.

"Not likely. Should have shot the driver, but there's no market for women. He could have fetched a good price as a labourer."

The two walked around the wagon and stood, silhouetted against the night sky.

"What have we here?" One man crouched down and turned Fury's face one way, then another as if he could see plainly in the night. "Not the prettiest face, but young." He dropped Fury's chin and peered at Nikay. "You're the pretty one. There's a market for pretty boys." He stood up and looked around. "Get Thun over here to salvage what he can from the wreck. Search the bodies for the keys for those chains, then bring them over to the rest."

Nikay put his finger over Fury's lips, and she nodded slightly. It was too early to plan their escape.

Thun was a big man who muttered curses as he poked about what was left of the wagon. The wheedler searched the woman as if she were a sack, not once a human being. Once he found the keys, he unlocked the chains and had Thun lead Nikay and Fury to a camp around three wagons. One made Nikay think of the Rehego, only it wasn't painted. The other two were cages. Fury was shoved into the cage full of girls while Nikay joined the men.

One of them made jokes about Nikay keeping him warm until the man with the rough voice ordered him quiet.

"Play with my merchandise, and I will cut you here and now." A knife glinted in the night.

From the whispered conversations in the cage, the men were from Belandria. Some of them were peasants, others criminals. He kept his ears peeled for clues about who was selling slaves to the south. After the almost-rebellion against his mother when she was regent, several nobles were hung for slave trading. There were obviously more who need punishing.

The days were brutal. The sun beat down on them, drying their throats. The slavers gave them careful rations of water. At night they were let out of the cages, still chained together to move around and eat the gruel that was their only meal. The men and girls were fed separately so Nikay didn't get a chance to talk to Fury. He worried about her. Not that she wasn't tough enough to survive, but each day her eyes flashed darker. One of the men always stood aside with a crossbow, drawn with a bolt in place.

One day they met up with other wagons. The others were loaded with grain sacks, except one which looked absolutely utilitarian. The man who rode in it walked like Sam, the Marshall. He wore what might have been a uniform which showed off his dark skin. The man looked disgusted each time he laid eyes on the slavers.

None of the owners of the other wagons spoke to the slavers, and they kept their eyes away from the slaves. It didn't seem to bother Gamble, the head slaver. He ordered his men to keep to themselves. Thun was huge and thoughtful. Nikay listened to him argue philosophy with the wheedler, Asam. Apparently if someone was a slave, it was because they deserved it and they needed to work it out. Nikay desperately wanted to argue the point, but as the youngest in the man's cage, he had to be on his toes. The men would hit him with casual elbows and, if Thun or Asam wasn't watching, steal his food.

For all the problems Nikay had, Fury had it worse. Asam took to grabbing at her every time Gamble's back was turned. Fury clenched her jaw and tried to stay in the middle of the crowd, but the other girls pushed her out because if Asam was pawing at Fury, he was leaving them alone.

One evening before it grew dark, Fury stared at Nikay, moving her fingers in odd patterns. He furrowed his forehead trying to figure out what she was saying. Two days later, he remembered lessons with the Marshall teaching them the basics of a finger code. Nikay felt like smacking his head against the bars of the cage, only it would draw attention. The meaning of the signs came to him quickly once he figured out what they were. He flashed an acknowledgement to Fury.

She rolled her eyes.

Finally.

Sorry.

Escape.

How? Nikay shook his head. They were in the middle of a desert.

Must. Die or go free.

Will report. Nikay couldn't think of anything else to respond, but she relaxed.

Nikay couldn't sleep but watched Fury's shape through the night. He couldn't see how she'd escape, but as he'd feared, Fury had reached her limit. It would depend on how the other wagon owners responded. The knot in his belly told him it wouldn't be good.

CHAPTER 7

CHASING RUMOURS

"While I am focused on Lusia, I can't ignore the troubles in the rest of the Empire." Striphona played with the goblet of wine but didn't drink from it. "I've sent messengers west to Hime and recalled the garrisons guarding the southern borders. We need to strengthen the line between us and the warring legions in the north. I haven't the strength to stop them, so the next best thing is to keep them out of the south."

"All of this is fascinating." Rodrigo sipped at his wine. "But none of your plans require my services."

"True." Striphona stared into his cup until Rodrigo gave up hope of him saying what he'd called Rodrigo here to say.

"You were a spy before the riots, though you did say I was your choice for emperor. I take that more as a compliment these days."

Rodrigo lifted his hook. "My spying days are over."

"What I have in mind is more like leading a reconnaissance mission than spying."

"Leading?" Rodrigo laughed. "The legions have little reason to love me."

"The men I've chosen will obey my command. If it means taking orders from a Rehego spy, they will do that."

"Right." He took another sip, then gave the wine up. It wasn't getting any better.

"Some of the crew have run into you before. In the Holy City, I believe."

"Oh great, they were some of the most inept spies I've ever encountered."

"Good thing you aren't spying then."

"Where do you want me to go?" Arguing with an emperor would get him nowhere.

"There are constant rumours of raids from the eastern plain on the towns in the northeast. Past the eastern range, there is nothing but grass between us and whatever is out there on the steppes. I need to know if they are getting worse. There is no need to be covert. You'll ride in as a representative of the emperor."

"That sounds like a good way to get killed," Rodrigo sighed. "If I'm going, I do it my way, no argument. If I don't like the way the men act, I will lose them."

"I will keep your family safe here."

"They go with me." Rodrigo put his hand flat on the table. "I'm done leaving people I love behind for stupid reasons."

"But they're a woman and a girl."

"A woman who is a force of her own. You don't want her angry at you. And my daughter, she kept up with us through everything. She's a lot tougher than you give her credit for, even if she isn't 4000 years old anymore."

"What?"

"Family joke." Rodrigo met the emperor's gaze. "They come or I stay."

"They are your family." Striphona dropped his eyes. "I am emperor with everyone except you."

"Every leader needs someone who sees through the image."

Rodrigo stood and bowed. "When I leave, find someone else who isn't afraid of you and keep them close."

"I will keep that in mind." Striphona flipped his hand so Rodrigo left, going straight to the rooms he shared with Milene and Aimee.

"Pack up, we're off again."

"Great." Aimee jumped up and started rooting through piles of clothes. "I was getting so bored. No one would talk to me."

"You did save the city from the plague." Milene began a more organized packing job.

"That was the Cup, not me."

"You'll want some warm clothes. Spring is here in the south, but it will be later in the north. We're heading for the eastern steppes. So anything we might be able to use in trade will be useful."

Their work was interrupted by a knock on the door. Aimee ran to it and threw it open.

"Long time, no see." Rodrigo waved the man in. "You still drinking macshka?

The man shuddered. "I can't get the taste out of my mouth. I'm Jorges, I'm your team lead. We've told the younger fellows about you. They're terrified."

"Right, a great help." Rodrigo shook his head. "Milene, my wife, Aimee, my daughter. If you think I'm scary…"

Aimee threw her shoe at him, which he caught and tossed back.

"Pleased to meet you." Jorges bowed. "We plan to leave in two days. If you have any suggestions for gear."

"Bring coin but also things you can trade in a pinch. Not everyone is impressed by the emperor's face. We'll stay at inns where possible but have camping gear along. For the start at least, you'll be our escort. We dress the part, and folks will assume we're nobles."

"So I should bring along the dresses." Aimee created a new pile.

"You'll want a couple of pack horses as well as a horse for each of us. Make sure the tack is nice looking."

"Can I have a white horse?" Aimee put her hands together to plead.

"You heard the lady."

Jorges laughed and nodded at Aimee before leaving.

***

They gathered in a courtyard of the palace. A white mare for Aimee, Rodrigo had a black gelding, and a bay for Milene. They were polished up to look higher bred than the men's mounts, but all of them were sturdy animals, unlikely to cause problems.

"Stand ready for inspection," Jorges ordered the group. The seven other men paused in their preparations and looked curiously at Rodrigo, Milene and Aimee. "This is our commander. Make no mistake, he's the real thing. You've heard my tale about the one who stole the commander's boots."

"Thanks for that rousing introduction." Rodrigo stepped forward. "Given our cover, you will communicate with Jorges. He will be the one to talk to me and my family. We are looking for information, not trouble, but if we find trouble, you will obey me instantly and without question. It could save your life."

Travel through the south was uneventful. Everywhere they went, they heard stories of how the plague had suddenly vanished one day. People were rebuilding and glad of news from the capital.

Aimee decided she'd join the training the men did every morning.

"You won't likely fight in formation or with a sword," Jorges told her. "With your father's permission, I can show you how to defend yourself in close quarters with a knife."

"Papa taught me a few things, but I'd be glad to learn more."

Rodrigo laughed when Jorges asked. "Be careful."

"I won't hurt her." Jorges looked insulted.

"I'm not worried about her."

While Aimee didn't have the strength of the grown men, she had a complete dedication to winning which gave her an advantage against the men who didn't want to hurt her. By the time they reached the northern province, not one of them hadn't felt the point or edge of the wood blade Jorges carved for her.

It kept Aimee from getting bored on the trip.

"We're entering uncertain territory." Rodrigo stopped the group. "There is no telling how people will take legionnaires entering their towns. If there has been fighting, they won't welcome us. Don't underestimate a farmer with a pitchfork."

The first few places weren't any different than what they'd seen, but they soon arrived at a village marked by burned out houses.

"Look sharp," Jorges ordered. "Keep your hands off your swords."

The inn was built of new timber. The stable stank of fire from the burnt beams.

"We are looking for a room for the night." Rodrigo climbed off his horse to speak to the innkeeper.

"Haven't enough for all of you." The man glowered at Rodrigo.

"One room for me and my family. The men can stay in the courtyard."

"A gold for the room, a copper for each of the men and for each horse." Jorges opened his mouth to argue, but Rodrigo held up a hand.

"I pay you the gold now, the copper when we leave. Bring bread for the men."

"Yes, my lord." The innkeeper took the gold coin from Rodrigo and led them into the building.

The food was plain but filling, bread baked the day before.

"I'm sorry, we have no bath. The well is blocked with rubble."

Rodrigo strolled outside.

"The well is blocked up, and the ladies would like a bath. Could you do something about that?" He returned to the common room leaving Jorges and the other men talking and waving their hands.

The inn filled up with men, but they nursed one drink. The innkeeper wouldn't be making much from them.

"Are there any musicians?" Milene asked the innkeeper. "If we can't have a bath, then perhaps some entertainment."

"I'll ask if they feel like playing."

A few minutes later three men pulled out fiddles. They weren't bad, but their heart wasn't in it.

"Do you know 'The Eastern Rose'?" Aimee wandered over to them. "It goes like this." She sang a few bars.

"Happens we do," one of the men said, and they launched into the tune. Aimee left a few coppers on the table for them. After a while, Milene made a request and left a few more coppers.

"My lord." The innkeeper came to stand shaking in front of Rodrigo. "The well has been cleared. There will be baths for the ladies when the water is heated.”

“I’m glad to hear that.” Rodrigo smiled at the man who bowed and vanished into the back. After another seven or eight tunes, a young woman came to take Milene and Aimee to the bath.

Rodrigo ordered another glass of wine, a surprisingly good drink. The ravaging legion must have missed it. The young woman returned to tell Rodrigo the ladies had retired to their room.

Jorges came in and ordered beer for himself and his comrades, then insisted on paying when the innkeeper was going to give it away.

Rodrigo went to join Milene and Aimee.

“Good work.” He stretched out on the bed. “The rumours will talk about a wealthy and overly generous noble. It is possible the people who burned the village will follow us to relieve us of our wealth.”

“You want that to happen?” Milene raised an eyebrow.

“It will tell us how fractured the region is and whether anyone at all has control. The band who came through here burned a few places down and blocked the well but then extorted goods. They were smart enough not to kill anyone. Someone knows they won’t eat without farmers planting the fields in the spring.”

They left in the morning. When they were out of sight of the village, Rodrigo stopped them.

“There’s a good chance someone will try to rob us over the next couple of days. We need scouts out front and back. These guys won’t be much for subtlety, so you should spot them easily enough.”

“What do we do when we spot them?”

“As little as possible. Ideally, we disappear and go around them. I’m looking for information, not a fight.”

Mid-morning the next day, Milene flashed a sign. *Trouble.*

Where?

Around the next bend.

Rodrigo nodded.

“We’ll take a break now.”

The men shrugged, dismounted, and made a fire to boil water for tea. The scouts slipped in.

“Ambush up ahead, maybe five minutes ride. Sloppy, they have a lookout but no scouts.”

"Good, that tells me a lot. We're going to cut across country and pick up a small track half a day east of here. We'll be camping for a few days."

They packed up their gear.

"You think the lookout will have seen the smoke?"

"If he isn't blind." Jorges put out the fire.

"There is a cattle track a few minutes back. We ride to that and head east. As long as they think we're coming, they'll wait."

Rodrigo mounted his horse and led the way back down the road to the muddy path he'd spotted.

"Scouts out all four sides. Trouble comes in more than one shape."

They rode for the next week along back paths and tracks, not seeing anyone else.

"We should be close to Hirnberg. It's the last major town before the steppes. I want to stop and get a sense of what we are dealing with." Rodrigo drew a map in the dirt beside that evening's fire. "If whoever is running the area is smart, they'll have a garrison there. I don't want to tangle with them. Here's the city wall, gates to the west, the river passes under the wall from south to north. Last time I was here, I got in that way." He pointed to a bend in the river south of the town. "You will wait for me here. Milene and I will enter the town and find out what we can. Aimee, you need to be ready to report to the emperor if we don't get back out."

She looked rebellious but nodded.

They rode in through the morning to the river and the bend Rodrigo talked about. He could already smell the smoke.

"Jorges, you're with me. Milene, ward the camp. I want scouts out. We're likely in enemy territory; act like it."

Rodrigo wound through the trees beside the river to a hill where he could overlook the town.

The gates and the wall were blackened by fire. Smoke rose from within the wall. Men stood on the wall, armoured with bows and shields. The gate stood open, and wagon loads of goods were being led out of the town and handed over to a mob of horsemen. The last wagon exited, and the town gates were pulled closed. The horsemen rode east, surrounding the wagons.

A first glance suggested an undisciplined mob, but watching for a while convinced Rodrigo they were riding in deliberate order which allowed them to travel quickly but keep scouts moving on all sides.

"Jorges, this is where we part ways. Legionnaires will not be welcome. You need to take information back to the emperor. They aren't taking that food just for that number of men. There's more of them, and that means a risk of invasion if they find out how weak the Empire is on this border."

"I've scouted the steppes people before."

"I know, but you need to get your crew home. The others aren't suspicious enough. Don't stop at any towns until you get to the south."

"Yes, sir." Jorges followed Rodrigo back to the camp.

"We're done." He separated one of the pack horses and moved Rodrigo's camp gear to that animal. "Orders are to return to the emperor and report." They mounted up. Jorges leaned over to Aimee and handed her something.

"This one's real. Be careful." They rode away.

"Time to become Rehego again. The steppes people may not like us either, but we aren't as dangerous as the legions."

A vision of a man on horseback pulled at Rodrigo. After everything they'd been through, he was back to the original purpose of his trip. He jumped onto his horse.

"There's a ford here. The water isn't high enough to make it dangerous yet. Stay in line behind me. Aimee first, then Milene."

They crossed the river, and the horses scrambled up onto a plain stretching east to the horizon.

CHAPTER 8

BAD NEWS

Harald paced through the room. It had been weeks since Arthuria and Nikay vanished without a trace. Half of the castle staff and guards had been down with a gut-wrenching illness. They'd all recovered, but Sam thought someone had poisoned the food.

"Anything new?" Harald spun as Sam entered the parlour.

"This showed up in the south near Lord Torrance's estates." He handed Harald a small ring. "I've sent a message to Lord Torrance asking him to come to identify it."

"It has the family crest. You're thinking Nikay dropped it?"

"Too valuable for the abductors to discard it, in more than one way." Sam sighed. "I have messages to all the communities in the southeast to watch for them, but I fear they may have left the country by now."

"What do they want?" Harald clenched his fist around the ring. "No ransom demands, no communication at all. If they are on a ship, they could be anywhere by now."

A knock on the door interrupted them.

"Pardon, Your Majesty. Two people are here insisting to see you immediately. They look like those people the Rehego man brought in."

"Very well. I'll see them in the Hall. Try to round up Cameto and his guests and bring them as well."

"Sam, if Lord Torrance arrives before I'm done, he may join me in the Hall or wait here."

"Yes, Your Majesty."

"Oh, send word to the queen. Any news at all may be welcome."

Harald strode through the halls making the guard beside him trot to keep up. The palace had changed since the children were taken. Guards stood at every corner staring suspiciously at the staff. The council hadn't met in the time since Fury's maid had come breathless and panicked to their door.

He tried to keep the business of the country going, but Sarandia had retreated to her chambers where she spent her time trying to read a clue from the tarot cards. The other children were never out of her sight.

Harald couldn't blame her and tried to spend as much time as he could with them.

The guard opened the door to his small chamber behind the throne. Harald walked without pausing to enter the Hall and sit on the throne.

A woman in white and a man in black and white stood surrounded by guards. The man's face was divided into halves to match his clothes. The Nekkest Cameto brought said it was something to do with choosing.

"Welcome to Belandria." Harald leaned forward. "We are told you wished to speak to us at once."

"You are gracious, Your Majesty." The woman bowed fluidly. "I am Xiuefa, and my companion is Mahaloun. I regret we do not bring good news. To be blunt, the White Queen of the Rehego has charged us to warn you that the Confederacy may be planning an attack on your borders. The Nekkest of the Oasis will do our best to stop such an attack through the desert, but we are only a few warriors. We can do nothing about the southern route."

Harald sat back trying to make sense of what she was saying.

"You mean the Confederacy wants to go to war with us?" Harald stood and paced in front of the throne. "We beat them back in my grandfather's time."

"My apologies, Your Majesty, but I have little direct information. A troop of warriors met one of our council to try to call a great power into the world. They failed, but the White Queen feared it meant a build-up of the Confederacy's forces. Belandria is the only reasonable target."

"Page," Harald looked at the young man kneeling off to the side, "we need a map of the south of the continent." The page's eyes widened, and his mouth opened and closed before he jumped up to bow and dash away.

"I fear it may take some time for him to return."

"Xiuefa," a voice called across the throne room. "What are you doing here?"

Lupji, the red-haired Nekkest, ran over to the woman, ignoring all protocol as he usually did. Harald had finally ordered his guards to ignore the man unless they saw a real threat. Cameto and the other two Nekkest entered more slowly and bowed toward the throne.

"Lupji, it is good to see you." The woman, Xiuefa, frowned slightly and Lupji blushed and turned to bow to the throne.

"Is there any word of my wife and son?" Cameto stood, his hands clenched together.

"They are healthy and pursue their course to the south." Xiuefa's hands stilled for a moment.

"Xiuefa has brought a warning from the White Queen about a possible new conflict with the Confederacy." Harald watched Cameto carefully, but the shock on his face looked genuine. Some of his advisors blamed the Rehego for the young people's abduction. Harald's instincts said otherwise.

"Your Majesty," Cameto hesitated and wet his lips. "If the Confederacy is planning an attack, they may be behind the kidnapping of your children. If I can meet up with Leandra in the capital, we may be able to learn more and rescue them."

Harald's heart leaped, and he bit down on his immediate response. Instead, he sat back on the throne and thought carefully about the proposal. There were political implications to sending such an expedition. The abduction was an inside job, so the likelihood of other agents close to him was high. If the enemy heard of a rescue attempt, it would endanger the children.

"We will do nothing in a rush." Harald forced the words out, making them sound cold and stilted to his own ears. Cameto frowned but bowed.

The page returned with a roll of paper.

"We will retire to my chamber to examine the possibilities." Harald turned and walked into the room. A month ago, he'd have been making tea. Today he stood at the end of the table, foot tapping in impatience.

The Nekkest were escorted into the room, and Sam took his spot in the corner. Cameto pushed his way, in followed by Lord Torrance.

"Everyone else out." Harald waved his hand. "I can hardly breathe for the crowd."

The guards left, closing the door behind them. One would be stationed at each door. The room was built to be private. They'd have to put an ear to the door to hear anything at all.

"Keep your voices soft." Harald looked at each person in the room. "We don't know most of you but have reason to trust you at this time. Do not betray that."

The people in the room bowed.

"Very well." Harald slumped his shoulders, all the worry and weight of the past weeks hitting him at once. "We are certain there are foreign agents in the palace and that they were responsible for the abduction of the Princess Arthuria. As such, we can't send a public rescue mission."

Cameto nodded reluctantly.

"However, certain of my advisors have been pushing us to shorten my welcome to the leader of the Rehego. Any time there is trouble, old prejudices appear. So, Cameto, you will be ordered to return to the lands granted the Rehego by the crown. Whatever you do from there is your own business. Do we have an understanding?"

"Perhaps His Majesty has grown weary of a certain Nekkest's disregard for protocol and will send the Nekkest away as well." Lupji raised his eyebrow, then flushed red.

"Excellent notion." Harald nodded. "We would like Xiuefa and Mahaloun to remain to give advice."

"If there is a party going to search for Nikay and Fury, I'd like to accompany them." Lord Torrance's face had new lines on it.

"We don't think that would be wise." Harald's gut clenched. He needed Lord Torrance and Marriette. "We have a different request of you."

Torrance stood stiffly, then nodded. "I am my king's to command, as always."

"Very well." Harald sighed. "We can't send troops to the border lest we start the conflict we seek to stop, but as you showed many years ago, our citizens are a force to be reckoned with. You have estates by the southern border of the kingdom. We'd like you and Marriette to travel to your estates and quietly ready the populace to defend themselves and their land. We will leave it to you how you accomplish that."

"You have my word." Lord Torrance bowed.

"Sam." Harald put out his hand, and his marshall put the ring in it. "Lord Torrance, this came to us this morning." He held it out to Lord Torrance. "You recognize it?"

"I do. I gave it to Nikay this year." Torrance bowed his head.

"I keep forgetting they are growing up." Harald hung his head and imagined Fury as he'd last seen her, dressed in training clothes and holding her staff triumphantly after defeating three of Sam's men. "I swear upon my crown, I will do everything in my power to get our loved ones back."

"Your Majesty." Torrance pushed tears off his face, then took Harald's hand. "Marriette believes Nikay left on his own. He wore his clothes, and we found his horse running free through the city."

"We know all this." Harald flipped his hand impatiently.

"If Nikay had one of his dreams, it would explain why he acted as he did. He'd give his life for Fury. It isn't a stretch to think he'd give his freedom."

"That still leaves them in enemy hands." Harald pulled his hand back.

"It does, but it would mean there is a purpose beyond what our enemies have for them."

The words struck like an arrow in Harald's heart. A mix of hope and fear.

"If anyone is prepared to accomplish that purpose, it is our children." Torrance sounded like he was begging. "Maybe is it time to trust them to God and their own devices."

"We have no choice, do we?" Harald put his hand on Torrance's shoulder.

Sam cleared his throat and nodded to the people at the other end of the table.

Harald had forgotten they were there. He closed his eyes. This situation was making him sloppy. The country couldn't afford half a king.

"Your Majesty," Cameto put his hand on his chest. "You have welcomed our people and made us friends. We will work on behalf of your kingdom down to our last breath. The Rehego trade all through Belandria. We can carry your messages to your people."

"Thank you." Harald nodded at the man. "Sam will show you out. Do not look like a man on a mission for the king." Cameto bowed and left through the Hall, the three Nekkest trailing after him. Lord Torrance bowed and left as well.

"Let's look at this map, and you will tell us what you can about the land."

Harald motioned Xiuefa and Mahaloun forward.

***

"Do you think Marriette is right?" Sarandia looked up at Harald hopefully.

"Haven't we been training them to take their place in the world?" Harald lowered himself into his chair. The other children were asleep, the queen's women watching over them.

"All I get is a muddle." Sarandia leaned back. "I'm sorry, I've left all the work to you."

"It is what you needed, but I need you back." Harald closed his eyes. "I feel like half a king. Our people deserve better."

"I had to learn to trust Fury once; I can do it again." Sarandia sat on Harald's knees and wrapped her arms around him. He held her until he was all but asleep, then carried her to their bed and crawled in beside her.

***

"Your Majesty." The guard looked pale. "There are people to see you."

"Send them to the Hall, and we will be there in a while." Harald turned back to the reports he had spent the last week trying to catch up on.

"My pardon, Majesty, but you'll want to see them now." He handed Harald a ring. "They carry an urgent message from Lady Prenny."

"What has that girl done now?" Harald slapped the desk, then followed the guard to the Hall.

He took his seat and examined the men in front of him. They looked exhausted. One wore leather and fur with short dark hair and piercing eyes. The other could have been a northman from his colouring though he was dressed like a fisherman.

"Your Majesty, Kel'aaka of the De'e'tcha and Garr'son from the North Coast." The guard introduced them.

"Speak." Harald softened his gaze.

The man in the leather and fur began speaking in the sing-song tones of one telling a story. Harald used the time to quiet his breathing and quell his annoyance. Lady Prenny's ring grew heavy in his hand. She was unpredictable but loyal.

The second man, Garr'son, began translating and Harald's hand shook.

"Your Majesty, I bring greetings from Lady Prenny. She has taken refuge with the De'e'tcha after northmen attacked our villages. Kel'aaka has come to speak the story of the treaty between his people and your ancestor who sat on a stone chair." Garr'son held out a roll of paper, and a page brought it to Harald.

"When the men in ships arrived on this shore...

The story sounded vaguely familiar. Something Harald had run across in the archives when he was young. A curiosity, a tale of long ago, but it lived in the tradition that the crown owned the northern forest, and no one could hunt or harvest wood there.

The crown didn't own it but had agreed to keep it out of bounds for settlement by Belandria. The council occasionally pushed for expansion, but it never came out as cost-effective.

The paper contained Prenny's account of the treaty and her report on the invasion. His fist clenched around the paper. The De'e'tcha man frowned.

Harald held up his hand, and Garr'son stumbled to a stop.

"We have no reason to doubt Lady Prenny regarding the invasion or the treaty. The treaty is in the archives. We will keep it as our ancestor agreed." He waved a page over. "We need paper, sealing wax, and send a message to the queen asking her to bring the royal seal." He looked back at Garr'son. "Our apologies for our rudeness. Please finish the story of the treaty." *If nothing else, it gives me time to think.*

When Garr'son had finished, Harald had them shown to rooms to refresh themselves and eat. He'd given Kel'aaka a sealed parchment in his own hand promising to uphold the treaty. The man hadn't looked impressed.

"I need duSarche here as soon as possible, General Huston too."

Harald paced in his room, massaging the ache in his gut. War on two fronts? How would they survive? It had taken all their resources to push the Confederacy back the last time.

"Your Majesty, Lord duSarche."

"Send him in." Harald took a deep breath.

"I received an urgent message." Lord duSarche looked pale. "My son is on the south coast resolving an issue in one of our ports. How may an old man aid you?"

"Please, sit down." Harald made himself sit though he wanted to pace around and kick things. "I have a report from Lady Prenny." He continued when duSarche had taken a seat. "Men from the north invaded the coast, burning the three fishing villages. Those who didn't escape were killed or taken as prisoners. She said the attack came from a Belandrian ship. An abandoned village has been taken by the northmen as a base."

"Your Majesty," duSarche fell to his knees. "We lost a ship late in the fall. We thought it was due to a storm. There are three ships in port. They are at your disposal. Forgive us, we didn't know."

"Did you know there were northmen on the coast?"

"There were rumours, but we thought it was rogues raiding from the other side of the ocean. It isn't as wide in the north. We should have reported them, fortified the villages…"

Harald sighed and rubbed his head. "I'm not here to cast blame. Take your seat. You were part of the ship blockade during the Regency. I'm looking for advice."

"It will still be winter up in those villages, marching men up the roads will be a nightmare with the snow."

"So what are you suggesting?"

"We attack from the sea. They won't expect it this early in the season."

"How dangerous will it be?"

"Your Majesty, only madmen would sail in the North Sea at this time of year. I will lead them myself. I have captains who've sailed those waters."

"We will not rush," Harald said. "They've had the winter to dig in. Surely, they will expect some response and have made preparations. My immediate thought is to send troops by land and by sea. It will take coordination. General Huston will be here soon. I would like you to speak with him and come up with suggested plans."

CHAPTER 9

ELDER COUNCIL

Prenny listened to Sa'menki name the trees as they passed. Without Garr'son, the only person who could translate was the elder, and they never left their fur in the longhut.

Sa'menki was a young woman, maybe Fury's age, and she chattered non-stop from morning to night. The only way to learn the De'e'tcha language was to listen. Prenny could pick out a few words from the torrent and ask for food or water.

Some of the trees had different names in winter than in the other seasons. The river changed depending on whether it was frozen over or not. There was a word for hunger, and one for wanting to eat when one wasn't hungry. Every relationship changed the words and their meaning.

A young man walked up to Sa'menki and spoke briefly. Prenny caught the word for elder. Maybe there was news. Her heart raced as he led them to the longhut.

"You will travel to the Elders." The old person looked up at Prenny with her sharp eyes.

"I will work on learning the language on the journey." Prenny sighed. It would be no use asking for any other news.

"The spirits brought you here. Trust them to carry you where you need to go."

"I will." Prenny dropped her head. It wasn't the first time the elder had talked about spirits, but she didn't understand. It wouldn't hurt to see how things went.

Outside there was already a group of men and women ready for the journey. Sa'menki hung on the arm of one of the men.

"Let's go." The De'e'tcha words tasted funny on her tongue. How did Garr'son hold three languages in his head?

They travelled west. If Prenny understood right, it would take at least a week.

***

As they crested a hill, Prenny had to stop to take in the view. A vast lake spread almost as far as she could see. Smoke from a village wafted into the air below them.

"Beautiful, yes?" Sa'menki stood beside her.

"Very," Prenny responded. The other girl giggled, so it had probably come out strangely.

"We sleep inside tonight." T'unkis waved them forward. He was silent the same way that Sa'menki talked.

The walk down the hill took them most of the afternoon, but they arrived in the village before the sun dipped below the horizon. From the ground, the lake looked like the ocean had frozen solid. Men pulled nets from a hole cut in the ice while women picked fish from the mesh and put them in baskets. The village had to be three or four times the size of the place she'd first visited.

"Welcome." An older woman, not yet an elder, came to Prenny. "I will help you prepare."

"Thank you." Prenny followed, wondering what she was preparing for.

After a series of baths in water of different temperatures from freezing to almost painfully hot, the woman gave her a set of clothes.

"You dress, new clothes." She wagged her finger at Prenny's discarded clothes beside the first bath. Bathing in front of the woman felt odd, but Prenny put it out of her mind. This felt tremendously important.

The clothes were marvellously soft. The woman helped to adjust them to fall right. When they were set to her satisfaction, the woman handed Prenny a cup. The contents tasted earthy, not unpleasant but strong.

When Prenny put the cup down, the woman offered an arm. The world spun a little, and Prenny was glad for the support. They walked a little way out of the village to a round house built of wood and furs. The woman led Prenny inside and with slight pressure on her arm sat her on a soft fur. When the woman left, darkness surrounded Prenny.

"You come from the people of the stone chair."

Prenny wasn't sure if they were speaking her language or De'e'tcha.

"I do."

"You know the treaty?"

"The elder taught me the story."

No response came. The silence curled around her, friendly, safe. Prenny told the story as the elder had taught her.

"Will the stone chair hold to the treaty?"

"I believe so. I have asked him to."

"Your word carries so much weight?"

"I am young and new to the king's council, but he will listen. Even when I have been wrong, he has listened."

"A wise man."

"He is my king, my elder. I put my heart in his hands."

"A great trust."

"He put people in my hands." Prenny saw a vision of the Rau'ch, of Thoms under her coach's skis and sobbed. "I fear I have failed him and my people."

"We were told you carry a heavy burden for one so young."

"I don't mind. I love my people."

"Don't you fear that carrying this burden will make your people weak?"

"I carry them, and they carry me and each other. We grow stronger together."

"Will you carry yet another burden?"

Prenny lowered her head in thought. Could she? There was so much to do, but her mother made it work because she had help. Prenny could create the same kind of council.

"I will try for the sake of your people and mine."

"We would make you the bridge between our peoples. The holder of the treaty. Alone of your people, you will be welcome to travel the forest, but you must tell the story of the treaty, so it is never forgotten. It is perhaps time we understand each other better."

"The De'e'tcha will always be welcome in my home."

"What of these invaders? Would you have us destroy them?"

"Do they deserve destruction?" Prenny stopped and imagined the village. There were families living there. Could she push families aside? Did one injustice demand another? "I would regain my people's homes, but perhaps there is space for a treaty such as we have to benefit both groups."

"You are young, but thinking such does not make you weak. Perhaps you will prevail. Go back to your people. Carry your burdens well."

Prenny sat for a long time, planning and hoping, until the wall of the building lifted, and she was led out into the evening light.

***

She journeyed east to where her people hid under the eaves of the forest. The weather warmed as they travelled. In some places, the snow had melted from the forest floor.

"The invaders of your peace will not be allowed in our forest. Any of the grey ones who escape will be kept safe."

"Thank you." Prenny bowed to T'unkis. "I hold the treaty." She lifted a woven cloth. "Travel well."

Prenny walked along the path the remaining distance to rejoin her people. Spring would be here soon. She didn't intend for them to miss the early run of fish.

CHAPTER 10

UNEXPECTED ALLIES

Tomak stared at the huge city. He'd heard stories of Lusia but never believed them. It made his home look like a hovel.

"Be ready for action." Deathsdotter leaned on the railing. "Don't be obvious, but blood will be shed before sunset."

"I see. Nothing helpful like a hint about who we are supposed to kill?"

"I will walk with you and point you in the right direction." Echoes of his sister came through her words in the edges of sarcasm.

"Very well."

"Men, Deathsdotter has said to be ready for battle. Thoric and Harik, you stay and guard the ship with your lives. Don't start any trouble, but if something starts, I expect you to finish it. The rest of you, mail and swords under cloaks, no shields or helmets. Be ready to march as soon as we dock."

They drifted into a dock where men jumped over and fastened the boat. The two guards stood at the rail, mostly looking annoyed that they weren't included in the coming battle.

"I'm coming with you." Heurfotter crossed his arms and blocked Deathsdotter's way.

"You are not a warrior."

"Neither are you." He frowned. "Why did I come if not to serve you?"

"Let him come. He is loyal." Tomak didn't even slow down as he headed for the gangplank. Her glare warmed his back, but she didn't argue.

Tomak led his men with Deathsdotter beside him along the dock. A man came out of a building.

"You have to pay the dock fee. You can't just park your ship wherever you want."

"Pay him, brother." Deathsdotter waved a hand.

Tomak handed the man a small bag of coin.

"If this doesn't cover it, I will pay the rest later." He left the stunned man peering into the bag. "I think I gave him the gold by mistake."

"No matter, money is the least of your problems." Deathsdotter's voice had taken on a definite rasp. "This way, don't run, but hurry."

They marched up the street, people running out of their way. The unmistakable sound of battle came from ahead of them.

"Go, there will be a man in white. Don't let him die." Deathsdotter pointed toward the tumult. Heurfotter stood fast beside her and lifted a club from beneath his cloak.

Tomak broke into a run, followed by his men. His wife had been stolen, he'd spent weeks at sea worrying about her, frustration at his helplessness building. Now he had a chance to work out that frustration the best way he knew how.

A mob of men surrounded one in white who had a few guards desperately trying to stop attacks from every direction.

"Keep the one in white alive. Everyone is an enemy." Tomak drew his sword and roared. The battle froze for a second until his men crashed into the back of the mob. None of the men wore armour. They fell under the northmen's blades like grass to a scythe. The mob broke and ran. Tomak held up a fist. "Hold up, don't pursue."

"Who are you?" The man in white came over to Tomak, ignoring the blood staining both their clothes.

"I am Tomak of Getthelm. Deathsdotter told me to preserve your life."

"Deathsdotter?" The man looked puzzled. Tomak pointed toward his sister who was sauntering through the carnage to join them, followed by her servant. At that, the man in white's eyes bulged, and Tomak wondered if he was going to run. At the last moment, he rallied and put a hand to his chest and bowed to Deathsdotter.

"I am told I have you to thank for my life."

"These," her hand waved at Tomak and his crew, "helped somewhat." An almost smile crossed her lips.

"I thank them as well. Will you join me for food and drink, and perhaps exchange more of our stories?"

One of the remaining guards stepped up.

"Your Majesty, we know nothing of these people."

"I know enough." The man pointed away. "Go and tell the palace to have a feast prepared."

The guard bowed and dashed away. A couple of other guards were nursing wounds.

"Alfric, see to the injured men." Tomak turned to the man in white. "You have my name. May I have yours?"

"I am Striphona, Emperor of Lusia."

"Sekwun, run to the ship and let your brothers know there will be a feast."

"Are you able to accompany him?" Striphona addressed one of the guards.

"Yes, Your Majesty."

"Prevent any trouble. Set a guard on our visitor's ship. I want it as secure as if it were my personal craft. Have the visitors escorted to the palace."

The man saluted, then ran off with Sekwun.

"Shall we?" Striphona nodded at Tomak. "While seeing the traitors' bodies in the street is a lesson for those who'd attack me, I believe I've been here long enough for the lesson to set in."

"Watch for bowmen on the roofs, men in alleys." Tomak signalled his men to treat the city as enemy territory.

"You are thorough. I like that." Striphona sauntered along the road while people stared open-mouthed at him and Tomak's men. "I've never been to the north. What is it like?"

"Cold," Deathsdotter said. "Dark, dangerous."

"Is she always like this?"

"Always." Tomak grinned at the emperor while Deathsdotter scowled at him.

The feast was beyond his imagination. Tomak regretted needing to stay sober but after a warning gave his men the freedom to eat and drink their fill.

"So you sailed all the way from your home because she told you to?" Striphona played with a gold goblet, not drinking much, though he made sure drink flowed like a river for everyone else.

"Something like that." Tomak stared into the distance. "She gave her life for me."

"But she's alive."

"She would have died for me, but the goddess wanted her life. The least I can do is listen to her."

"I'm glad you did." Striphona leaned forward. "Not all the nobles are happy to have a strong hand running the country again. Chaos is profitable for some."

"We have people like that as well."

"The men you killed were paid to attack, but the real villains remain hidden behind false smiles."

"Until Deathsdotter says otherwise, our mission is to keep you alive."

"If the emperor of Lusia dies, chaos will seem like a child's dream compared to what will happen. Everything is connected." Deathsdotter ate neatly but mechanically. Heurfotter filled her cup with water. Of all of them, he looked most relaxed.

"I didn't think I was that important." Striphona smiled at Deathsdotter.

"You aren't." She frowned at him. "It is the stability you give. Like a rock in river, you shape the flow. The river cares not which rock."

"A man I admire told me I need someone close to me who isn't impressed by who I am."

"Why not keep him close?" Tomak sipped at the wine, better than anything they got in Getthelm.

"He has his own part to play. He will put another rock into the river. You want to be careful, Emperor, that it doesn't crush you." Deathsdotter met his gaze.

"Since you are appointing yourselves as my guardians for now, will you stay in the palace?" Striphona glanced over at Deathsdotter.

"I would be delighted," Tomak said. Deathsdotter went back to eating.

***

"...so Your Majesty, he sent us back to report."

"Thank you, Jorges, I'll expect your written observations in the morning."

The legionnaire stood, saluted and left the small hall Striphona used to meet with people.

The northmen stood around the outside of the hall, with Tomak behind the emperor.

"Your thoughts, Deathsdotter." Striphona looked over at where she sat like a statue in the corner, her shadow beside her.

"You can't hold Lusia against what is coming. Don't overreach."

"That's what I was thinking. If they invade, they'll be forced to deal with Lusia. Maybe I can broker peace for my people."

"I said not to overreach." She glowered at Striphona.

"Point taken." Striphona sighed and relaxed in his chair. "All I can do is what I'm going to do anyway. The legion will go out into the countryside surrounding Lusia. We need the crops planted. They will keep the peace and protect the farmers."

"The nobles will still hate you."

"The nobles would hate me regardless of what I do." Striphona slashed with his hand. "They may as well hate me for doing good."

"The end will be the same."

"Not for the farmers."

It might have been Tomak's imagination, but he thought Deathsdotter rolled her eyes.

***

"Is life really so gloomy?" Tomak asked his sister as she played with a chess piece from the set in her room.

"I speak what I'm given to speak." Deathsdotter held up the chess piece. "I'm allowed to see a slightly larger portion of the game. The game doesn't care about people or their loves and desires, only their actions."

"Yet those loves and desires drive their actions."

"I'm not sure." Deathsdotter put the piece back on the board. "Everyone dies, and I see far too many of those deaths. How does love and desire help then?"

"We all will die. I hope to leave the world a better place. Does that change my actions?" Tomak walked over to stare out the window at the city. "Even if I must give up my life to preserve the work, I am content." He turned to see the glistening of tears on Deathsdotter's cheeks.

"Sister," Tomak knelt in front of her. She stiffened and pulled back. "Sister, I know you have a hard path to walk. Do not worry about me. Do what you must, and I will be fine." He brushed fresh tears from her cheeks. She threw her arms around him and sobbed into his shoulder.

Tomak held her until she regained control.

"I'm a fool. I should be stronger." She scowled at him.

"It is not weakness to care." Tomak looked up at her. "It may make our lives harder, but it is also what gives it meaning."

"We are both fools."

CHAPTER 11

BREAKING POINT

Low, scrubby bushes began appearing beside the track, but the air grew hotter. Watching out through the bars of the cage, Fury saw the landscape distorted and moving.

I'm killing him the next time he touches me.

You need a plan, or you will die alongside him. The voice of the being in her head sounded like crushed rocks.

So, what's the plan?

Pay attention to where Thun is with the crossbow. It will take a few seconds for him to reload.

That's not much help if I have a bolt in me.

Don't let it hit you.

Fury watched and schemed. Asam sat in the heat and complained as he drove the cage wagon with the men ahead of the girls. Thun didn't do much more than occasionally wipe sweat from his eyes.

Gamble's coach had an awning which shaded him from the worst of the sun. He had a jug he drank from constantly. Occasionally his head would drop as if he were falling asleep.

Far ahead, a pinnacle of stone rose out of the desert. The caravan pulled in, and the wagon owners jostled for shade. The slavers parked half in the shade, but it would cover them as the sun set.

"Double rations of water," Gamble ordered Asam. "Thun, take the water barrels and refill them." The big man drove Gamble's coach away around the rock, and Gamble held the crossbow. With his boss watching, Asam kept his hands to himself. Fury let the tepid water ease the dryness in her throat. She held the last mouthful of water in her mouth as long as she could until her tongue felt normal again.

The girls were pushed back into the cage, then the men given their water. Thun returned with the coach, the back end sitting lower with full water barrels.

With all the slaves locked in the cages, Gamble vanished into his coach with the jug while Asam and Thun lay beneath the wagons in the shade.

At mealtime, Thun nudged Asam awake but ended up kicking the smaller man's leg. Asam cursed and yelled until Gamble stuck his head out to shout at them both.

Thun retreated to the shade of the coach, frowning at Asam as he cocked and loaded the crossbow. It didn't take long.

Fury let the girls push her to the edge of the crowd as they scuffled for their daily gruel. There was no one between her and Thun when Asam came up behind her and reached between her legs.

She called to the being whose name she shared, *Fury,* and strength flowed into her. Spinning around, she gripped Asam's arm then completed her turn with him not quite blocking Thun's shot. He yelled at her and hoisted the crossbow while the girls screamed and fought to get away from the fight.

Asam's arm snapped in Fury's hand, and he screamed at Thun to shoot her. The crossbow snapped as she pulled Asam in front of her and let go of him to charge across the sand. A grunt and more screams came from behind her as Thun cocked the weapon and fumbled a bolt in place. He fired when she was still three paces away, but she'd dodged to the side as his finger tightened.

Her left hand snatched the bolt out of the air, twisting it to keep it in her grasp. Thun was still gaping at her when she drove it through his eye into his brain.

Gamble tumbled out of his coach and swung a sword at her. Fury slapped it away and waited to see what he'd try next.

"You're dead." He took a breath and settled into a fighting stance, not much different than the guards in training at home. A jump over the front of the coach put him on the ground and gave him space to attack.

Two poles held the awing over the seat. Fury leaped up and ripped one away. It was much too light and flexible, but she'd make it do. A thrust at Gamble forced him back and gave her room to get back on the ground.

He lunged forward to cut at her. She pushed him away with the pole. Attempting to strike only ended up slapping him ineffectively. He slashed at her weapon, cutting off several hand's spans of length.

Fury danced just out of range of his sword, analyzing his attack. Gamble had training and kept up enough practice to be proficient. Against any normal person, he'd be deadly. Even she'd be in trouble if the fight went on much longer. The lack of food sapped her energy and even with Fury's help, she was rapidly weakening.

As her weapon shortened, it gained stiffness, not enough to do damage, but it gave her an idea. The next slash of the sword she blocked and at angle with the pole. The blade cut through it like it wasn't there, and the point of the sword drew a line down her right arm. Fury dropped the half of her weapon in that hand and stepped in closer, catching his arm. Gamble wrenched it away before she could break it, but with her left hand, she drove the pointed end of her remaining weapon into his throat, using the last of her strength.

He gurgled something and dropped to the ground. Fury reached for the sword to finish him off.

"Hold."

She looked up to see the owner of this new voice. The man with the plain coach and uniform. Even in this heat, he looked immaculate.

"It is death for a slave to hold an edged weapon." His hand rested on the hilt of his sword. Fury shrugged and stepped away from

Gamble. She doubted he'd live until sunset.

"I have decided to commandeer you." The man relaxed when she'd moved back.

"There's two of us." Fury fetched the keys from Asam's body, the girls shrinking away from her. The men crowded the door. "Get back and I'll give you the key when I'm done." Fury glared at them. They reluctantly moved. "Nikay, I'm bringing you with me."

He squirmed to the door. The men muttered as they had to shift around to give him slack in the chain. The girls weren't chained, fortunately. After searching through the keys, she unlocked the door, then the cuff holding him to the chain.

Nikay put his arm around her and helped her walk to the man in uniform. Fury tossed the keys on the ground.

"What are you doing about them?" Nikay nodded his head at the men fighting to get out of the cage.

"They have the keys; they can figure it out. Maybe drive back to Belandria. I'm too tired to care."

"I need your promise to not run away." The man frowned at Fury.

"You're taking us where we need to go." Nikay tightened his arm around Fury.

"Good enough." The man led them back to his utilitarian coach. "It will be crowded but better than the cage."

After helping Fury up, Nikay climbed into the coach

"I am General Sambian." The general didn't offer to shake hands. "You will call me Master."

"I'm Nikay, she's Fury."

"You will learn the language of the Confederacy nobility while we travel."

"At least we won't be bored."

Fury leaned against the wall at the end of the coach. The master handed them bread and cheese which she ate slowly, then curled up beside Nikay and let herself sleep.

***

When they rolled into the capital of the Confederacy, Nikay and Fury understood the master's commands and could respond with one of the limited phrases he said slaves needed.

The coach rolled to a stop beside a long low building.

"Out."

"Yes, Master." They clambered out and stretched. He'd only allowed them brief periods out of the coach to care for their bodies' needs.

"Follow me, no talking."

"Yes, Master."

They walked through doors guarded by big men on the inside and along a hallway to a room.

"Wash. You must be completely clean. Throw your clothes in the corner. You will be given appropriate attire."

"Yes, Master."

At first, Nikay tried to keep his eyes away from Fury's body, but it was too much work to wash and worry about privacy. She didn't look like she cared. They scrubbed until their skin was red, scrubbing each other's backs as the Master watched and pointed out places they'd missed.

"Dress and wait here." He pointed to neatly folded garments, then strode out of the room

The clothes were loose grey pants and shirt, light enough that Nikay didn't feel properly dressed. Fury's fingers moved in code.

Enemy territory.

Play along.

For now.

"I thought I said no talking." The Master frowned at them. A man with a leather apron over his grey clothes walked around peering at Nikay and Fury.

"You want him cut?" The man scowled.

"I wish to breed them later. They have interesting characteristics."

"Collars then, full training?"

"Regular collars. I don't wish to fuss with them later. They are already trained."

The man pulled out two leather collars with black stones set in them. He wrapped one around Nikay's neck with a brief flash of heat, then attached another to Fury. The master flicked a hand and the man left.

"While we have a moment, I will give you your orders. You are not to disclose them to anyone under any circumstance."

"Yes, Master."

"You are a gift to a young woman. She is to be protected at all costs. If you fail, you die. If you reveal these orders, you will die. If you run away, you will die."

"Yes, Master."

"Be careful with your finger speech. Others in the army may recognize it for what it is." He led them out of the room before they could respond and walked them back to the coach.

After a short ride, they stopped, and he ordered them out.

"When you meet your mistress, you will kneel and remain kneeling until she orders you otherwise."

"Yes, Master."

Nikay and Fury followed him along an opulent corridor, floored in polished stone with richly grained wood walls. The general opened a door and waved them in, then closed the door behind them. Compared to the hallway, the room was plain, empty of all decoration except filigree over the only window.

The door opposite opened, and the general went to his knees. Nikay knelt, and Fury's heat warmed his left arm.

"Uncle, you of all people should not kneel to me." The girl's voice was cultured and rich.

"I have brought you a gift. Slaves from the cold north. They are a set."

"What do I need with more slaves?" The voice became petulant.

"They haven't passed through the slave house." The general's voice had an odd tone in it.

"Really?" The girl stepped over to Nikay. Her feet and legs weren't quite as dark as her uncle's, but they'd been dusted with gold. "Stand up."

Nikay stood, keeping his head down. This girl tied his gut in knots much more than her uncle had. A finger under his chin lifted his face. Her brown eyes assessed him. Her cheeks had been reddened slightly and gold dusted her face. Gold cloth wrapped around her, leaving her arms bare and her legs just above her shins. Her hair was braided tight against her head, tied with gold threads and dangling with beads.

"What interesting eyes. I've never seen such blue before."

She twisted her hand, and fire burned around Nikay's neck. He couldn't breathe past it and fell to his knees. The pain ended as suddenly as it started.

"Are you angry that I tested your collar?" His mistress tilted her head.

"I will serve you with my life if you ask it." Nikay's voice grated his throat.

She turned to Fury and twisted her hand. Fury looked up at the mistress with a blank face, hands shaking. The girl relaxed, releasing Fury.

"You are an interesting one. More angry that I tested your mate than you." She looked up at the general. "I had to test them."

"Of course." The general sounded pleased that she didn't trust him.

"Thank you for the gift." The girl shuffled her feet. "When will I see you again?"

"I am kept busy. I am here only because I arrived a day early."

"Visit me when you can." She spun toward the door. "Come, both of you."

Nikay stood and swayed on his feet, still dazed from the 'test.' Fury took his hand to steady him, and they followed the girl out of the room.

***

"I am Queen Mathial." The girl pointed at herself. "You will refer to me as mistress."

"Yes, Mistress."

"Ugh, only do that annoying 'yes, mistress' when there are others present."

Fury nodded her head. This girl had to be no older than her and Nikay. An odd mix of pride and insecurity, then a surprising flood of jealousy warmed her. The odd stolen kiss in the dark of the wagon had been interesting but nothing more. Nikay's heart raced, but hers had beat as it always did.

"What are your names?"

"I am Fury, and this is Nikay."

"Tell me how you came here." The queen tilted her head with a tiny smile. "Do not lie."

"I was stolen out of my bed, then Nikay and I were smuggled out of the country. The slavers killed the kidnappers and put us in the cages to bring us here."

"How did my uncle come to own you?"

"He took us from the slavers," Nikay said. *Probably a good idea not to explain about killing the slavers.* Fury put them out of her mind. She'd done what she had to, just like years ago when she was just a kid. At least now her body could keep up with her.

"Are you nobles?" Queen Mathial put her hands to her cheeks. "You are, aren't you?"

Fury nodded.

"I am queen. I should be served by nobles." She put her finger to her lips. "You will tell no one. If they ask, you will lie and deny it. Only I can know."

"As you wish," Fury said.

The queen pirouetted and laughed, suddenly sounding much younger. Under other circumstances, Fury might have been friends with the girl.

The queen tugged on a rope, and a few seconds later an old woman appeared through the door. She wore the grey clothes but had a gold sash across her chest.

"A male slave?" The woman frowned. "He will ruin your reputation."

"That's enough." Mathial made a slashing motion with her hand, and the old woman winced. "You will say nothing bad about my uncle's gift."

"Yes, Mistress." The woman glared in Nikay's direction. "What may I do for you?"

"Fetch colours for my new slaves. There will be no confusion as to who owns them."

"Yes, Mistress."

The woman left while Mathial scowled at the closed door. "She's been my nurse forever and thinks she may tell me how to live. I had to threaten to kill any slave who listened at my door to get this room to myself." She pointed at Fury, then Nikay. "You will never repeat anything I say in this room, no matter who asks. You will die before you speak."

Fury bowed, and Nikay copied her a split second later.

"You're funny." Mathial clapped her hands, her anger forgotten. "Is that what you do in the north?"

"It is." Nikay smiled.

"Are you laughing at me?" Mathial rushed over and gripped Nikay's chin.

"It pleases me to see my mistress happy."

"Really?" She dropped her hand and reddened.

"How can we serve you properly if we don't wish to please you?" Fury asked.

"Nobody except uncle cares if I'm happy," Mathial said.

A knock on the door interrupted her, then the old woman walked in. She fit a sash on Fury, then a belt on Nikay.

"That is all." Mathial flipped her hand. She waited until the door closed behind the woman before clapping her hands. "We are going for a walk. I want to show off my new toys."

CHAPTER 12

ONCE FREE

The dust from the horsemen clogged Rodrigo's throat, but he wanted to maintain a balance between falling too far behind and losing them or getting so close so they decided to capture him.

"Pfah." Aimee spat dust from her mouth. "Do we have to ride right behind them?

"For now." Rodrigo handed her a cloth. "Bind this over your face."

Aimee did as she was told, and they started up again.

He'd expected to ride at least a few days, but the group sped up toward evening, and Rodrigo spotted the glint of fires in the distance.

"I don't know much about the steppes tribes other than they make a horrible drink called macshka and they are very particular about rules. Breaking any of the rules can mean anything from banishment to death."

"So what are these rules?" Aimee pulled up beside Rodrigo.

"Don't know. Watch the people, where they step, how they walk, how they eat."

"Wonderful." Aimee sighed, and Milene chuckled.

"The Rehego will camp toward the outside. We don't like being hemmed in." Rodrigo pointed to the side, "We'll wait until it is a little darker, then circle around until we find them."

Rodrigo had almost given up when he spotted a Rehego wagon. They rode over to where it and a dozen others were parked in a circle.

"May I come to the fire?" Rodrigo called softly. Voices argued in the dark before a woman called out.

"Welcome to the fire."

When he walked into the light, the muttering began. People stared at him, some like he was their last hope, others like he was the devil himself.

"I'm Rodrigo, my wife, Milene, and daughter, Aimee."

"What are you doing here?" The woman who'd invited them to the fire stood with hands on her hips. "I'm Hallith, as if that matters here."

"I was called." Rodrigo sat and stretched his legs out in front of him, right arm at his back for support. Aimee sat close beside him and huddled against his side. Milene stood behind.

More muttering and arguing. Something was wrong, but he couldn't put a finger on it yet.

"Where are the children?" Aimee asked. The Rehego looked down, not one meeting Rodrigo's eyes.

"Asleep, as they should be," Hallith said, and Rodrigo's skin crawled. Milene's hand tapped on his shoulder. *Trouble.* Men with bows stepped into the firelight.

"Dhovo said there were people following him. Don't know that we need more horsekeepers." A man with gold woven into his hair looked Rodrigo up and down.

"Just visiting my cousins." Rodrigo put his left hand on Aimee's head. She was trembling.

"Did your cousins tell you the rules?" He waved his men forward. "Slaves don't get to keep their children."

"Go, don't fight. I'll find you." Rodrigo tapped the message on Aimee's head, and she slumped. A man hauled her up and threw her over his shoulder.

"Might have some fun with this one." He laughed and Aimee whimpered.

"Bhotta hears you and you'll get staked." The leader frowned.

"Bhotta don't need to know."

"Bhotta knows everything." The leader pointed to another man who lifted Aimee away from the man who'd turned pasty.

"Obey and no harm will come to your daughter." The leader walked away followed by the rest of the men.

"So now you know our shame." Hallith slumped to the ground. "We dare not disobey in the slightest for fear they'll hurt our children."

"How do you know they are not?" Rodrigo asked. "Do they let you visit? I'm guessing not."

Hallith went even paler.

"Some tried to leave. They were hunted down, and their bodies paraded in front of us. What can we do against so many?"

"Who knows?" Rodrigo sighed and pulled his feet in. "Nothing, as long as there are those who aid the enemy." He scanned the circle of shamed faces. "I will sleep in the dark." They turned away and went to their wagons. Rodrigo slipped away from the fire and sat down, letting his eyes adjust to the dark.

Tents stretched as far as he could see. There was no clear order to them, making it hard for attackers to push into the centre of the camp. Somewhere in the gloom was a group of larger tents holding the people who ruled this horde.

***

"I followed them to a fenced-in area. Children crying on the inside of the fence, some Rehego, some other languages." Milene leaned against him. "It just about killed me to leave her there."

"It was let her go or maybe watch her die here." Rodrigo put his arm around her. "I need you to put a seeming on my right arm to make people think I have two hands."

"Shouldn't be hard. It is what they'll expect to see." Milene murmured and drew runes on his claw hand. "Unless someone is sensitive to the runes, they will only see a hand, bandaged so they won't wonder why you don't use it."

He helped with the horses for the next week. He could brush them with his left hand and hold their feet up with his hook. It had been a long time since he'd spent a lot of time with horses, and he would have enjoyed it except for the worry about Aimee.

Milene checked on her every night. Aimee was one of the oldest inside the fence and took care of the young ones.

By the end of the week, Rodrigo had spotted three people who informed on the Rehego to the horsemen. It would be easy enough to remove them, but then someone else would be forced to take their place. Better to use them to his advantage.

He made friends with the most eager of the informants, easy enough to do since no one else would talk to the man, Pantiro.

"...and the merchant never knew who'd lifted his purse. I could have taken his cloak and pants if I'd wanted," Pantiro bragged about his exploits as a thief. Every tale centred around him duping the people of the towns and villages he passed through.

Each evening Pantiro slipped out of camp, thinking no one saw him, to report to the horseman who treated him with contempt.

Rodrigo whispered in worried tones that he'd overheard a legion commander planning an excursion to punish the steppes people for their raiding.

Two nights after that, horsemen came and took Rodrigo away for questioning. The man who asked the questions had gold and ivory beads in his hair and wore several rings.

"Tell me about this legion?" The man looked bored.

Rodrigo told his tale the same as he had to Pantiro.

"You're the new one?" The man shook his head. "Doesn't matter, you're here now and there's no leaving. A scouting group has gone to check your story. If you're lying, I'll stake you out."

He waved Rodrigo away, and they locked him in a hut and left him alone. When night fell, he slipped out of the hut and went to listen at the questioner's tent.

"Carry this to the horde leader. I expect this slave is lying, but we should be prepared."

Rodrigo followed the messenger to a much larger tent, this one with guards at the front. He sliced through the wall near the ground and rolled through into the dark.

"Legion? They couldn't find their butt with both hands, but you'd better carry the message to Bhotta, just in case. Hurry, he was bragging about some new girl he'd chosen from the slave pen, gold hair if you believe him. Once he starts, you'll not get sense out of him until morning."

Rodrigo's gut ached. He wanted to run to the fence and take Aimee out, but that wouldn't help. Iy766666t would just put the camp into an uproar. The messenger jogged through the camp, the tents further apart and the guards more plentiful. The man was stopped three times, but the last pair of immense guards waved him in.

"Your funeral, the girl's been washed and prepared." The guard pointed toward a round hut on a raised platform. Rodrigo detached his hook and tied the thin line he carried around his waist onto it. Balancing on the edge outside the tent, he listened to a woman giving Aimee orders.

"Don't care what you do."

"What if I kill this Bhotta?" Aimee snarled at the woman.

"Go ahead if you can, but we took all your toys. Stronger people than you have tried, and they weren't tied to a post."

Aimee yelled at the woman as she left, showing a remarkable vocabulary. More shouting came from below. Rodrigo expected the poor messenger was giving his report.

He cut through the tent near the centre pole and dropped into it, knife at the ready.

"Papa!" Aimee threw her arms around him, then pushed him away and punched him. "It took you long enough."

Rodrigo looked at the rope lying on the floor and laughed.

"Up the pole and outside. I'm going to have a talk with Bhotta. Don't make a sound."

Aimee scampered up the pole and vanished. The tent was lit by several lanterns and piled with furs and cushions, but nothing hid the stink of fear. He extinguished all but one lantern then stood in the shadows.

A large man pushed through the curtain into the tent and frowned at the unlit lanterns. He looked like he used to be muscular but had gone soft. A knife was stuffed in his belt, but otherwise, he only wore a robe. Rodrigo ran past behind him as the man spun to look at the tent.

"I know you're still in here. I'm going to find you, and we're going to have a great time, at least I will." He laughed until Rodrigo put the point of the man's own knife against his back where it would pierce the heart if he pushed it in.

"You have a choice," Rodrigo hissed in the man's ear. "Listen to my words or call your guards and die."

"You're going to kill me anyway." Bhotta's muscles tensed, then he spun around, but Rodrigo danced out of reach back into the shadows. Bhotta took in breath to shout as Rodrigo jumped forward to land his heel just below the fat man's rib cage. Bhotta crumpled to the floor. Rodrigo dragged him to the centre pole, then bound. He crouched behind the man.

"You aren't going to die yet, so listen. The Rehego are cursed. Try to kill them off and you're cursed. Make slaves of them and you're cursed. You are going to lose everything you value, little by little."

"I'll have them all killed," Bhotta groaned.

Rodrigo put the knife to the man's throat. "Then what purpose do I have in letting you live?"

"Wait, wait." The evidence of Bhotta's fear puddled on the floor. "What do you want?"

"You figure it out. Guess wrong and I'll be back. There's nowhere in the world I won't find you. You've angered the Rehego Champion, and now you're doomed if you don't make it right."

He dug the blade into the wood of the pole holding the point against Bhotta's neck, then climbed out of the tent to join Aimee on the roof. She had her hand over her mouth to smother her giggles.

"Come on, time to move." Rodrigo dropped to the platform and caught Aimee, then sent her down the rope before removing it from his hook. The hook back in place, he dropped beside her and wrapped her in his cloak before leading her away to Milene.

In the morning, the man with the rings flung the door to Rodrigo's cell open. Rodrigo peered at him blearily.

"What?"

"Get out of here."

The camp buzzed with rumours as Rodrigo walked back to the

Rehego wagons.

"She's safe," Milene whispered as Rodrigo hugged her. "I don't know what you did, but she giggled all night."

"I'll tell you about it later."

***

"What do you know about the Champion?" The guard glared at the Rehego.

"He's the one who warned us to leave the Empire." Hallith crossed her arms. "Holds the Balance now."

"Why would he be in this camp?"

Hallith's face lit up for a second before her grumpy expression returned.

"The Champion's got more magic in his little finger than I'll have in my life."

"Magic?" The guard paled. "It doesn't matter. We'll catch him and stake him out."

"Might as well try to steal a shadow." Hallith shrugged and picked up a bucket. "If you don't mind, we've got work to do."

The guard didn't quite run away.

Rumours spread through the camp, each one wilder than the next. Rodrigo flitted through camp at night gauging the temperament of the people. Most of the stories he heard were accompanied by quiet laughter, as if Bhotta was feared but not respected or liked.

The platform and the tent vanished, but the rest of Bhotta's compound stood, crammed with guards. The guards became a subject of ridicule and Bhotta banished them all, reportedly sleeping in full armour. Rodrigo paid a visit and left a note pinned to Bhotta's blanket. The guards returned.

Through all the commotion, Rodrigo worked with the horses and listened to Pantiro's lies.

CHAPTER 13

ACROSS THE RIVER

Lydia had prepared herself to be eaten by the hunfish, but she wasn't prepared for the icy cold of the river. It hit her like a blow, stealing her breath so she couldn't even scream.

Still, she flailed her way to the surface and fought the current to stay afloat. Something splashed beside her, then Shu burst from the water. He put her on his back and swam across the river. The rock walls of the gorge blurred past, then he surged forward to heave her onto a rock ledge before rolling onto the rock himself.

As soon as he left the water, hunfish boiled as if angry they'd been denied their prey.

"I should have known you were god-touched." Shu shrugged off his shirt and wrapped it around Lydia. "It will keep you a little warmer. This way." He climbed up the rock. She watched where he put his hands and feet, ignoring the increasing distance from rock and water.

She squealed when he reached down to grab her wrist and lift her onto the stairs.

"Wait here." Shu descended the steps and vanished, only to reappear rowing the boat across the river. The strain on his muscles made them bunch and cord, but he made it to the far side. Two of the men climbed into the boat along with Vakate. One of them helped row back. After rowing three times through the current, Shu barely looked tired. Vakate brought Lydia her clothes, so she dressed quickly, leaving Shu's shirt for him.

They climbed the stairs to the plain. The snow covered the ground in patches, and already shoots of green were visible.

The men lined up and saluted Lydia, then knelt in front of Shu.

"Command us."

"I have a curiosity about how Bhotta is doing." Shu pointed to the south. "We should go pay him a visit."

"We just escaped that place and you are going to go see your cousin?" Vakate shook her head.

"Isn't that what you wanted?" Shu peered at her until she threw her hands in the air.

They walked south. Wen dug up roots which they gnawed on as they walked. They didn't taste as good as the hunfish, but they kept Lydia's stomach from growling.

At night they huddled together for warmth, not one man putting a hand out of place.

After a week of walking, Shu pointed ahead of them. "Horsemen, eight of them."

"Your orders?"

"Hide and wait."

Lydia looked around at the flat plain and wondered where they were supposed to hide, but the other men had already vanished.

"Don't look for them. The horsemen will only see what they expect to see." Shu brushed his hand against Lydia's arm. Vakate stood on the other side of her, arms crossed, wearing the frown she'd had since they were captured.

Surprisingly quickly, the horses arrived and pranced in a circle around them. Shu stood waiting until one of them spoke.

"A ghost." He pointed his lance at Shu. "Bhotta said you were dead."

"Bhotta has a bad habit of lying." Shu shrugged. "He hoped I would die but feared the curse too much to kill me with his own hand."

"There is no curse when there is a challenge." The man frowned. Shu stared up at him until the man shifted uncomfortably on his horse. "You are a ghost, no matter if you die a second time." He thrust the spear at Shu, but Vakate darted forward to push the jab offline. Shu leaped up and kicked the man from the horse. When Lydia looked around, the horsemen lay dead and Shu's men stood waiting for orders.

"At least you got out of my way." Shu looked at Vakate, who glared back at him.

"Mount up. Wen, you take the god-touched. Vakate will ride with me."

They jumped onto the horses. Lydia put her arm up, and Wen lifted her in front of him.

"You aren't taking the weapons?"

"Who wants to hold a fool's spear?"

Lydia shrugged and concentrated on getting comfortable. She ended up leaning back against Wen and letting the motion of the horse rock her to sleep.

***

Shu held his hand up, and Lydia sat back to stop her horse. She'd insisted on learning to ride as the steppes people did. Vakate appeared content riding with Shu, though they sparred verbally every night.

Haze in the distance revealed a large encampment. They'd meandered across the plain to avoid other groups. Shu's only explanation was that they didn't need any more horses.

"We'll not be able to avoid the scouts from here on." Wen rolled his shoulders. "I'd rather not meet Bhotta's murderers alone on the plain."

"If you hadn't left them behind, you'd have spears." Vakate turned to glare at Wen.

"We gallop in and arrive before Bhotta can send anyone out to stop us. Once we're there, he can do nothing." Shu kneed his horse into motion.

Lydia expected to gallop the whole way and worried about

holding on to her mount, but they started at an easy lope.

"We won't charge until we're close enough for them to identify us." Wen looked over at her and grinned. "I'd love to see Bhotta's face when he's told that ghosts are invading."

The camp was huge, like a city of tents filled with activity. Off to their right, riders left the camp on a course to intercept Shu and his group.

"Just relax and hold on. The horse won't drop you!" Wen shouted to Lydia as they surged forward. Lydia clung to the saddle and let her horse run as it wanted. Without thinking, she let out a yell, and then they were all whooping and shouting.

They arrived at the camp and wound between tents, leaping over abandoned wheelbarrows. A toddler wandered into the path, and the horses split to pass by on either side. The roar from the crowd lining the path might have been excitement or rage. Lydia didn't look to the side for fear of falling from the saddle.

The narrow path opened into a broad circle. They rode around the outside of the arena before stopping in the centre. Lydia leaned back and laughed with delight. Shu glanced over at her and nodded, then stood in his stirrups.

"Bhotta!" His bellow made the horses prance in place.

Around the arena, people gathered, pointing and whispering. Some climbed on wagons for a better view. In front of them stood a building that looked half-tent and half-castle. *How could they move that?* Of all the camp she'd glimpsed on the wild ride, this was the only thing that looked permanent.

The double doors on the wooden façade burst open, and a big man rode out. He wore full armour and carried a lance.

"You dare return?" Bhotta pointed the lance at Shu. "You gave your word."

"I thought to return and see how my people fared." Shu looked around. "Where is my family? I would like to see my children."

"My men are sharpening their lances at this very moment." Bhotta grinned nastily. "You have doomed them with your oath-breaking."

"An oath coerced is no oath." Shu frowned. "Even you should know that much of the law." He pointed at the building behind

Bhotta. "But clearly you have no care for our laws. I must challenge you."

A rumble travelled through the crowd like a wave.

"Kill him!" Bhotta shouted, but the guards holding spears and bows shook their heads.

"I will kill you and all your family and stake your corpses out for the vultures." Bhotta rode at Shu. Wen and the other men rode out of the way, and Vakate leaped from in front of Shu to run away. But Lydia's horse refused to move, and her limbs turned to water as Bhotta hurtled at them.

If she was going to die, she'd do it with dignity. She straightened in the saddle and glared at Bhotta. The big man glanced at her and licked his lips. In that moment Shu charged, standing on the back of his horse. He jumped high in the air. Bhotta tried to bring his lance around, but his opponent was already inside its reach. Shu landed a kick, sending Bhotta out of his saddle. Shu rolled to his feet as his horse trotted to the side. Lydia's followed it, huffing its annoyance. She slid off and put her arm around the beast's neck while she watched the fight.

Bhotta had retained his lance, and for all Shu's disgust at the man, he looked like he knew how to use it. They circled, Bhotta jabbing with his weapon, Shu weaving out of reach.

People near her were placing bets.

"Fifty beads on Bhotta," one man said. "He's armed and in full armour."

"I'll take that bet." A woman responded. "He's facing Shu."

Others jumped in on one side or the other. Lydia tried to ignore the beast clawing at her gut. Even when she was young, she hadn't liked watching bouts. She felt movement within her, and she put her hand on her stomach, feeling the roundness under the many layers of clothing. *Tomak.* The name didn't bring the stab of pain she'd expected. God's purpose drove her. It brought her here, to this moment.

The lunge looked to Lydia like all the others, but this time Shu wrenched the lance away from Bhotta. The big man's face paled, but Shu didn't use it to attack. Lydia recalled Wen sneering at the weapons of cowards. He threw it at the wooden front of the building where it stuck ten feet from the ground.

The people who'd been betting on Bhotta groaned, even as he drew a knife almost long enough to be called a sword. He slashed and jabbed, but even Lydia could see the big man was holding back, not getting close enough to truly threaten Shu.

Shu wove and dodged, his expression never shifting from the mask of calm.

Bhotta stumbled and swung wide. Shu lunged faster than Lydia thought anyone could move and slapped Bhotta on the side of the head. Bhotta staggered and went to his knees, waving the knife in front of him. He struggled to his feet, but his attacks were wilder, more desperate. Shu darted in to land blows though none of them incapacitated his opponent.

He's making a point. Lydia shook her head. He's teaching his people.

The end came suddenly. After a slice at Shu missed and buried the point of the knife in the sand, Shu took hold of the knife arm and wrenched. Bhotta squealed as his hand fell open, dropping the knife.

"Kill me with the blade," Bhotta gasped, pointing at the knife on the ground.

"You haven't earned a warrior's death." Shu gripped Bhotta's head. "You sneer at the laws of our people and have brought a curse upon them."

Bhotta turned grey. "The Champion warned me."

Shu twisted hard, and Lydia could hear the snap from where she stood.

Shu turned and stared at the crowd cheering his name, then raised his hand.

"Do you accept me as King of the World?" The response made Lydia's head ring.

"Sire." A guard knelt on the sand. His armour had blood on it. "I went to rescue your family as soon as I'd heard your name spoken." A huddle of women and children grouped behind him. Other guards surrounded them, their focus on the crowd. "I failed to save your oldest son. He died protecting his siblings."

"He died a warrior's death." Shu might have been carved from stone. "See that he is honoured as such. We move now. Anything which cannot be taken is to be burned. I will not sleep in a cursed place.”

The crowd vanished, and shouts echoed through the camp. Shu came over to Lydia.

“You didn’t move out of the way.” He frowned at her.

“I was tired and knew he was no match for you.” Lydia put her head against the horse’s neck. “I can’t believe I need to ride more today.”

“You may ride in a wagon.”

“I will ride.” Lydia straightened, then grinned. “Though you may need to tie me into the saddle.”

“I will ride with her and keep her safe.” Vakate stood behind Shu. “Go greet your family.” She pushed Shu toward the huddle of women and children. He hadn’t taken a step before the children ran forward in a mob and surrounded him, crawling onto his shoulders. The women followed more sedately.

“Let’s go find something to eat.”

***

Lydia stood by her horse ready to mount, Vakate beside her. Shu was answering a steady stream of questions. He was interrupted by a familiar figure.

“The Rehego need horses to pull their wagons.”

Shu turned to look at him, a frown on his face.

“Wait here.” Lydia handed the reins to Vakate and ran over to where Rodrigo confronted Shu.

“They can use their own horses.” Shu turned away.

“Bhotta stole their horses like they stole their children.” Rodrigo rasped, and Shu froze.

“Shu,” Lydia gasped in a breath. “May I introduce Rodrigo, also known as the Champion of the Rehego.”

Shu sighed and rubbed his head. “Bhotta’s crimes have no end. I have no time to deal with this. Hoárr, see to it, command in my name, whatever you need.” He turned to the next questioner.

“Lydia?” Rodrigo put his hands on her shoulders. “I never thought to see you again. You’ll have to tell me all about it.”

“Later.” Lydia headed toward a man with plenty of gold and beads in his hair. “Shu has ordered me to see that the Rehego have what they need to move camp."

"I don't deal with slaves."

Lydia grabbed his cloak and pulled him close. "Shall I tell Shu you have refused his direct order?" The man paled and stammered something. "Sorry, I didn't hear you."

"I will order their horses returned to them."

"Immediately." Lydia didn't release the man.

"Immediately."

Lydia straightened the man's cloak. "I knew you would be reasonable. I will be sure to report your ability to Shu." The man left, already yelling orders to subordinates.

"Take me to where the children are."

Lydia walked after Rodrigo through the chaos of people. Already most of the tents were down and being packed on wagons and horses. They arrived at a wooden enclosure with no one around. Children's voices called from the inside.

Rodrigo had the door open in seconds, and they walked in. Children sat in cages, some shaking the wooden bars, others weeping in corners.

"There are more than Rehego here." Rodrigo bit off the words. Lydia had never heard him angry before.

"Take them all. We'll find the other's families later." They opened every door and checked every corner until they were sure no child was left, then Rodrigo led the mob and Lydia brought up the rear.

People scurried away from Rodrigo, but occasionally a glad cry would come from the side and a child would run to their mother or father. The word must have spread because more men and women lined the path looking hopefully at the mob of children.

When they arrived at the Rehego's wagons, the horses were in their traces. The Rehego children surged forward to glad shouts. The others hung back.

"Come, you will travel with us tonight, and tomorrow we will find your families." Rodrigo waved them forward. "No child will be left behind. If we must, we will walk and carry them."

"I will leave you here." Lydia smiled at the bustle as children were piled into wagons. "Shu may have other work for me."

"I will walk you back," Rodrigo said. "The camp is confusing at the best of times."

"Papa, aren't you coming with us?" Aimee appeared leading a black and a white horse. Milene led a bay.

"Why don't you come with me?" Rodrigo jumped up on the black horse, and Aimee mounted the white.

"You can ride with me," Aimee said to Lydia.

They rode through the camp to the arena where Rodrigo pulled up.

"This is as far as we go. I would like to give Shu some time to forget my face."

"I will come to see you. We must trade stories." Lydia slid off Aimee's horse and headed over to where Shu still stood surrounded by people with questions.

"Hoárr," he yelled, "would you believe my family has no tent? Deal with it."

She waved in acknowledgement, then scanned the crowd for someone with gold in their beard.

CHAPTER 14

EVIL MULTIPLIES

Leandra wiped her forehead, but the cloth was already so wet it made no difference. Even Raphael had ceased his running back and forth between Hojiam and his mother.

"We should reach the capital by evening." Hojiam turned back and shrugged. "I can't say if it will be cooler."

"Wonderful, any more of this and I'll melt into a puddle."

"Don't be silly. People can't melt," Raphael laughed.

Other than feeling like it was underwater, the jungle was beautiful. Brightly coloured flowers competed with the birds for attention. Monkeys howled and chattered in the trees. They'd glimpsed larger animals too - a strange thing like a pig with a long nose, another covered with armoured scales.. At every stop, they found a print from a jungle cat.

"What do we do when we get there?" Leandra started forward again.

"I think we should find the Nekkest." Hojiam dropped back to walk with Leandra and Raphael. "We don't know for sure what is happening. They will know."

"Won't the Nekkest in the city be more likely to favour the war?"

"Not necessarily. Many work as guards or in other jobs, and war would hurt them."

"Why is there so much need for guards? Isn't the Confederacy at peace?"

"The Confederacy is a loose union of tribes under the royal family. They are always jostling for position. Sometimes it gets rough; hence the need for warriors."

"Right, so we need to worry about getting caught up in the wrong faction." Leandra rolled her eyes. The Rehego's history was of getting caught between factions.

"The Nekkest are politically neutral, though the royal family came from the Nekkest generations ago."

Leandra picked a fruit from a tree and checked it over before taking a bite. "Just how much weight does the royal family carry?"

"The stories from before the split tell of factions using the family for their own ends."

"So mostly symbolic. Who actually runs the place?" She wiped juice from her face.

"There is a council formed from all the tribes."

"Our first step will be to find out how that council plays out."

"The Nekkest will know."

Hojiam handed a fruit to Raphael and bit into another. They walked on. The strain in her legs told Leandra they were climbing. The slope stayed steady throughout the day until they broke through the jungle onto fields of crops. A city sprawled over a hill past the fields.

The air was marginally dryer out of the jungle. They hiked along fence lines to a road, then followed the road past a maze of farms to a larger road with carts loaded with food and goods heading toward the city.

***

In the city, the air was dry enough Leandra no longer felt like she'd been swimming in her clothes. The people in the street were a mix ranging from midnight black to pale with blond hair. Her blood ran cold at the first person she saw wearing Imperial clothing, but they didn't even glance at her.

If the Rehego fled across the ocean, who's to say people from the Empire didn't as well? As long as they weren't people with ambitions of recreating the Empire on this side of the world.

Hojiam stopped each Nekkest who wasn't busy and asked where they should head. Some frowned at them, but most pointed along the road. When they turned a corner and saw a building which looked like the Hall in Home, Leandra guessed they'd found the right place.

"It's a copper a night, a small silver a week if you pay in advance." The woman at the door barely looked up from her ledger. "You have three days to find work and pay your way, then you're out on the street until you pay your bill."

Leandra dug into her pouch and came up with a few coins. She handed them to the woman who pulled out a scale. After some fussing, she announced Leandra had paid for a week for the three of them if they shared a room. She handed Leandra a token with orders not to lose it.

A youngster barely older than Raphael led them to a room. She held her hand out.

"I think she wants something for her trouble," Hojiam said. "I have nothing."

"And I gave my last to the doorkeeper."

Raphael reached into his pocket and pulled out a handful of stuff and picked through it until he found something he liked and dropped it in the girl's hand. She peered at it and huffed but put it in her pocket and ran off.

"Let's check out what the last of my money bought us." Leandra walked into the room and shook her head. "Not much."

The stone walls were bare, only a tiny slit allowed light in from the outside. The mat looked like mice were nesting in it. Raphael stood over it and sketched a rune, no exodus of vermin happened.

"Did I do it right?" Raphael looked back at Leandra.

"You did." Leandra dropped her bag against the wall.

"You and K'nekket take the mat. I'm more comfortable on the floor."

"I'm hungry." Raphael rubbed his stomach.

"Let's see if they have a mess hall like at the Oasis." Leandra took his hand, and they head along the hallway. Soon she could follow her nose to dinner. Others were showing their tokens, so Leandra did the same, then filled her and Raphael's plates They sat at a long table. The girl who'd guided them ran up to Raphael.

"You have any more rocks? I traded that one for sweets."

Raphael emptied his pocket onto the table. He'd collected rocks, seeds, beetle shells and things Leandra couldn't easily identify. They put their heads down and pushed the collection this way and that until the girl picked out a pinkish stone.

"You get half," she said and Raphael nodded.

"Looks like you've found a friend." Leandra watched as he carefully returned his treasure to his pocket.

"She hasn't seen my other pocket." Raphael looked pleased with himself.

"Did you pick up stuff to trade deliberately?"

"Uh huh, the kids at the Oasis were always trading stuff. I wanted to have something when I got back."

"We may not get back there for a long time."

"I know, but we're here now, so that's all right."

They'd finished most of their food when the girl came back holding a stick covered with ants stuck in something like honey.

Raphael took it and peered at it closely. He licked some of the honey stuff off a finger, then eagerly munched at the rest of it.

"You were hoping he wouldn't like it." Leandra took a better look at the girl. She stood a hand taller than Raphael and was lean and hard. Her hair had been roughly cut off at her shoulders. She looked down.

"Don't be ashamed. It is trading, and that's what you're good at, isn't it?"

"The adults call me Trader." The girl puffed out her chest. "It's how I pay to stay in the Hall."

"You have to pay your own way?" Leandra's admiration for Trader went up a notch.

"Mom and Dad are working in the south. They said it was dangerous, so I stayed here."

"Alone?" Leandra tried to get her mind around parents who'd leave a child who could be no more than eight to fend for herself.

"No, but Uncle got beat at the Arena and couldn't pay the bill. I didn't want to live on the street with him."

"Your parents should be proud of you."

That earned Leandra the flash of a brilliant grin.

"I can show you everywhere, in the Hall and outside."

"I bet," Leandra said.

In the morning, Trader waited for them in the Hall.

"You need a job." She waved at them to follow. "Morning is best. You can eat anytime."

She wove through the crowds on the street, smiling and talking to people. A few of the merchants asked her opinion about something and seemed pleased with the answer. Leandra could only follow about one word in three since they talked so quickly.

"Come, if we run, we will make it in time." Trader bolted down the street, never missing a step but not bumping into the crowd. Raphael tried to keep up. Leandra stayed with him and waved Hojiam to keep up with the girl.

It was easier to follow Hojiam, and they soon pulled up in front of a stall.

Trader was deep in discussion with the owner of the stall, pointing back at Hojiam. The owner finally nodded and handed Trader a few coins.

"You'll work here for the week," Trader explained to Hojiam. "Her regular is off somewhere. You guard the stall and take the money when she's away. All right?"

"Is the pay good?" Hojiam raised an eyebrow.

"She pays fair, even after my finder's fee." Trader nodded her head vigorously.

"I will accept the offer." Hojiam smiled and bowed to the stall owner. "Show me what I need to know."

"Come on," Trader tugged at Leandra's hand. "I think I can get you a job too." She didn't run as fast this time, and Leandra and Raphael were able to keep up easily.

The streets got emptier until Trader knocked on a door where only a few people carried crates about.

"What do you want?" The man who looked out at them was the first person to frown at Trader.

"This woman is looking for work."

"The last one you brought me broke a load of pottery, then ran off."

"How about you don't pay me the finder's fee for this one, then we're even."

"I'm still out all that pottery."

Trader shrugged expressively. "Can't help you with that, sorry."

"What about the kid? I can't have a kid breaking things in my shop."

"Put him to sorting buttons or something. He'll work for free."

The man rolled his eyes and threw his hands in the air.

"If they don't work out, this is the last time, you hear?"

"They'll be great, I just know it." Trader bobbed in the briefest of bows, then dashed away.

"Poor kid." The man waved them into the shop. "Her parents died in a fever in the south, her uncle is a drunk and a loser. I'm Theniar."

"She didn't say her mom and dad were dead." Raphael crossed his arms.

"It's her way of coping with being alone, pretending they'll come back and they'll be a family again. She's not being malicious."

"That's a good word," Raphael said and tried it out a few times. "I like it."

"I'm glad." Theniar pointed at the shelves. "All this is breakable, so no running in the shop, not for any reason. You can clean up here." He pushed Raphael into a room full of broken parts of things. "There's water in the jug and a plate of biscuits for lunch. You going to be all right here?"

"Sure." Raphael looked around the room like it was a cave full of treasure.

"He can't do any harm in there, and you can check on him occasionally."

Then Theniar led Leandra away from the room. "You'll be

unpacking and putting things on the shelves. Slow and careful is the way."

***

Raphael poked around the debris in the room. It looked like hundreds of smashed pots and chunks of stone that might have been tiny statues. He sorted the broken pieces by colour, then found two that fit together. Raphael looked around, but the man had said to clean up and didn't sound like he cared what Raphael did. He drew a rune to join the pieces, then another to find the rest of the pieces of the jug. There were still a few holes when he'd done, but Raphael tilted his head and nodded. It looked good. He picked up a piece of stone next.

***

Leandra came running at Theniar's shout, expecting the worst, but he stood pointing into the room his mouth hanging open.

"What, what?"

"Sorry." Raphael hung his head. "You said to clean up."

"Sorry?" Theniar waved hands. "What do you have to be sorry about?" He picked up a jug seamless but with a few holes. "Just what you've done here has saved me hundreds of coppers." Theniar replaced the jug and picked up a strange-looking animal. He shook his head. "How did you know what it looked like?"

"The pieces go together. I did a rune of finding..." Raphael looked up at Leandra. "You said I need to practice."

"I did." Leandra looked around the room. "You've done very well. I'm proud of you."

"Runes?" Theniar stared at Leandra. "The boy does magic, is that what he's saying?"

"He's learning."

"And I suppose you are a master?"

"In some eyes, yes. In others, I'm a beginner."

"You even sound like them." He smacked his head. "Why are you working for me when you could be earning gold as a magician?"

"I don't do magic for pay." Leandra crossed her arms.

"Right." Theniar leaned against the wall.

"Please don't tell anyone." Raphael tugged on Theniar's sleeve. "Mean people might take me away."

"Good grief." Theniar tried to push himself into the wall. "Your eyes."

"The big cat gave them to me," Raphael said.

"Of course, he did." Theniar shook his head. "I need a drink."

Raphael carefully poured a cup of water and handed it to Theniar.

"Thanks, kid." He drank the water down and handed the cup back. "You just caught me by surprise. I won't tell anyone, promise." He put his hand out, and Raphael took it solemnly.

"If you want to work for me, I'm not going to turn you away, but I can't just take what the kid's done and not give him something for it."

"Can I keep this?" Raphael held up something that looked like a jaguar in black glass.

"Of course." Theniar grinned. "You keep practicing. If you get bored, come see me. I may have something else for you to try."

"Thanks." Raphael put the jaguar on the table and crouched down by the pile of pottery shards.

***

"Did people really kidnap him for his power?" Theniar counted Leandra's wages into her hand. Over the course of the week, Raphael had worked his way through the pottery and stone in the room and started experimenting with bent and broken pieces of metal.

"They did. I was lucky to get him back." Leandra put the coins in her pouch.

"Here, give this to Trader. It's her finder's fee." He gave her another smaller pile of coins.

"I will." Leandra smiled. "I've never seen someone who worked so hard."

Trader was ecstatic with the finder's fee.

"I knew he'd like you." She leaned close to Leandra. "I have almost enough to start training."

"Training?"

"I'm a Nekkest. I need to be a warrior. There is a warrior who said he'd train me if I paid him a gold coin."

"I'd like to meet this warrior." Leandra's gut twinged. What would happen to Trader if the warrior took the money and didn't give her any training?

"Come on." Trader bounced up and down in excitement.

"Kitten better stay with Hojiam. It's a rough part of town."

"I'll let him know and meet you back here."

Leandra returned from her errand in a few minutes. Raphael was asleep on the mat, worn out from a mix of practicing his runes and trying to keep up with Trader.

For once, Trader walked. She talked the whole way about how she'd train to be a great warrior.

"There is more than one kind of warrior." Leandra looked around at the people. She should listen to her own advice. A week and she hadn't begun to look for the imp.

"Really?"

"There are strong warriors who protect the weak. That's what most people think of when they hear *warrior*."

Trader nodded her head.

"However," Leandra held up a finger, "some warriors don't look strong, but they challenge people to do the right thing. My brother is one like that. There are others whose fight is just to get by day-to-day. They have surprising strength, but very few people notice."

"I want to protect the weak." Trader walked in silence for a block. "Can I tell you a secret?"

"Of course."

"My mom and dad are dead. They died of a fever in the south. Uncle got a letter. It said they caught the fever trying to help people who were sick."

"That was brave."

"I want to be like that."

"I'm sure you will be." Leandra smiled at Trader. The girl could teach the Rehego something about trading: she strove to give the best value.

"Here." Trader ducked down an alley and led Leandra to a tiny courtyard.

"Zanfe," she called out.

An old man came out. He leaned on a stick, but Leandra didn't think he needed it. The grace of his movements made a lie of his age.

"Hello, little warrior. Introduce your friend."

"This is Leandra. She's staying at the Nekkest Hall."

"But she isn't Nekkest." The man tilted his head and studied

Leandra. "Many years ago, when I was a foolish young man, I went to the Empire to fight in one of their wars. I met a woman who felt like you do. Called herself Rehego."

"I'm impressed." Leandra nodded at the man.

"I almost have the money." Trader held up a hand with finger and thumb almost touching. "I'm this close."

"I look forward to training with you." He looked up at Leandra. "You're wondering why I ask such an impossible amount of a young girl. I won't work with someone who isn't dedicated. I've had too many spoiled nobles quit after a week."

"Trader is the hardest working person I know," Leandra said. "She'll get you your money."

"I am hoping she does."

They returned to the Hall, where a man staggered forward.

"Give your uncle a kiss."

Trader put up her hand. "You stink."

Her uncle moved to slap her, but Leandra caught his hand.

"Go inside." Leandra pointed with her chin. "Your uncle and I have something to discuss.

"Unless you plan to bed me, I have nothing to say to you. The ungrateful brat works for everyone except me. But I have a sure thing. I'll soon be rich as the queen." He laughed and staggered away.

Trader came running out and crashed into Leandra.

"It's gone, it's all gone." Tears ran down her face, and she vibrated with rage. "I'm going to get it back from him."

"I will go." Leandra held the girl until she relaxed in defeat. "You find Raphael, ask him to show you his other pocket."

Trader slouched back into the Hall. Leandra sketched a rune of finding and headed after the uncle. She caught up to him handing the bag of money over to two men radiating with menace.

"He stole that money from a child." Leandra walked up to them. "I expect you don't care."

"You got that right." One of the men pulled a knife and advanced on Leandra.

She tossed a rune at him, knocking him back against the wall. "I could break you into pieces."

"Perhaps you could." The other man appraised Leandra. "But

our associates would be very displeased, and that would cause trouble for you and this drunkard's niece." He kicked the uncle down. "It is regrettable that he took her money. We've heard how hardworking she is. I'm sure you would try to protect her, but however powerful you are, there is only one of you."

Leandra released the man with the knife who put it away.

"We have a proposal for you." The second man hefted the bag of coin. "This is a bet he is placing against a sorcerer who will lose. The man is a fool. However, it is also enough to pay the entry fee for a contestant. If you win, we pay the girl her money back."

"When I win, you will pay her two gold coins and swear you will never trouble her again."

"Very well, two gold coins and we leave her alone."

"Swear it on whatever god will listen to you."

"Very well, we swear on this bag of coin."

Leandra drew a rune in the air, and it flared brightly before fading.

"What was that?"

"I have sealed your oath. If you break it or allow anyone in your organization to break it, ruin and disaster will follow you and your associates until you die."

The man paled. "I may have misjudged you." He shook himself. "Well then, shall we go? The matches will start soon, and I'm sure you don't want to miss the opportunity to recover the dear girl's coin."

Leandra followed the men to a building that looked like a copy of the arena in the Oasis. They took one of the men guarding the back door aside and whispered to him. He finally shrugged and took the coin.

"You're up first," he said to Leandra as the others vanished. They walked through the door and into the gloom under the arena. "The crowd likes it flashy. Keep them happy and they'll cheer you. Disappoint and they have ways of showing their displeasure." The man clipped something to her belt, but she ignored it.

"I'm sure." Leandra tested the air. It was full of power travelling along threads, probably to the contestants. She sealed her energy in and prepared a few runes in advance.

"Through this door. Wait until you're lifted into the arena, then you can move anywhere you want on the floor of the place. The match begins when the white flag drops. It ends when the red one drops. It's considered bad form to kill your opponent, but it happens. Hope you don't have anyone waiting for you."

Leandra waited for the door to close and the floor to lift. Her red-hot anger had faded. She was a fool, but now that she was here, winning was her priority.

No one paid any attention when she appeared on the sand. The crowd roared when the other contestant showed up. Apollos, according to the announcement. She was dismissed as 'the challenger.' He waved and made a show of it. Power flowed from the crowd to him.

High in the stands, a man dressed as an Imperial noble stood watching. Sitting on his shoulder whispering in his ear was the imp. It grinned at Leandra.

The flag dropped and the match began.

CHAPTER 15

RISING STORM

Prenny paced up and down her room in the longhut. Close to four hundred villagers occupied sites set up by Kel'aaka and his tribe before he'd been sent south. Food was a constant concern since the game in the area had been eaten quickly.

Petan's response was a plan to raid the villages held by the Rau'ch. Careful scouting showed only a small force holding each village, no women or children. The men spent a lot of time drinking.

The plan itself was simple. They'd wait for a storm, then ride dogsleds to the merchant's warehouses in each village, empty as much food as they could take, then burn the rest. The biggest problem at the start was choosing from the volunteers.

The wind whined outside the hut. The men had left at dawn as they would have from the other sites. Travel in the poor weather would be hazardous, but it would hide their tracks. The Rau'ch would know there were survivors, but finding the sites would be hard. They'd have to stumble over the longhuts to know people lived there.

"Peace, Prenny Tha'sinre, you wear a track in the floor." Se'anics, the De'e'tcha who acted as intermediary between the villages and the tribe, looked up from where he sat on a blanket

She looked down, then laughed at herself.

"It is easier to risk my own life than that of my people."

"You are their leader. If you didn't worry, you wouldn't be worthy, but you also need to trust."

"Yennet is with them." Prenny took a deep breath. "The Rau'ch will be in trouble if they face her. I need something to distract myself." She dug around until she came up with needles and a ball of wool. "Let's see if I remember how to do this."

***

Thumping at the door resolved into the code for friendly visitors. She was a long way from knitting a sweater, but it wouldn't be a bad scarf if she could find more wool. Prenny put down the length of knitting and went out into the main room.

"Went easier than we thought." Petan shook the snow from his cloak and hung it up. Yennet followed him into the longhut. "The others are putting the goods away."

"Using the storm was a good idea." Yennet straightened her cloak on the peg. "I did some scouting while the men were loading up the sleds." She frowned. "I fear the situation isn't as simple as we first believed."

"Simple?" Prenny raised her eyebrows. "An invasion from the north is hardly simple."

"We assumed they were acting from population pressure or lack of resources." Yennet sat at the table and poured tea from the pot that sat ready day and night. "I was curious when I understood the conversation of the invaders. They should have been speaking Rau'ch. There was a man with them who, I'm guessing, was inspecting the villages and was caught by the storm. He and the leader of the invaders in Tansent's Arm were arguing. The invaders were expecting support from somewhere else to solidify their gains. That it hadn't shown up yet was a matter of concern."

"Complicated." Prenny put her hands on her head and thought about the news. "If someone wanted to draw a lot of resources away from the rest of Belandria, an invasion in the north would work. Travel is slow and communication difficult. It's a trap, and we fell right into it."

"Not much we can do now." Leohl looked up from where she sat with some of the other women.

"We can't push the Rau'ch out on our own. But we can make life less pleasant for them." Petan clenched his fist. He'd become leader of the Tansent's Arm survivors while Prenny and Garr'son had wandered through the forest.

"Burning their stores will go a long way to accomplishing that, but they will be more alert now." Yennet sipped at her tea and made a face.

"Any action we take can't lead back to the villages," Prenny waved her hand, "but we can't count on convenient storms. How many do you think were in Tansent's Arm?"

"At least twenty, maybe thirty," Yennet sipped her tea, "from the number of houses they occupied. I expect they are all unattached young warriors. Eager to make an impression, but expendable."

"A series of traps." Prenny held up a hand. "A couple of bowmen shoot from cover and retreat. When the Rau'ch find the trail, they'll follow it and we have a more serious attack planned. Hit them and retreat again to a new ambush site."

"It won't be easy to hurt them." Yennet shook her head and played with her cup. "They have armour and shields. We'd be vulnerable to return fire."

"There must be something we can do." Prenny clenched her fist. "We don't know when anyone will come from the south, and that is if Kel'aaka and Garr'son made it to the king and they decide to send support."

"Trust." Se'anics looked over at her.

"Right." Prenny sat back and stared at the wall. "The weather is breaking. I'm guessing we won't get a lot more storms to hide behind."

"So any help from the south will be coming soon." Petan grinned, "We'll have our homes back before summer."

"It isn't easy to pry warriors out of houses. The village could end up burned to the ground." Yennet sighed and looked over at Leohl and the women.

"Were the men you were listening to in the Inn?" Prenny asked.

"Yes, I hope you're not thinking of trying to attack through the tunnel."

"Not me." Prenny grinned. "If we get some of the soldiers in there, then draw the Rau'ch to the windows. The king's soldiers will have armour."

"It is a possibility, but that presumes we can let them know about the tunnels."

"I think I should go south and meet the army, update them on the situation."

"Don't think they will give you command." Yennet waggled a finger.

"Wouldn't want it." Prenny held up her hands. "Mom had Suze advising her before her battle. Still, giving the commander up-to-date information could be useful, right?"

"You just want out of the longhut." Petan poured himself tea.

"That too."

"I could guide you along the forest tracks," Se'anics said. "You've been given the rights of the forest, Prenny, Treaty Holder."

"That's another thing. They need to know they can't go into the forest."

"Garr'son and Kel'aaka will tell them."

"Honestly, do you think the commander will listen to a fisherman and De'e'tcha?"

"Probably."

Prenny tried not to pout.

"I will go with you." Yennet stood up. "We should leave in the morning."

***

Travel in the winter was uncomfortable; in the spring it was miserable. Everything was damp and cold. No matter how many layers Prenny wore, the air chilled her.

They stopped at the other sites and learned the men from Sham's Harbour hadn't returned from the raid. It made Prenny sick, but they were beyond her help. She wrote out orders for the other villages to share their food and sent them with a hunter.

They left in the morning, the villagers wishing her well and making her feel guilty.

"We're south of the villages," Prenny pulled up her memory of the map of the coast, "and the forest moves away from the ocean. We should stay closer to the road. It will help to spot any sentry posts the Rau'ch have put out."

"True, but it heightens the risk of them catching us." Yennet checked her weapons. "Be alert and don't hesitate."

Toward evening, Se'anics spotted two Rau'ch skiing north rapidly.

"They must have something to report." Prenny strung her bow. "We need to get to the road and stop them." She headed across the open land to where a hill overlooked the road.

"Careful or they'll spot you," Yennet hissed at her.

"If they do, I expect they will come after me rather than leave an enemy behind them. Be prepared to attack."

"They are carrying bows." Se'anics pointed to the men. "They have yet to string them."

Prenny arrived at the brow of the hill. It would be a long shot, but there was no cover between the hill and the road. She readied her bow. As they skied along the road, they didn't look up.

"Yennet, scream and flop through the snow helplessly." Prenny set an arrow to the string. "I need them closer. They've spent a winter with no women. They'll come after someone they think is helpless."

"Very well, my lady." Yennet rolled down the hill, squealing girlishly. As Prenny had hoped, the men stopped and pointed. They argued on the road before one shoved the other aside and skied toward Prenny. The other stood on the road yelling, then much more slowly followed his companion.

She stood, aimed carefully, then released the arrow at the reluctant one. It struck him on the side of the neck. He shouted and scrabbled at the arrow. Her next shot bounced off his helmet, and his yelling grew louder as he gave up on the arrow and pulled up his own bow to string it. Her third arrow deflected off his bow and buried itself in his cheek. He dropped the bow and flailed at his face.

The first one had his bow out and aimed at Yennet who was

caught in soft deep snow. Prenny didn't take time to aim but drew and released her arrow, followed by a second and a third. She reached for another, and her hand found nothing.

The first hit his shoulder throwing off his own shot. The second bounced off his helmet. As he turned to see where the attack came from, the last pierced his eye and he fell back into the snow.

Two men skied into sight, then held up their hands.

"We're Belandria skirmishers."

"I don't think the one near the road is dead!" Prenny yelled back. She backtracked and climbed down the side of the hill where the snow wasn't as deep.

By the time she made it to the road, followed by Se'anics, Yennet had fought her way out of the soft drift and stood beside the men.

"We weren't expecting any resistance from the villages," one man said while the other checked the Rau'ch, disarming and tying him. "You saved us a bit of a chase. The beggars are fast on those skis."

"It is good to meet you. I need to speak to your commanding officer." Prenny took her arrows back from the man on the road. "Blast, I'm down to two. I hope the road is clear from here."

"Look, missy, we appreciate the help, but..." He stopped and peered at Prenny. "Just why are you here?"

"I have come to meet your commander." Prenny pulled her hood back. "I'm Lady Prenny, Countess of the North Shore."

"She's the real thing," the other man said. "I recognize her from the palace."

"My apologies, my lady." The first man bowed. "We're advanced scouts for the main force. It is at least a day behind us."

"Then we should get on our way." Prenny sighed and put her hood back up. "I was hoping for a warm bed."

"You've been sleeping cold?" The first man shivered. "I'll never get used to that."

"It's been a long winter." Prenny shook her head. "We may make it to the old lord's mansion before dark."

"The commander is heading for there. You could wait and meet him."

The second man handed Prenny arrows from the Rau'ch's quiver. "They're shorter than yours but should do in a pinch."

"Shean, go with them, then bring back something to haul this fellow. I don't fancy carrying him."

"Yes, Corporal."

They headed south on the road, following the ski tracks and the scout's trail. Shean pointed up the hill where the ski tracks came down. "They had a good setup. If they'd waited to ambush us, it would have been messy."

"We suspect they are mostly younger warriors, not a lot of experience," Prenny replied.

"You have been busy. We were told you were with the Deetcha."

"De'e'tcha," Prenny corrected him, "and I headed for the coast soon after Garr'son and Kel'aaka left."

"Good to know. They're with the main force. This Garr'son says he can speak the Rau'ch lingo?"

"It's a long story and his to tell."

"Right."

Prenny wouldn't let Shean slow down though she was staggering with exhaustion when they came into sight of the mansion.

"It's occupied. Let me go ahead and check it out. It's my job, my lady."

"Very good, Shean." Prenny crouched on the road. "I will wait for you here."

Less than half an hour later, Shean returned with two men pulling a sled.

"If you will, my lady, we'll haul you to the house, then head out to bring in the prisoner."

"I don't think I could take another step." Prenny clambered onto the sled and let them drag her to the mansion. She was nodding off before they arrived.

"Commander Vuntil will be here with the main force tomorrow." A sergeant whose name she didn't catch showed her to a room with a fire burning in the grate. "Rest for the night."

Prenny curled up in her cloak and went to sleep.

***

Knocking at the door woke her.

"My apologies, my lady, but breakfast is hot."

"No apology necessary." Prenny rolled out of her cloak and

stretched until her joints popped. Yennet was already standing by the door. "Lead on."

The men stood as one when she entered and saluted.

"Your fame precedes you." Shean came over and handed her a cup of tea. "The prisoner is in one of the rooms. Corporal's been telling the story all morning."

"Thank you, I think." Prenny sipped at the tea and sighed. "I needed that." Shean sat her at the table.

"I refuse to sit and eat while you watch. Sit down and have your meal." Prenny pointed to the chairs. The men didn't need to be asked a second time.

"Corporal Kanset is one of the toughest men I know." Sergeant Smithson piled bacon on Prenny's plate, then handed her a huge bowl of porridge. "If you impressed him, then I'm impressed."

"I did what I needed to do." Prenny tried the bacon and had to hold back a moan of pleasure.

"That's what makes a good soldier." Sergeant Smithson smiled at her. He'd be old enough to be her father if her father had lived.

To everyone's surprise, Prenny polished off the bacon and the porridge. Yennet sat on her other side watching the room with sharp eyes but saying nothing. Prenny took that to mean she hadn't embarrassed herself yet.

After breakfast, the sergeant took her on a tour of the mansion showing where they'd repaired walls and made space for the coming army.

"I know this is yours, and we should have asked permission first." He led her into the ballroom. The windows were covered with tarps and bedrolls covered the floor in neat rows.

"I have no intention of living here, so I'm happy you could make use of the place." Prenny blinked in the sun when they stepped outside.

"The well is still good, which helps a lot, and they left a huge amount of wood behind."

"Good." Prenny looked around. "This will make a good base to work out of, though a bit far away for a permanent garrison. We'll need to build on, probably in Seal's Bight, keep a smaller force in each of the other villages."

"You think that will be necessary?"

"If they tried this once, what's to stop them from trying again?" Prenny sighed and leaned against a wall. "Unless we invade them in turn, and I don't think that is the best use of our strength."

"What would you have us do?"

"Make a treaty, give it enough teeth to let them know we mean it, then trade with them. If they need us for their survival, they won't be invading."

"Sergeant," Shean ran up and saluted. "The main force has been spotted on the road."

"Very good, let's make sure to welcome them properly."

CHAPTER 16

LONELY QUEEN

Nikay followed Mathial two paces back, flanked by Fury. The slaves stopped and knelt as she walked past and glared at Nikay.

"You are my personal slaves," Mathial said. "You answer only to me. The rest are palace slaves, and most of them report to someone about everything. That makes you higher status and a danger to their ambitions."

She spoke in conversational tones as if she didn't care who heard her. As far as Nikay could tell, everyone else in the palace was a slave. They wandered from one exquisite room to another, but Mathial paid no attention to them.

"Here we are." Mathial turned to them. "Speak to no one without my permission."

Nikay and Fury bowed. Mathial smiled and pushed the ornate

door open. The room could have been the palace archives and library combined. Books and scrolls were everywhere. Slaves scurried about carrying books to people in brightly coloured clothes sitting at tables. The people stood when Mathial entered but showed impatient faces as if they were humouring the queen and not paying her due respect. She waved them to their seats, her face blank. They walked through the library to a table with a grand chair set at one end.

An elderly slave appeared and knelt. Mathial fussed with her robe until the slave clenched his teeth, then sat regally on the chair.

"I wish to read about the country in the north." Mathial tapped the table with her finger. "I tire of reading of the Empire's tales of grandeur."

"Yes, Mistress." The slave ran into the rows of shelves. He returned with a heavy book he thumped on the table. He opened it and stood by her side.

"You may read for me."

The slave launched into a boring account of shipping manifests. Nikay could read the writing from where he stood. It told the story of the choosing of the king and the formation of the noble's council.

"Why are you lying to your queen?" Nikay made his voice as hard and cold as he could, imagining his father dealing with a liar.

"I, I would never..." the slave stammered and slammed the book shut.

"Nikay, read for me and I will judge." Mathial tapped the table. *Watch him.* Nikay signalled to Fury, then stepped into the slave's spot to open the book and began reading. This was his favourite part of the history of his home. He heard a scuffle behind him but kept reading.

"Hold." Mathial turned to glare at Fury. "What are you doing?"

"This one tried to leave. I have kept him here so you may decide what is to be done with him."

The slave paled where Fury held him kneeling on the floor.

"You lied to your queen." Mathial held his eyes until he wilted. "Report your failure to your master and do not trouble me again." Fury let him go and he crawled away.

"Continue reading." Mathial sat straight in her chair.

Nikay had read several pages when a man wearing white clothes sauntered up to them.

1

"My servant reports you dismissed him for lying." The man's voice made Nikay's skin crawl. "My apologies, my Queen, but the council wishes you to learn the stories of its allies, not its barbarian enemies."

"Phenos, the council may hem me in all other things, but what I do for entertainment is mine alone."

"Sadly, everything you do affects your ability as queen. If people were to hear you were listening to such tales..." He let the sentence trail off suggestively. Phenos turned his gaze to Nikay. "Allow me a word with your slave."

Mathial nodded slightly, and Phenos led Nikay away to a small room with a single desk in it.

"The queen is a delicate girl." Phenos held Nikay's gaze, and something moved behind the man's eyes. "As her slave, you are in particular position to preserve her wellbeing. Report to me everything she does. If you do not, I will find a way to have you and your mate removed."

"Yes, Master."

The thing in Phenos' eyes tried to invade Nikay's mind, whispering horrible things that would happen to Nikay and Fury if Phenos was disobeyed. He let them slide off him but put on a scared face. How he knew what to do was beyond him, but he trusted his instincts much more than this oily man from the council.

"Return to your mistress and say nothing of this conversation. Tell her I was ordering you to take special care for her."

"Yes, Master."

Phenos walked out of the room, and Nikay took a long breath before he went to find the queen.

***

"Did Phenos order you to report to him?"

They stood in Queen Mathial's room. Fury leaned against the door. No one would listen there. She'd check the rest of the room for spyholes and passages later. Finding them in the palace at home had been a game of hers for years.

"He did," Nikay said, and the Queen frowned. "I will report to him, just not the things that matter."

Mathial's eyes widened. "You would lie to him?"

"I am yours, Mistress. To deny him would simply give him cause to remove me, but if he thinks I am making him privy to your deepest secrets, he will fight to keep us by your side."

"You are brilliant." Mathial jumped forward and hugged Nikay. Fury held her face still. Aas long as she didn't hurt him, she'd tolerate it. "What will you tell him?"

"I will spin a tale of a lonely girl with no power to control her life, one who is so lonely she shares her deepest thoughts with her slaves."

"But that isn't a lie." Mathial reddened and stomped her foot.

"The best lie is most of the truth." Nikay tilted his head. "What I won't tell him is how you plot to gain control over your fate."

She stared at him wide-eyed.

"Is it possible?"

"I believe so, Mistress." Nikay bowed. "If I may, the first thing we should work on is your reading."

"Reading?" Mathial frowned.

"Would it not be useful to know when someone is lying to you about a document? What if they ask you to sign something?"

"But reading is hard."

"We have time." Nikay smiled at Mathial. "And you are a queen.

"

At that, nothing would do but to start immediately. Nikay used the liner from a drawer and a stub of an eyeliner pencil to draw out the letters. She learned them quickly. They put the liner back and hid the pencil.

A knock on the door came after the evidence had been hidden.

"My Queen, dinner is about to be served. Will you attend?" A woman called through the door.

"I am tired." Mathial opened the door. "Bring a meal for me and something for my slaves."

"As you will." The woman left.

A short time later slaves appeared carrying a table on which they set a feast for Mathial. Two bowls they put on the floor for Nikay and Fury.

"Bah, they try to insult me." Mathial scowled at the bowls. "The palace slaves eat better than that.

Fury sniffed at them. The being inside her stirred.

Poison.

"They are poisoned." Fury put them down. "Let me check your meal, Mistress."

Mathial stepped away from the table, turning pale.

"All clear." Fury bowed to her. "They dislike your slaves, not you."

Someone comes, behind the wall.

"Throw a temper tantrum, mistress, and throw the poisoned food against that wall." She tilted her head slightly. "Do not mention the poison."

"How dare they insult me by feeding my slaves slop!" Mathial shouted and stomped about the room. She picked up a bowl and heaved it against the wall where the contents slid messily to the floor. The second bowl followed, and a muffled curse came from the other side.

"What was that?" Mathial screamed.

"Rats, Mistress," Fury said.

The rest of the food followed the bowls as Mathial ranted. She would have thrown the table if she could have lifted it.

A timid knock at the door stopped the destruction.

"Mistress." The older woman slave knelt in the doorway. "How have we angered you?"

"My slaves will eat from my food." Mathial pointed to the mess. "Bring me a proper meal and do not think to insult me again. I heard rats in the walls. Send someone to deal with them."

The woman crawled out of the room, and Fury closed the door behind her.

"Well done, Mistress." Fury put her finger to her lips. "Someone was sent to spy on you, but they have left."

"Spy?" Mathial turned white. "This is the only place I am free from the slaves, and now you tell me they are spying on me?"

"Mistress, just as Nikay will lie to Phenos, we are going to lie to the spies."

"Knowledge is power, Mistress." Nikay surveyed the wall. "No one can approach without Fury knowing." He flashed a finger sign. "This is a sign telling you someone is listening. Say nothing you wouldn't wish Phenos to know."

"Who are you?" Mathial looked at them wide-eyed.

"We were sent to help you." Nikay got that faraway look he did when talking of his dreams.

"It is his gift," Fury said. "He knows things sometimes."

"Gift?" Mathial sat on the bed.

"People come." Fury held up a hand. She walked over to the door and threw it open. "Clean up that mess, Mistress should not live with such." The slaves scrambled to shovel up the food, then wash the wall and the floor. When Fury was content not a speck of food or shard of pottery remained, she ordered the slaves out. Soon after, another group of slaves brought trays of food. Once Fury declared them safe, the three of them ate.

When they came to remove the food and table, three slaves stayed to help Mathial get ready for the night. Nikay inspected the wall until the three had left.

"I could not find a spy-hole, but there is a thin place where one could hear what is being said in the room."

Mathial had been tucked into the huge bed.

"I hate going to sleep. My parents disappeared while I slept as a child, and I have been a prisoner ever since."

"We are here to guard you." Fury looked around the room. She could find no other passages or spy holes. The ceiling was hung with gauzy fabric. Someone could listen from above but not spy. She didn't think there would be a passage there.

"Sleep on my bed." Mathial patted the covers. "One on each side of me."

"Very well. Mistress." Fury climbed up beside the queen, and Nikay lay on the other side.

"Fury will watch," she whispered to Nikay. He nodded.

Mathial had already fallen asleep, Nikay slept soon after. Fury lay awake thinking about her family. She wished she could send a message to them. For a moment in the dark, she allowed herself to be weak and tears swelled in her eyes.

CHAPTER 17

A NATION ON THE MOVE

Lydia rode beside Shu through the night. Vakate had found a horse and rode on the far side from her.

"What's next, Shu?" Vakate turned in her saddle.

"We stop when we can no longer see the flames behind us." Shu didn't look back.

"And after that?" She asked. "Do you plan on conquering the world? They call you King of the World, after all."

"I will do what I must." Shu sighed and rolled his head on his neck. "Since before my grandfather's time, we have moved east as drought kills the land behind us. If you rode east for two weeks, you'd come to desert. There are some who live there, moving from spring to spring, but there is nothing for the steppes people there."

"So you will move into the Empire." Lydia stretched to stay awake.

"I will do what I have to for my people."

"You mentioned the number of tribes when you explained why you speak Imperial."

"Far to the east, long ago, tribes wandered the plains. When they met sometimes, they fought; sometimes they feasted and exchanged brides. Then people from the south began moving north. They were disciplined warriors, and no tribe could stand against them, so they wandered west. They met men in black who spoke a strange language and talked of a god who loved everyone. This was strange to us, for why should our God care about our enemies?

"The men were persistent, and some of the tribes began following that western god. Wars were fought. The followers of the western god banded together and spoke the language of the men in black to each other. The god must have blessed them since the tribes they fought gradually either joined them or moved north into the forests or south into the jungles.

"There was a plague and many people died, including the men from the west. Our people forgot much of what they learned, but the language stuck."

"Their God is my God." Lydia felt strange claiming God after all this time. She'd almost forgotten how, through the years, the certainty of her fate gave her peace.

"Really?" Shu sounded curious. "There are laws which remain from that time. An enemy must be given a chance to join the tribe. If they do, they start fresh. If there is an argument between two parties, they must try to work it out, and they make offering to God to help them."

"Some other time, I can answer questions." Lydia looked down.

"You don't want to convert us? The stories said the men in black clothes were always trying to convince the people to believe in their god."

"You believe in God, or you don't. It has little to do with me."

"But you believe, don't you?" Vakate asked from the darkness beyond Shu.

"I married a man and was happy. Then people he'd banished betrayed him. They abducted me and killed him. They tried to force me to guide them to a treasure an ancestor had found in the south.

They are dead. I tried to warn them, but they didn't listen."

"You are called Hoárr, after one of the northern gods." Vakate sounded angry. "Then you followed the spirit of the forest."

"Hoárr talked to me, as did the spirit, but does that mean my God doesn't exist? Shu rides beside me, yet there is an emperor in Lusia."

"I don't understand."

"I don't understand much either." Lydia stared into the darkness. "I grew up knowing God and my fate. Then all that changed, and I tried to leave my God behind. God stood with me until I was ready to return. He welcomed me and comforted my tears."

"Gods are demanding," Shu said. "There is always something they want from us."

"Are you saying you want nothing from anyone?" Lydia asked.

"I tried that, and it didn't work well."

"I'll say," Vakate said. "It took the god-touched to leap from the rock, and you followed within seconds. I thought I'd lost both of you."

"I didn't expect to survive, but my body acted on its own."

"God preserved us in the river." Lydia closed her eyes and tried to recapture her thoughts at the time. "I think I was a little mad. I challenged God to keep me alive."

"More than a little mad," Vakate snorted. "I have followed the forest spirit all my life, but I would never put my life in her hands."

"I never gave the gods much thought," Shu said. "Maybe I need to consider them."

"There is a place in the world for you to fill," Lydia said. "You are a light, and how you shine will change things. God doesn't coerce. You choose and God will take that choice and do what He will with it."

"Me a light?" Shu laughed.

"Not all light is gentle."

Shu rode in silence for the remainder of the night.

***

"My king, there is a legion formed up outside the walls of Hirnberg." A scout knelt in front of Shu.

"What do you say, Hoárr?" Shu raised an eyebrow.

"Why not start with a parley?" Lydia's gut churned. She didn't want to be his sounding board, but Shu never let her stray far from his side for long.

"It will have the advantage of confusing them," Vakate laughed. "It is the last thing they'll expect from the barbarian horde."

"Then we will parley." Shu nodded firmly. "Hoárr, Vakate, you will come with me. Wen will lead my guard." He looked down at the messenger. "Arrange the parley."

"What do I do?" The man's eyes widened.

"Leave your weapons aside and ride with your hands spread until they can see you. Then wait for them to come ask what you think you are doing." Vakate put her hands on her hips. "Tell them they can send their leader plus a few men as a guard. We meet in the open where everyone can see us."

"You heard her." Shu turned to the next person who wanted to speak to him.

***

"I hear you're off to a parley." Rodrigo came up to Lydia. "You think Shu would mind if I tagged along?"

"I'll ask. Wen is putting together the guard. I can probably convince him to include you."

"Thanks." Rodrigo put his hand on her shoulder. "Come by and visit. Aimee is dying to talk to you."

"After the parley, I'll come, and Shu can live without me or tag along."

"He's going to make you one of his queens." Rodrigo frowned slightly.

"No, he won't." Lydia fought back a surge of grief. "My husband died in front of me. I will have no other."

"You're young yet."

"I'm also supposed to become the Holy Mother." Lydia shivered. "I'm not sure anymore if I'm ready for that."

"Good, hang on to that uncertainty. You might not think so, but it is a gift."

"If you say so."

Rodrigo laughed and waved before vanishing into the crowd. Lydia went to find Wen.

"Rodrigo wants to be in the parley."

"Why?"

"He didn't say, but he's the Rehego Champion, so he might be useful."

"As long as he stays out of the way."

"I'll let him know."

Lydia found Rodrigo talking to one of the commanders not far away.

"Well?"

"Wen says you can come if you stay out of the way."

"Fantastic." Rodrigo smiled broadly. "By the way, ask Shu if he has a plan for if things go wrong."

"You are a pessimist." Lydia rolled her eyes.

"Expecting treachery is why I'm still alive. Then if things go well, it's a pleasant surprise."

"Lovely, I'll pass on the message, but I'm sure he's thought of it."

Shu grumbled as servants dressed him in fancy armour.

"The Champion will be joining us." Lydia spoke brusquely. "He asks if you have a plan for if the parley goes bad."

"He's a suspicious sort." Shu closed his eyes as the servants tried to arrange a tassel on his helmet. "I like that. The men will be horsed and ready. We are meeting mid-way between the armies. Our people will arrive before the legion." He tapped one servant on the shoulder. "See that Hoárr and Vakate have armour."

By the time the servants had fitted her, she understood Shu's impatience.

***

They rode out to where a legion soldier and the steppes rider stood waiting.

An equal number rode from the legion, arriving at the same time. The one in the officer's armour took his helmet off and scowled at Shu.

"If you don't turn and leave, the Legion will crush you."

"The Shung aren't easily crushed," Shu replied calmly. "You are welcome to try."

"If that man is a general, then I'm a dancing girl," Rodrigo whispered in Lydia's ear. "Be ready to get back out of the way. It's going to get messy."

"Die then!" the one in officer's armour shouted, his voice

breaking.

The men behind the officer reached down to put up loaded crossbows.

Rodrigo vaulted off Wen's back and kicked the closest of the bowmen off his horse. The motion distracted the others who turned to aim at Rodrigo who'd already jumped to the next horse and dragging his claw across the man's throat. At the same time, Vakate pulled up a short bow and shot the officer in the eye. The messenger was down with the legion soldier's sword in his armpit, but Wen rode down the soldier. Shu charged into the line of bowmen as they were caught between Rodrigo and the enemy in front of them. Seconds later the legion soldiers lay dead on the ground.

Lydia hadn't moved, even when a bolt glanced off her breastplate. Thunder sounded behind them as the horse archers swarmed past the failed parley.

Shu escorted Lydia and Vakate back to safety in the camp.

"The men know what to do without me yelling at them." He climbed onto a Rehego wagon and looked over the battle.

Lydia followed him with Vakate not far behind.

"Who are you?" Aimee frowned at Shu.

"I am Shu."

"Oh, Lydia's friend. Welcome to our fire." She widened her eyes as she took in Lydia's armour. "The metal suits you."

"Thanks, I think." Lydia sat with her legs over the side of the wagon. "This is Vakate, also a friend."

"You are welcome too." Aimee smiled then turned back to the battle. "You see papa?"

"If you are speaking of the Champion, he retreated after the horsemen passed us. He is a wise man."

"He's my papa. You want to hear what he did to that idiot you killed?" Aimee lowered her voice. "Mama doesn't want me telling the story, but it was so funny."

By the time she'd finished her tale, Shu had run the gamut from rage to helpless laughter.

"I'm going to have to pay more attention to that one. I want him on my side."

The rear of the legion collapsed, and the horsemen moved in for the kill.

"The legion expected us to attack by horse," Shu chuckled. "The parley gave us time to get around behind them."

"You said your people were the Shung?" Lydia asked. "I didn't know the people had a name."

"We don't. We've always been *the people*, but I needed something to say to that sheep in wolf's armour."

"Sounded good," Vakate said. "It is a new thing. It will bring your people together."

"Hey, you got room for one more up there?" Rodrigo stood below.

***

Lydia followed Shu into the tent the Shung had turned into a hospital.

"The legion broke and ran," Wen reported as Milene bandaged his arm. "As you ordered, we didn't pursue."

"We have to protect our people. We can't do that if we're chasing after cowards." Shu looked around the tent full of casualties. "They did some damage. We can't underestimate them."

"The council of Hirnberg wish to meet with you." Wen shook his head. "A lackey came out shaking in his boots while we were mopping up."

"Tomorrow will be soon enough." Shu turned away. "Well done, old friend. Get some rest."

Lydia nodded at Wen and followed Shu.

"What do you think about meeting with the townspeople?"

"They aren't warriors." Lydia rubbed her temple. "The legion can retreat and fight another day. The town can't move. Their fields have been trampled. They'll be worried about having enough food."

"I can't leave enemies behind me." Shu stretched his hand and clenched it.

"What if they aren't enemies?"

He stopped and stared at Lydia.

"All they want is to survive. Give them an option for survival which doesn't leave them hating you. Are you really going to drag all the women and children with you through your war with the Empire?"

"They can stay on the steppes."

"Hunger is already an issue. If Bhotta hadn't taken the food from

Hirnberg, it would be worse."

"There you are." Vakate walked up to them. "Sorry, don't like seeing wounded. I was reassuring your family you were fine."

"Lydia is suggesting we make peace with the town."

"It would be great if it works, but you'd have to leave some people to keep them thinking the right way."

"There will be those who don't want to leave the steppes." Shu paced in front of the women. "But the word has spread, and tribes are coming from all directions."

"Why not just leave the ones who want to stay behind? Appoint a good leader and let them work with the town? Make staying just one choice, not a matter of cowardice." Vakate folded her arms across her chest. "There were times in the forest when a tribe split because they wanted to go in different directions. We made sure we parted as friends. We even have a ritual where we trade tokens."

"See to it." Shu stopped in front of Vakate.

"Just like that?" Vakate didn't move. "Something like that needs authority. Everyone knows Hoárr is your left hand. What am I but the woman who nags at you?"

"If you have such a low opinion of yourself, do you wonder why I keep you nearby?" Shu put his hand on Vakate's shoulder. "You have a sharp tongue but a wise mind behind it. I value your presence."

Vakate stared at him mouth open.

"If I make you a part of my family, will that give you the knowledge of your authority?"

"A part of your family?" Her mouth dropped further open.

"Become my queen." Shu didn't move his hand. "My family likes you. You think of them at times like this."

"In my tribe, a man gives a woman a gift before she becomes his wife."

"What gift would you have me give you?"

"Freedom for my people in your midst." Vakate lifted her chin. "Let them decide to stay or go like any other of your people."

"Very well."

"Then I will become your queen." Vakate trembled under Shu's hand. "I can't change who I am. Are you sure you want me?"

"I have an entire people who worship the ground I walk on." Shu pulled her to him. "You treat me like a man. I need that."

He looked up at Lydia.

"Organize the wedding for tomorrow."

"Of course." Lydia couldn't restrain her grin.

***

Lydia moved through the camp ordering the feast, spreading the word to gather at the open space at the edge of camp, the only place big enough for everyone to witness the event. She talked to Shu's queens and Rodrigo and Milene.

Late in the night, she fell into her bedroll in the tent she shared with Vakate. The other woman was already asleep.

In the morning, women descended on the tent to dress Vakate. She chose to wear leather and furs like her people but decorated with beads and paint. Lydia left her getting ready and went to find Shu.

"You need to dress carefully for the wedding. Show your respect for your bride."

Out on the plains, a wagon had been set and decorated. People were already gathering. Musicians played lively tunes and children ran through the crowd.

"Wen, escort Shu to the wagon."

Shu's children came out and surrounded the wagon. They laughed and played, some of the older ones trying to impose some order.

The other queens would lead Vakate to the clearing, making their blessing clear.

Lydia mounted the steps onto the wagon and checked that everything she needed was on the small table.

Shu arrived to the raucous cheers of his people. He wore plain clothing, but it was of the finest quality. Gold threads were woven through his braided hair, beads glittered in the sun.

Vakate's arrival made the crowd go silent. She looked exotic in the midst of the Shung queens. They walked her to the wagon, then joined the children. Vakate climbed the stairs to stand beside Shu.

"Welcome." Milene had drawn runes on the wagon to spread the words spoken there across the crowd. "Shu takes a new queen. She has agreed to give herself to serve at his right hand."

Shu lifted an eyebrow but said nothing. Vakate blushed.

"It is the tradition of Vakate's people for a husband to give a gift to his wife." Lydia looked at Shu. "What gift will you give your bride?"

"As of this day, all slaves are free. Each family will be given a tent and a horse. They will have the right of any of our people to come and go as they please. If they choose to stay, they will be paid for their service. This is my gift to my bride."

Lydia had to wait for the cheering to die down before she continued.

"Shu and Vakate join not just as king and queen but as man and woman. In token of this, I give them these blades so they may guard each other's backs." She handed each of them exquisitely made blades, a matched set.

"They will become one blood." She had them prick their fingers with the knives and mingle their blood. Slowly through the afternoon, Lydia worked through the symbols on the table, weaving the bond between the two.

"May all gods and spirits bless you, king and queen, husband and wife." She finished by joining their hands. Wen led a horse to the wagon, and Shu picked up Vakate, jumped onto the horse and rode through the crowd into the camp.

"Now we feast!" Lydia called out and the people cheered.

The party lasted all night and all the next day. Just as it looked to be slowing, Shu and Vakate appeared. The celebrations started up again.

Late the second night, most of the people wandered off to bed. Riders converged on the now-empty space surrounding the wagon.

"You have chosen to honour your king by guarding his safety." She passed bags to the leaders of each squad who'd spent the last two days patrolling the steppes. "In token of this, there is a bead for each of you to weave into your hair." The men took their beads then returned to their tents. Other riders gathered and rode out.

Lydia stumbled down from the wagon. Rodrigo met her on a horse. "Let me take you to your tent to rest."

She slid off the horse in front of her tent, now hers alone, and walked in to collapse on her mat. Everything she could do to ensure her friend's happiness, she'd done. Now she let the grief flood from her heart and the tears from her eyes.

CHAPTER 18

BATTLE ON THE SAND

Leandra's opponent sent his first attack before the flag had finished dropping. A blast of flame came at her, then split to go around. She didn't trap much of the power from it, but the shield didn't take much to maintain.

Her response was simulacrum that dragged themselves out of the sand to clutch at his feet. He danced around. stomping on its hands, then glared at Leandra. Now he'd have to waste power shielding beneath him.

The response was a fist of sand rising to hammer down on her. She let it crash into the ground, then released the seeming which put her image twenty paces to the right. The gasp from the crowd reached her on the floor of the arena. A blast of air struck the man from behind, but it did little more than flutter his clothes. He sent another fistm and her wind curved around to strike beneath it, shattering it to dust.

When the dust cleared, Leandra had sent illusions of herself across the floor of the arena. Some of them waved at the crowd, others made cryptic motions with their hands.

While her opponent destroyed the illusions, Leandra sent a thread of power toward the imp, but it stuck its tongue out at her. The man watching spun on his heel and left. He looked to be little more than a puppet for the thing.

Her opponent had crushed the last of her seemings, so she used the thread to tap on his shoulder, making him spin around. Apollos pointed his hand at her and sent a tight beam of power at her. This time she had a broad shield for it to splash against and pull power from his attack. A pittance compared to what he got from the cheering crowd, but she'd take it.

Before she could respond, his next move made the sand of the arena boil. Litter from the crowd sunk beneath the surface. The shield acted like a boat letting her float on the sand.

She pushed a pillar of sand up beneath him, and as expected he'd shielded, so he lifted on the sand. With a wave of his hand, Apollos dismissed her pillar, then walked down through the air as if he was descending stairs.

Impressive.

Leandra had run through most of the runes she'd prepared ahead of time and hadn't touched him yet. Raphael's work in the pottery shop came to mind. She threw up walls of sand but filled them with the moisture from the air, then baked them with a blast of flame. This time she added a roof to hold him in. As quickly as she could build them, she threw more walls and roofs at him.

Then he appeared out of the sand in front of the heavy block. She'd reminded him earlier of the space beneath his feet. Monsters reared out of the earth and roared. They charged at her from all directions.

Now he was using illusions. She let them dissolve against her shield, stealing the little bit of power he'd put into them. Then a heavy blow struck against the back of her shield, sending her to her knees. *Stupid.* One of them was a golem. The power of the name on its forehead heated her back. She liquified the sand beneath the creature. It wouldn't hold it for long, but it gave her a second to think. She laughed and used the lure of solid footing to move the creature where she wanted it.

It erupted from the floor of the arena and shook the block she'd made to trap Apollos.

He clapped in her direction. Then his face went blank.

After all this, he was just now getting serious.

Leandra cursed her overconfidence as she drew runes and dropped them at her feet, needing to add or erase one stroke to activate them.

A bird formed from fire swept over the arena, and the sand steamed as it passed close to the ground. It banked at the far end of the open space, and a barrier briefly glittered. The audience was shielded so she could stop worrying about her work overflowing into the crowd.

The fire roared as the thing raced toward Leandra. She kicked up a rune and slashed at it. Ice spikes sprang from the sand, piercing the bird through the body. Cutting at another rune created a ball of ice around the thing. It flamed against the ice, but she'd put a power sink into the rune. The hotter it got the more power she drew from it.

Another bird swooped across the space, but no heat came from it. She flipped a hand and dismissed the illusion. Since she'd been working ice, Leandra encased Apollos with pillars of ice, remembering to freeze the ground beneath his feet.

He exploded the ice, sending blocks high into the air. For a second, he staggered on the sand, unused to the cold most likely. The golem broke through the cube and roared, stomping toward her. Apollos stumbled away, catching the attention of the thing and it lunged forward to attack. Leandra blew him back with a blast of wind, then reached out to catch an ice block. She made it as hard as rock, then brought it streaking faster than an arrow to smash on the golem's forehead. One of the letters in its name chipped, and the thing fell to pieces.

Apollos was on his feet and sent wind around the arena gathering sand and lifting it high into the air. Shivers ran down Leandra's spine as she remembered a similar move by Lichou, one which had destroyed the arena.

She couldn't see him through the storm, but his magic was a bright light in her mind at the far end. Throwing a shield that far would use up just about all her remaining power, but her fear overruled her mind telling her this arena wouldn't collapse.

The shield would stop the flow of power, disrupting his concentration just enough to let the sand drop harmlessly to the floor.

It worked exactly as she'd planned, only she hadn't realized how much sand had been hoisted into the air. It landed on her with a crushing weight making it impossible to breathe. She had one chance. Her fingers drew a rune she'd promised herself never to use.

Power flowed into her. She burst from the sand and released the rune. Landing lightly, Leandra looked around for the next attack but couldn't see Apollos.

There at the far end, he was buried in the sand, not moving. Leandra ran toward him, then pushed the sand away. His face was blue. Using the thinnest thread of wind, she filled his lungs, then drew the air out. The arena spun around her, but she repeated the action until he breathed on his own.

The announcer was shouting, and the crowd screamed and shouted, stomping their feet. Power flowed into her from something at her waist.

Apollos opened his eyes, and he strengthened quickly.

"You saved me." His voice was a rasp.

"I was told it was bad form to kill an opponent." Leandra shrugged.

"I'll be back, and I'll beat you next time." He pushed himself to his feet and walked off the sand.

"There won't be a next time." Then Leandra thought of the man with the imp on his shoulder. She needed to find out who he was. The only way was to come back and battle again. With a grimace, she lifted her hand and waved to the crowd.

***

Leandra walked into the Hall, exhausted, but with two gold coins in her pocket. She found Trader slumped in a corner of the hall with Raphael trying to get her to talk.

"Something's wrong, but she won't talk."

"It's all right, kitten."

"Did you call me?" He looked at her quizzically and guilt struck her.

"I did, I'm sorry."

"That's all right." Raphael shrugged and pointed to Trader. "What do we do about her?"

Leandra dropped to the floor beside Trader and held out the two coins.

"I had a chat with the men your uncle bet your money with. I convinced them to give your money back."

"I don't want it." Trader pushed her hand away. "Those people are trouble. I won't touch anything to do with them."

"They promised never to bother you." Leandra leaned her head back. "They will keep their promise."

"They're liars."

"They are, but I am not."

Trader looked at her with pity in her eyes.

"They have their claws in you. They will ignore me because you are more valuable. I will not take their money." She sighed and pushed herself up. "I will start again tomorrow."

Leandra stared at the coins in her hand.

"When did an eight-year-old become wiser than me?"

***

Leandra worked at Theniar's pottery shop, thinking about what Trader had said. The girl had returned almost to her normal self, finding Hojiam a new position and running about with Raphael trading the curiosities he'd collected in his pockets.

"You aren't paying attention." Theniar stopped her. "Something will end up broken." He led her back to the tiny room he had his stove in and made tea.

"I disappointed Trader," Leandra admitted, "and it's bothering me more than it should."

"Perhaps it should bother you." Theniar handed her a cup. "If disappointing our friends made no difference to us, are they truly friends?"

"I'm learning wisdom from everyone these days." Leandra hung her head.

"At least you're learning." Theniar tilted his head. "I heard rumours of a challenger in the arena who destroyed Apollos, then saved his life. That wouldn't be someone I know would it?"

"I got angry and let myself be manipulated. It won't happen again."

"I'm sure it will." Theniar smiled. "I keep vowing to never hire strays again, but..." He shrugged. "I expect you were trying to help Trader. I heard about her uncle placing a bet close to a gold coin."

"She's afraid they have their hooks in me now."

"I'm sure they think they do." Theniar sipped at his own cup. "They live by manipulation and fear, so they don't understand anything else. If you're going to rid yourself of them, you'll need to speak their language."

"I see." Leandra sat back and took a long drink from her tea. "I may not be able to work here much longer. Certain people will want me to perform for them."

"I will miss you." Theniar shook his head. "But I do have to wonder who Trader will bring me next. Kitten will have to find a new place to practice, though I don't think there is much left for him to do."

"Thank you for your kindness."

***

The men waited for her along a deserted stretch of road. Leandra was sure the emptiness was no accident.

"Lovely boy you have there." One of them reached out to pat Raphael's head and drew his hand back with a curse.

"Surely you didn't think I would let him wander unprotected." Leandra smiled at the man. "What do you want?"

"The crowds want to see the person who defeated Apollos back."

"Crowds are fickle." Leandra waved her hand, letting a rune float down on the man's hand.

"They are, but entertaining them is profitable."

"I don't use magic for money. It corrupts the user." Leandra waited until their frowns deepened. "But it happens that I have some unfinished business there."

"You will compete tomorrow." The men turned and left.

"The arena?" Raphael frowned at Leandra. "That's where

Trader's uncle got hurt."

"I will try not to get hurt." Leandra put her hand on his shoulder. "But I saw the imp there. No other method has shown me where it is."

"I can help."

"I know." Leandra smiled at him. "And you will."

They walked the rest of the way to the Hall.

"Papa!" Raphael shrieked and ran over to Cameto who swept the boy up in his arms. Hojiam was talking with Pounjou, Teekja and Lupji.

"Let's get inside and find a place to talk."

"There is the matter of paying the bills." The doorkeeper had her arms on her hips.

Leandra dropped some coins on the counter.

"That should cover a week."

The doorkeeper handed out tokens and made notes in the book.

"I'll room with Pounjou and the rest." Hojiam grinned at Leandra. "You catch up with your husband."

"That's great. Make sure they talk to Trader about jobs."

Cameto followed Leandra to her room, still with Raphael holding on like a burr.

"This is a pleasant surprise." Cameto leaned against the wall. "I thought you were up north by the Oasis yet."

"I have a mess to clean up." Leandra sat beside him and felt his strength. She told the story from the beginning, sparing herself not at all.

"Let me see those eyes of yours." Cameto held Raphael out at arm's length. "They are quite something when you look carefully."

"People see what they expect to see, I don't think many people aside from Trader have noticed."

"Trader?"

"Friend of Raphael's." Leandra put her head back.

"She's your friend too. She's just worried about you."

"I know, kitten." Leandra sighed. "Another mess for your mama to clean up."

"If you weren't cleaning up your mess, you'd be working on someone else's." Cameto put his hand on her knee. "You were fighting for your son's life. I'd say you did well."

"Now, I'm back in the arena, hoping to see the Lusian carrying the imp."

"I will have to come and watch. I've never seen magic on the scale you're describing."

"Be careful. I can't put a protection rune on you like Raphael. It would drain you too quickly."

"I have my own ways of protecting myself." Cameto grinned.

"Don't underestimate them." Leandra swivelled to look at him. "They are going to get very angry before we're done."

"I'll keep that in mind."

"I've told my story. Why are you here?"

"Someone abducted Nikay and the princess. Indications suggested they were being taken south." Cameto shook his head. "Met some people who'd been taken as slaves heading north. They told a wild story about the slavers being killed. None of them could agree on anything."

"Fury in action?" Leandra snuggled closer to Cameto. "I don't know her well, but it doesn't sound like her."

"Being made a slave would get anyone riled up, but why abduct them to make them common slaves? There's no political purpose to that."

"So, we're looking for those kids too." She sighed. "I don't know enough about them to do a tracking rune. We'll have to do things the old-fashioned way. I wish Rodrigo were here."

***

The Lusian didn't show up for the next match, but Cameto picked up some gossip about the booth. It was reserved for highly ranked Lusians, those who'd arrived years ago when the Empire fractured.

"It would make sense if one of them wanted to recreate their power base in the Confederacy. Even the biggest pile of wealth will disappear after a while." Cameto rubbed Leandra's back. "I will see what I can learn on the street. People are always willing to talk about those at the top of the heap."

Leandra drew out the matches, making them dramatic for the crowd. Her keepers always made sure to recover the gem at her waist which collected the power from the crowd. The flow of power was intoxicating, and she stored as much as she could hold at the same time refusing the high.

The rune she'd planted on the man who thought she worked for him had done its work. She had a map of all the places in the city he travelled and, more importantly, the spots he returned to consistently.

Trader's efforts to earn money worried Leandra. The girl had taken on a hardness. She didn't laugh much and no longer spent much time with Raphael.

Leandra followed the route to Zafre's courtyard.

"I'm concerned that Trader's ambition is destroying her." Leandra had explained about the money and most of what came after.

"She is losing her centre," Zafre said. "It happens. The harder she works, the further she will be from her goal until she forgets the goal entirely. Then she won't be worth training."

"Isn't there something you can do?"

"I train them, but I can't fix them." He sighed, looking his age for the first time. "There may be only one person who can reach her, if it isn't too late."

CHAPTER 19

CONSPIRACIES

"I dreamed about trouble last night." Nikay rolled over and looked at Fury across the sleeping queen.

"Any details?" Fury wrinkled her nose. "Trouble could be a lot of things."

"Sorry, it was pretty fuzzy." He climbed out of bed and walked around the room. The dreams always left him restless.

"We'll deal with it." Fury stretched like a cat and sat up. "What do you think of our queen?"

"She's never been allowed to grow up," Nikay said. "No one's taught her the least bit about ruling, so she is the perfect pawn. That Phenos drinks up everything I say about her weakness, but as long as she's obedient, she's safe from him."

"Teaching her to read and think is going to put her in danger."

"It will only be a different kind of danger." Nikay stopped in front of Fury. "They will either breed her to get an even more compliant queen or recognize that the council holds all the power and kill her."

"Which would be worse for Belandria?"

"I don't know. I don't think either would be good. Somebody wanted us for a power play, and I don't think they've given up on that."

"We need allies." Fury jumped off the bed. "Three kids don't have much chance of changing anything."

"What about her uncle?"

"I got the feeling he's on a tight leash. We need to find a way to help him slip the leash."

"We're back to three kids against who knows what?"

"What are you talking about?" Mathial moaned and sat up.

"Plotting, Mistress," Nikay said. "We need to do more than walk around the palace."

"What can we do?" Mathial scrubbed her face. "I'm not allowed out of the palace for my own safety. It's been like that forever."

"Maybe that's where we start." Fury looked toward the door. "People coming."

The slaves came in and dressed Mathial for the day, then left promising to send something for breakfast.

"I hate it when they do this." Mathial minced across the room. "They've wrapped it so tight I can barely walk."

"I don't like it." Nikay moved his head trying to catch a piece of the dream. "Can you fix it, Fury?"

"I've been watching them long enough, probably." Fury fiddled with the cloth wrap.

"That's better." Mathial heaved a deep breath.

"Walk like the dress is still too tight." Nikay put his hands to his head.

"You are my slave. Remember your place." Mathial's face reddened.

"Apologies, Mistress." Fury spoke in the background while noises clashed in Nikay's head. "He gets like this when he dreams."

"His dreams come true?" Mathial asked in wonder, anger vanished.

"Always."

"Then I will forgive him this time."

Someone knocked at the door, and slaves brought in the table full of food and left.

"Don't eat the yellow fruit," Fury warned them. "There's something wrong with it."

"If we don't eat it, they'll be suspicious." Nikay shook his head, dismissing the conflicting memories of his dream.

"I'll eat it. It is supposed to slow us down. Fury will take care of it."

"I thought *her* name was Fury?" Mathial asked as she reached for the bread.

"It's complicated." Fury started on the yellow fruit sticking her tongue out. "Tastes disgusting. You can complain about the taste." She spat out her mouthful and threw it on the plate.

"You're scaring me." Mathial looked from one to the other.

"Just remember, we're here to protect you no matter what happens."

They finished their meal.

"What did you have planned for today?" Nikay asked.

"There's a special flower blooming in the garden. I want to go see it."

"Who told you about the flower?"

"One of the slaves said something while they were dressing me."

"That will be it then." Nikay looked around the room. "We haven't been in the garden before."

"It is in the middle of the palace. I used to go there a lot."

"Let's go then."

"But if something bad is going to happen?" Mathial clasped her hands together.

"We are here to stop it." Fury took the queen's hands. "Trust us."

They left the room, Mathial taking short little steps and breathing too fast. Slaves knelt as they passed. Nikay made note of the ones who looked concerned. There were more than he expected.

They arrived at a long hallway, open on the left to the garden below.

"This is it," he whispered. Fury nodded and Mathial's breathing quickened again.

Two concealed, two more ahead. Fury's fingers moved rapidly. Nikay nodded.

The attack still came as a surprise to Nikay. A section of the wall they'd just passed swung open, and two men with swords jumped out. Nikay dragged Mathial away as Fury went on the attack.

The first man she slapped the sword away from her and kicked him over the rail into the garden. The second hung back.

"Push him. Back the others are coming." Nikay held Mathial upright. Fury nodded and charged at the man, kicking and punching. He retreated and Nikay carried Mathial into the secret entrance. The attacker charged ahead before he could close the door. Fury spun and kicked out behind her sending a second man over the rail.

The two remaining attackers kept out of reach of Fury's hands and feet. Hanging on a hook was a lantern. Nikay grabbed it. As an attack pushed Fury away from the open door, one of the men lunged into the passageway and Nikay threw the lantern into the man's face. Flames burst over the attacker. He opened his mouth to scream, but no sound came out. Even on fire, the man tried to swing his sword, but it caught on the low ceiling. Nikay turned and kicked like a mule to send the man staggering back. Fury reappeared, holding the last attacker's sword arm and throat, then slammed him into the flaming man sending both over the rail.

She ran into the passage and pulled the door closed. Only a tiny hole allowed light in. Chaotic shouting sounded on the other side of the door. Nikay couldn't tell if the newcomers were more attackers or coming to the rescue. He tugged on Fury's arm, and she nodded.

Her squeezing past him holding the unconscious queen was tight, but then she put a hand on his shoulder and led him along the secret passage. Other passages opened, but he only felt them as changes in the air. Fury kept going straight until she hit the end.

"Going to check for a way to get out," she whispered. Her hand moved away, and knocking and scratching sounds filled the cramped space. Then a click and the wall in front of them swung away letting in light.

They crept out of the tunnel and looked around. It had opened into an alley. The buzz of many people floated from the open end.

"What do we do?" Nikay asked. "We can't carry Mathial out onto the street, and we can't go back to the hall over the garden either."

"There's a lamp by the door," Fury said. "We go back and try the side passages until we find a way out."

"I guess." Nikay took a last look at the open air. "We remember this." He carried Mathial back into the passage. Fury found flint and steel and lit the lantern, then closed the door. Nikay passed Mathial over to Fury and took the lantern. The passages were labelled, but not in a script Nikay recognized. He tried to remember the turns he took memorizing the name of the passage to the alley. Mathial moaned and twisted in Fury's arms.

"If she wakes up in here, we won't be able to keep her quiet," Fury whispered.

"If the next exit is clear, we'll take it." Nikay held up the lantern. "I've seen a lot more spyholes than doors."

Fury nodded.

When Nikay heard voices, he held up a hand and Fury hung back.

"...who ordered an attack?" Phenos sounded like he was in the passage with them. The reply was muffled.

"Find out and eliminate whoever is responsible. Locate the queen and make sure she is secure. We need her for a while yet. Bring her male slave to me."

Another muffled reply and Phenos muttered under his breath. A door slammed, and a locked clicked. Nikay started forward again. The passage ended, but with the lantern it was easy to find the mechanism.

"We clear on the other side?" Fury nodded and Nikay opened the door. He examined it as Fury carried Mathial out. "Ah," he pushed a section of the panelling. "So we can get back in." The door closed with the softest of clicks. "They are looking for Mathial. We need a good story."

Mathial moaned again and flailed in Fury's arms. Fury put her on her feet.

"We were attacked, but other men came and saved us. You ran away and don't remember how we ended up here." Nikay held her gaze until she nodded. "You are the queen. Be strong."

***

"My mistress saw the attackers and ran. I think others were fighting too. I stayed with my mistress." Nikay trembled as he reported to Phenos. "Every time we heard people ahead, she ran down a different hall. I was completely lost until the other servants found us."

"How is your mistress?" Phenos sounded sincerely concerned.

"Terrified, Master. She huddles in her bed and refuses to do anything. She won't even eat until we've tasted all the food."

"I will find those responsible and have them punished." He flipped a hand, dismissing Nikay.

Nikay walked back to Mathial's room where she shivered on the bed while Fury held her. *Listeners.* Fury warned him. He nodded and sat leaning against the wall until she said they were gone.

"What do we do?" Mathial asked. "They're trying to kill me."

"I think it is time to leave the cage." Nikay sagged against the way. "I'm not sure Phenos bought the whole story, but he's not ready to move yet. If we get the queen out of his reach, then maybe we can find more people to help."

"Leave?" Mathial shook harder. "How will I survive?"

"You'll have us." Fury squeezed gently.

"First thing we need is more clothes. Mistress can't go out dressed like the queen. We'd get caught right away." Nikay rubbed his eyes.

"Something to prove who she is to whomever we talk to would be helpful."

"We go to my uncle," Mathial said. "He'll know what to do."

"First we need to get away."

***

The clothes turned out to be simple. Mathial demanded more clothes for her slaves. She wanted to dress them up more, she said.

The outfits were still based on the grey fabric all slaves wore, but they had tunics, which left Nikay's legs uncomfortably bare, and a dress, which Fury pronounced suitable for fighting.

Mathial wanted to bring all her jewellery, thinking to sell it. While Nikay approved of the pragmatism, trying to sell her jewellery would tell anyone searching for them where to look. He'd counted on that same thing when he'd dropped his ring. They'd bring the stuff to keep Mathial happy and think of something.

More importantly, she had a disc on a chain which was proof of her status as queen. She insisted anyone not of royal blood who wore it would die. He'd seen enough strange things to believe her.

The last issue was the slave collars. He expected they could be tracked, and even if not, they were a weakness. Any citizen could give an order, and they'd have to obey unless Mathial was there to override the command. She needed to be kept out of sight.

"We head out after supper." Nikay sat facing Fury and Mathial on the bed. "Fury tears the wall open where the listeners hide. We escape through the secret passages. I am reasonably sure I can find my way to the door in the alley."

"They'll know to come after us." Fury frowned.

"I expect they will, but it will give us a lead. There is too much risk going through the halls. One wrong person sees us and Phenos will be after us."

"What if we dress Mathial before we leave?"

"She is instantly recognizable." Nikay put his head in his hands. "Why don't we do a test run?"

"What are you thinking?" Fury leaned back.

"Mistress, have you ever seen the stars?" Nikay looked over at Mathial who sat shaking.

"No, I would like to."

"Great. If we go to the garden, we'll be able to see some of the stars from there. It gives us an excuse if we get caught. After a few visits, no one will think twice about it."

"I like that better than wandering in the passages." Fury nodded and grinned. "If I wear the dress, I can put on more clothes under it."

"I will carry the jewellery in my wrap. I used to sneak treats away from functions that way." Mathial's eyes were bright.

"Tomorrow night we become stargazers." Nikay leaned forward. "We must act completely normal, or it will create suspicion."

"They all think I'm a fool." Mathial frowned. "It will be a pleasure to trick them."

"Let's get some rest." Fury pulled back the cover for Mathial, then Nikay lay on one side and Fury on her other side as they had since the first night.

They passed the day in the library, Nikay reading from the

history texts Phenos approved for her. That evening, Mathial waved off the slaves who came to prepare her for bed.

"I wish to see the stars." Mathial clapped her hands. "They were mentioned in the history."

"Mistress," one began to object. Mathial slashed her hand, and the woman paled.

"Come, we will go to the garden." Mathial swept out of the room, Nikay and Fury following, the women servants brought up the rear.

"You may go. Fury will dress me for the night." Mathial flipped her hand and the servants scuttled away.

"Be prepared to speak to Phenos," Nikay whispered softly.

Mathial nodded without ceasing her chatter about seeing the night sky.

He waited for them in the garden.

"My queen," he bowed slightly. "It is late."

"Of course, it is," Mathial craned her neck to look up. "How else can we see them?"

"There is a better place to view them over here." Phenos led them to a platform raised above most of the trees. "I am told your mother was also fond of the stars." He pointed up. "That one, the brightest in the sky, your people call the Cat." For the next hour, he pointed out star after star, drawing the constellations with his finger.

"I have to admit, the stars make me homesick. They are the same over the lands where I once lived."

Mathial yawned, then blushed.

"My apologies, I will retire for the night. Thank you for sharing your knowledge of the heavens with me."

Nikay walked ahead of her and Fury beside her, deep in thought.

"That was unexpected." Fury threw herself on the bed.

"I may have underestimated Phenos." Nikay leaned against the door. "I have a better idea of how he plans to use our mistress."

"I'm too tired for this." Mathial rubbed her eyes. She pulled at the cloth wrapping her. Nikay closed his eyes while fabric rustled and the girls muttered.

"All right, climb into bed," Fury said. Nikay opened his eyes as Mathial crawled under the covers, then he joined them on the bed.

For the next week, Phenos joined them every night in the garden. His knowledge of the night sky was prodigious, and he never repeated anything unless asked by the queen.

"He is different," Mathial said while getting ready for bed one night, "almost civilized."

"He is wooing you," Nikay said from his position at the door. "His plan is to marry you and become king."

"That's impossible." Mathial flipped her hand. "He's not of the right lineage."

"He must think it possible." Nikay rolled his eyes. Mathial stormed over to him and slapped him.

"Don't argue with me." She raised her hand to hit him again. Nikay caught her hand and went to his knee.

"Forgive me, Mistress. If I anger you, punish me, but take care not to hurt your hand."

Mathial pulled her hand away, turning deep red.

"I'll forgive you this once." She stomped over to Fury and yanked at her wrap. It fell to the floor leaving Mathial wearing only a gossamer-thin shift. Before he could close his eyes, Nikay saw the scars marking her back.

CHAPTER 20

INVASION

Shu ordered the people to gather at the wagon where he and Vakate had married a week back. Lydia replaced the wagon at its spot and had Milene check the runes on it.

Now she stood on the wagon with Shu and Vakate, along with his oldest queen.

"The Shung are moving from the steppes."

Lydia looked at the people. Some were excited, others hesitant. This could fracture his people.

"I am your king. I could order all of you to follow me to the new world on the other side of the river. But I will not." A rustle went through the crowd. "I freed all slaves. I will not treat you as slaves." A cheer interrupted him. He waited until it died down and then continued as if there had been no interruption.

"Hanshu will rule those who remain on the steppes until her son is old enough. She speaks with my voice." He crossed his arms and scanned the crowd, then nodded and waved the older queen forward. "Give your loyalty to your queen!" The crowd shouted and waved their fists.

"Those who come with me, you will be broken into cohorts. I will go ahead with the warriors and make the land safe for you. Of the families who come after, some will settle here and some there. Be good neighbours to the people who live there. If you wish to live in peace, you must bring peace with you. If you do not desire peace, then ride with me and there will be blood enough to sate you." The people talked with a rising buzz, some waving their hands as if arguing.

"Whether you ride with the warriors or follow with the families, you are my people. I am Shu, King of the World, and I tell you this." He climbed down from the wagon and jumped onto a horse which might have been the wind given flesh. He rode with no saddle or reins and galloped in a wide circle as his people cheered him.

"If he falls and breaks his neck, I won't take care of him." Vakate stepped up beside Lydia.

"Little danger of that." Lydia smiled as she watched.

"I will ride with his warriors." Vakate folded her arms. "Someone needs to keep an eye on him."

"I will rest easier knowing you are with him."

"You are not coming?" Vakate turned to look at Lydia.

"I am, but I am not truly Shung." She looked up at the blue sky. "To be honest, I'm not sure who I am anymore."

"You are Hoárr." Vakate looked back at Shu, a smile curling her lips.

"Maybe now, but not in times to come."

"Let that time come when it may."

***

Lydia went to find Rodrigo. Maybe he had some wisdom for her. With all the commotion going on she felt lost.

She found him talking to Hallith.

"I, at least, will be staying on the steppes." Hallith had her hands on her hips.

"It isn't my place to tell you where or how to live." Rodrigo leaned against the wagon. "I am Champion, not king, and even if I were king, I wouldn't order you to do anything."

"We need stability for the children. Many of the ones you brought are still here."

Rodrigo sighed. "I suspect nothing I say will convince you, but you need to find your own path. It will be different from what the Rehego were in the Empire, but that is a good thing. The exile is ended, not because we have returned to our homeland, but because we have learned we are Rehego without it. Perhaps someday Rehego will travel across the world to learn from each other. Move forward toward that day. Don't look back to what was."

He stepped forward and put his hands out.

"Give me your hands."

Hallith slowly placed them into his.

"Close your eyes and feel the Balance." Rodrigo's hands glowed. "I didn't understand until I felt it."

Hallith's eyes widened and her mouth dropped open. For a brief moment she shone in the sun, then she was just Hallith again, pragmatic, wise, caring.

"Welcome, Grandmother." Rodrigo smiled crookedly. "Maybe someday you'll forgive me for this."

"I don't know whether to thank you or kill you." Hallith wiped at her face.

"Mother had a vision for the Rehego, and she raised her children to fulfill it. It is time to bring new visions to bear."

"Go in peace, Champion. You will be always welcome at my fire."

Lydia wandered away before either of them noticed her.

***

Lydia stood on Shu's left, Vakate on his right as they met the delegation from Hirnberg.

"We hear that you have taken another queen." The man in well-made but worn clothes stepped forward with a box. "Please accept a small token of our congratulations."

Shu took the box and opened it. Within were two cups, formed of gold twisted about what looked like enormous eggs.

"These were made by one of our goldsmiths from eggs laid by a giant bird in the far south. The box is carved from local wood by one of our master carvers." The man pointed at each item as he talked.

Shu handed the box to Vakate who peered at it curiously.

"My thanks for your good wishes." Shu smiled a flash of sunlight on his face before his normal emotionless expression returned. "About your city. I have no interest in ruling it. I know nothing of cities. I ask that you welcome my people who come to trade, and your people will be welcome on the steppes."

The man stared at Shu.

"You don't want tribute?"

"If we have need, we will ask as friends. If you have need, ask."

"Our gates will always be open to your people." The man straightened. "The legion took many of our young men, and the fields need planting. If any of your people wish to help, we will share the harvest."

"Vakate, see to it."

She nodded, a smile on her face. A week ago, it would have been Lydia who was just as happy to let Vakate do the work.

"If that is all." Shu nodded to the man.

"My people will be happy that they no longer need fear destruction." The man bowed deeply.

They returned to their camp, now just on the far side of the river.

"I will speak to Hanshu," Vakate said, "then join you for our meal." She walked away toward the centre of the camp.

"I was surprised that you required no tribute or loyalty from Hirnberg." Lydia walked beside Shu.

"You once suggested I leave behind friends, not enemies." Shu glanced over at her. "Are you upset that Vakate has replaced you?"

"Say relieved," Lydia laughed. "She takes joy in being your right hand."

"Good." Shu stopped to face her. "We ride at dawn. I would have you ride with us."

"I will be there, Shu."

"Do you wonder that I never tried to make you queen?"

"I would have said no." Lydia let the stab of grief pass through her.

He walked away. Lydia headed toward her tent. She'd switched it for a much smaller one, but it still felt lonely.

"I still haven't decided if it is an act, or if he really is that straight-forward." Rodrigo stepped up beside her.

"I think he is much more complicated than he appears." Lydia didn't slow.

"I have no doubt he is complicated," Rodrigo laughed. "I'm so devious, I have to see it in everyone else."

"You are honest in your own way," Lydia snorted.

"Now you wound me." Rodrigo put his hand over his heart. She laughed and slapped his arm. For some reason, she felt better.

The warriors assembled as the sun lifted above the horizon behind them. Lydia couldn't guess how many there were. Even more would follow in the days to follow bringing families and everything they own. It wasn't an invasion as much as a migration.

The world was changing this morning.

They rode out at an easy pace. Vakate had given orders not to ride across any planted field. Skeins of riders followed the border between the forest and fields, others rode in the ditches on either side of the road. Even so, Lydia expected it would take hours for the cohort to pass the gates of the town. As promised, the gates were wide open, and people filled them watching the spectacle. Some of them waved.

Shu wasn't in a hurry. He'd made it clear he'd rather be slow than spread out the cohort and make it vulnerable to attack.

"If it comes to battle, the fields will get trampled." He looked over at Vakate.

"Of course." She rolled her eyes. "But no reason to destroy what we need before time. If you want people to see us as a force for stability, we must create stability."

Lydia thought he might have smiled just a tiny bit.

A week into the ride, they'd passed villages burnt out and hopeless. Shu left men to help rebuild until the next wave arrived. They would join the tail of the ride. Word spread ahead of them, and people came out to welcome the host.

"The legion is trying to deny us the food of the land." Shu clenched a fist. "We send scouts out in the morning to find them. They will not destroy more of my land."

The legion had fortified a village a day's ride ahead of them. Shu sent riders out to gather the host's commanders.

"We will surround them and destroy them. Any who wish to surrender will pledge allegiance to the Shung."

"Not all the men will be willing to fight," Lydia said. "Remember they took the young men from the towns and villages."

"If they fight, we will fight. If they surrender, we will spare them."

"Shu, if you allow, I will ride ahead and pay a visit to the legion." Rodrigo smiled. "I think the men will be much more willing to defy their orders if they know your intentions."

"Take care I've come to value your opinion." Shu nodded at Rodrigo.

***

He rode into the evening and Lydia retired to her tent. A young girl waited for her and helped her undress. She'd appeared the first night they'd camped.

"Thank you, Shyzu." Lydia felt lighter with the armour off. She'd had to loosen the straps to make room for her growing belly.

"How was your son today?" Shyzu put the armour on its rack and draped a soft robe over Lydia's shoulders.

"I think he must like riding; he doesn't kick while we're on a horse."

"A true Shung." Shyzu set out tea and a light meal.

"Lydia?" Aimee called from outside the tent.

"Let her in."

Aimee ducked in and paced around the tent.

"Papa has gone somewhere, and Mama won't tell me where."

"Then I will not either." Lydia let Shyzu help her down on a cushion. "But stay and drink tea with me. I could use the company."

"When is the baby coming?" Aimee flopped bonelessly on a cushion.

"I've lost track of the time since I was abducted from my husband's home." Lydia sighed, "That was the depth of winter. It is now well into spring."

"Likely when summer gives in to the fall." Shyzu poured tea for Aimee. "Babies come when they feel like it."

"I can't imagine waiting that long." Aimee sipped at her tea and tore off a piece of bread.

"Your time will come." Shyzu smiled. "Such a beautiful young woman."

"Not any time soon." Aimee held her hands out between her and Shyzu.

"No, I don't expect any time soon." Lydia smiled behind her teacup. "You are young yet."

Aimee looked caught between wanting to be older and younger. She finally took a bite of bread.

"You think Papa will be all right?"

"I do." Lydia took a piece of bread for herself. "He is the essence of what it means to be Rehego."

"He is the Champion." Aimee sighed. "I think being Champion is hard on him, but it doesn't stop him."

"Lives worth living are hard at times." Lydia heard a faint chuckle in her heart. *I may be a slow learner, but I do learn.*

"I guess." Aimee put her cup down and sprawled on the cushion. "In some ways, I was born just six years ago. I look thirteen or maybe fourteen now. At one point, I was also 4000 years old, not anymore. The Cup is gone, and I don't know why I'm still here. I think Papa called me back."

"Golden One," Shyzu bowed to her, "perhaps your work is to shine like the sun and bring hope to people."

"I did that as the Cup." Aimee shook her head. "But the Cup is gone."

"Yet here you are," Shyzu said. "You are special. Many children remember your kindness inside the fence. It isn't magic, but it is real."

"There aren't any children here." Aimee rolled over and buried her face. "It's boring."

"There are children. Some of the servants brought their families. My daughter is also bored."

"Your daughter?" Aimee sat up. "You don't look any older than me."

Shyzu laughed. "Maybe you can meet her one day."

"I'd like that."

"I'd love to sleep here, but Mama would worry." Aimee dragged herself to her feet.

"I'll walk you back to your wagon." Shyzu bowed again.

They left chattering about Shyzu's daughter.

Lydia curled around her stomach.

"Sleep well, dear one."

Her baby kicked as if she'd heard.

***

"I won't promise they will mutiny," Rodrigo yawned widely. "But given an opportunity to lay down their arms, they might be eager to do so. The problem is the hard-core legionnaires who will cut down any whom they see as cowards. Those will be placed behind the conscripts to push them forward."

"They would be foolish to come from behind their walls." Shu frowned. "Even if we were to break through, they would be at an advantage. They've chosen their ground well."

"You are fighting their way." Vakate waved her hands. "The Shung have taken cities before."

"How do you suggest we fight then?" Shu looked at her. "Tell me your plan, and I will give you command of the battle."

Vakate paled and got up to pace around Shu's tent.

"If the problem is the wall, then we need to remove the wall."

"The legions are experts at building such fortresses." Rodrigo spread his hands out, "They are hard nuts to crack."

"We have oil for fire arrows." Vakate spun about. "How did you get in?"

"Climbed over the wall. The posts are buried in the earth and tied together. The wood is green, so it won't burn easily."

"If the rope is cut, could horses pull the posts down?"

"Probably, but it will be hard with the legion shooting arrows at us."

"Then we have the legion go elsewhere."

"A feint." Rodrigo rubbed his chin. "We'd only have a short time until we're discovered and have to fight our way out."

"We attack at night with fire, setting the gates aflame and putting arrows over the wall. In the dark we can look like more than we are. Others will climb the wall opposite of the fire and weaken it, pull it down if we can."

"Even if it fails, it will show we can attack at will." Shu nodded and saluted Vakate. "You will command."

"My husband, I will need to draw on your wisdom." Vakate looked at her feet. "It is a great distance between plan and command."

"See, you show wisdom already." Shu put his hand on her cheek. "I am yours to command in this."

"Very well." Vakate straightened. "Champion, I won't ask you to take the wall, but will you guide our men to where you entered? Your knowledge of the enemy will be invaluable."

"You couldn't keep me away." Rodrigo grinned. "Milene may have a few tricks to add to the chaos."

"I will leave that in your hands." Vakate put her hand on Lydia's shoulder. "Will you prepare the tent for the wounded?"

"Of course." Lydia stood and bowed. "I will gather the supplies together now."

"Husband, please choose those who will attack the gate and those who climb the wall. You know your men best."

Shu saluted.

They waited for the moon to set, then the force attacking the gate dragged the wagon forward with ropes held as they rode. Riders around them sent volley after volley of arrows over the wall, some flamed, lighting the field with a ruddy glow. As Rodrigo predicted, the gates and wall didn't burn well, though flames and smoke appeared from inside the wall.

At the last possible second, the riders pulling the wagon split, letting the thing crash into the gate. Fire arrows lit the oil in the wagon. The riders returned, if at all, with arrows in them. Men carried them to the hospital tent while others helped the horses.

Lydia turned away from the battle and headed for the tent. Aimee waited there.

"I can't do much, but what I can do, I will." She lifted her chin.

"Very well, we fight our own battle here against death." Lydia sent the healers to examine and treat the wounded. Some were beyond help and lay to the side, staring up at the tent.

Aimee crept over and spoke to the men. Some laughed; others cried. Lydia sighed and turned back to her work. The training from years ago in another part of the world guided her hands. She prayed as she removed arrows and bandaged wounds, and each time she looked up to see another silent figure covered with a blanket.

***

Rodrigo crept through the dark, a hundred men behind him, though he couldn't hear them. Milene was at his side.

He took time to check that the sentries hadn't changed their routine. Experienced legionnaires would. Once he was satisfied the timing hadn't changed, he signalled down the line. Half the men would follow him up the wall. The rest would bring horses to the wall. As Rodrigo and his men swarmed up the wall, Milene drew runes on the posts along the wall on either side of where they climbed.

Men clung to the wall, sawing at the heavy ropes. Only ten topped the wall to climb over onto the catwalk. They spread out down the walk watching for sentries or people walking by below. Flame lifted into the sky on the far side of the legions' camp. The roar of battle would hide their activity for a short time.

Ropes came up to the catwalk, and Rodrigo looped them over three posts. He slapped the ropes and the horses pulled. The wall creaked but held.

A shout came from below, cut off as an arrow killed the person, but the damage was done.

"Shoot quickly, then get over the wall. It will do no one any good for you to die here."

Rodrigo ran back to the ropes. They hummed with tension but refused to move.

"Go, Champion. We have this." One of the men slapped his back.

Rodrigo climbed down the wall, cursing. He'd had his doubts but hoped he was wrong. Men still cut rope, not worrying about noise now.

Milene's runes were sinking into the wood, but too slowly. He had a rune he used to put on his knife to give it speed. If he could get it right. Rodrigo drew the rune with hurried swipes of his hand, then pushed at the wall.

The wall shuddered.

"Run!" Rodrigo bellowed and sprinted away followed by others who jumped and rolled. A section of wall, six posts on either side of the three with the rope pulling on them, splintered and crashed to the ground. The catwalk hung crazily in the gap. Shung warriors still knelt and picked their targets. *Idiots.*

Rodrigo stumbled and hands picked him up and threw him up on a horse.

"What did you do?" Milene held him tight. "I'd be dead if I tried that."

"I never could get them right."

They rode into the night, passing others who rode to battle to take advantage of the gap they'd made. The flames in the distance leaped higher.

"Looks like the gate went down." Milene pointed. "It isn't our fight now."

Back with the Shung, Milene helped him into their wagon. Aimee wasn't there.

"She said something about helping in the tent for the wounded," Milene said as she pushed Rodrigo onto a bunk. He pulled her down for a kiss but fell asleep before their lips touched.

***

Aimee couldn't stop her tears, but she refused to leave her post at the side of the tent. More men came as others ceased breathing and were covered with blankets. She talked to them and listened to their stories about their families, the hopes that would never be fulfilled. Some of them joked about fighting death when she came.

The last of the men died before she realized no more were coming. Trying to walk wasn't a good idea. Her legs went rubbery, and she collapsed into someone's arms.

"You been here the whole battle?" they asked.

"Someone had to be," Aimee whispered through tears she was sure would never stop.

"Golden One," the person said. Shyzu had called her that too. The camp was silent as she was carried through. Blurry people turned to look at her. Maybe they waved; she couldn't tell.

They arrived at the wagon she called home.

"Shu!" Her mama came out. "Is she hurt?"

"Exhausted," Shu said. "She spent the night with the dying."

Shu? Shu carried her through camp? If she weren't so tired, she'd die of embarrassment. He placed her on her bunk and brushed a hand across her forehead.

"Rest."

Aimee nodded, but the grief wouldn't let up. Her mama came to sit beside her and drew a rune on her forehead. A familiar one from other nights when she couldn't sleep. She fell into unconsciousness.

***

Aimee woke to a memory of sadness. The night had carried away the weight on her soul. She sat up. Her papa still slept in his bunk with a smile on his face.

Must be dreaming of Mama. A gold cloth cloak lay bunched over her legs. It was trimmed with fur, and there were gold clasps. Shu must have left it behind.

"Ah, you're awake." Her mama climbed into the wagon. "There's tea and soup in the pot."

"I am hungry." Aimee's stomach growled. She lifted the cloak. "Did Shu leave this?"

"Vakate brought it early in the morning. It is the commander's cloak."

"I'm no commander."

"She commanded. It is hers to give as she pleases." Milene brushed her hand over the fur. "She told me she heard what you did for the men last night, and it touched her so much she needed to acknowledge your deed."

"All I did was talk to them." Aimee looked down at the cloak. "I didn't do anything really."

"Shu said you cried tears for the dead all the way from the tent to here. According to him, you eased the passing from this world to the next for those men. That is a task which carries great honour for the Shung."

"Oh." Aimee stroked the fabric, the softest she'd ever touched. "Did we win? The battle I mean."

"Yes, Vakate is very much the hero of the day. The legion fell apart. The conscripts fought to get free. The legionnaires couldn't fight them and us."

"So the wall thing worked."

"Your papa had a hand in that. He'll be sleeping for a while yet."

Aimee tiptoed over and kissed his forehead.

"Let's get that food."

She filled herself with soup and bread.

"Golden One." Shu waited beside the wagon. "The men would like to see you."

"Thank you for bringing me home last night." Aimee's face heated. "You didn't have to carry me yourself."

"You are displeased?"

"No, no." She put her hands up. "But you're Shu, and I'm just..." she trailed off.

"The Golden One, the peace for the fallen." Shu put a hand on her shoulder.

"I will come." Aimee stood and fetched the cloak from the wagon. It should have sat heavier on her shoulder, but it floated as light as air.

Her white horse waited, saddled and ready. She climbed into the saddle and followed Shu. A mass of men knelt on the ground guarded by a few Shung. A much smaller group was guarded by more men.

"Who are they?"

"Prisoners." Shu pointed. "Those surrendered after they fought free of their captors." He frowned. "The others are the survivors of the legion."

"So few." Aimee rode toward the larger group. "What will happen to them?"

"These we will send home. They didn't wish to fight us. They will live good lives. The others, if they give us their word, we will release too. They will carry my message to the legions in the north. I will not tolerate destruction of my land. If they stay out of the way, I will let them be. Now they know I can crush them."

The prisoners in the large group gaped at Aimee and Shu.

"Have you told them yet?"

"I am about to."

"Men." Aimee didn't raise her voice, but every head she could see stared at her. "Listen to Shu's words, then live in peace."

"You will be released." Shu stood in his stirrups. "Go home. Do not take up arms against the Shung again."

"All right, on your feet!" one of the Shung shouted. "We aren't going to send you away hungry." He pointed to a wagon on the far side of them. "Line up, and you will be given bread for your journey."

The prisoners cheered.

"You need not speak to the others," Shu said. "Follow me." He rode further away from the camp to where bodies were lined up on the ground. A few had people gathered around them. Most were alone.

"I show you this so you know you can't guide everyone to the next life."

"I will still do what I can." Aimee lifted her chin and rode up and down the rows. They tugged at her heart but did not leave a weight on her soul. "Now, let's visit the living."

She and Shu rode aimlessly through the camp. A few people stopped him to ask a question. He answered as if he had all the time in the world for them. Most stared at her. She couldn't identify the emotion on their faces. They ended up at the hospital tent. Aimee slid off her horse and walked in. She stopped to talk to each one of the wounded, whether Shung or legion. A few lay to the side. Aimee took a deep breath and went to speak to them. They smiled and thanked her even as they gave up the fight to breathe.

The weight of their deaths made her tired for the first time in the day. Aimee left the tent and felt the warmth of the sun on her face. She turned to it and lifted her arms until the last of the heaviness on her soul had passed.

CHAPTER 21

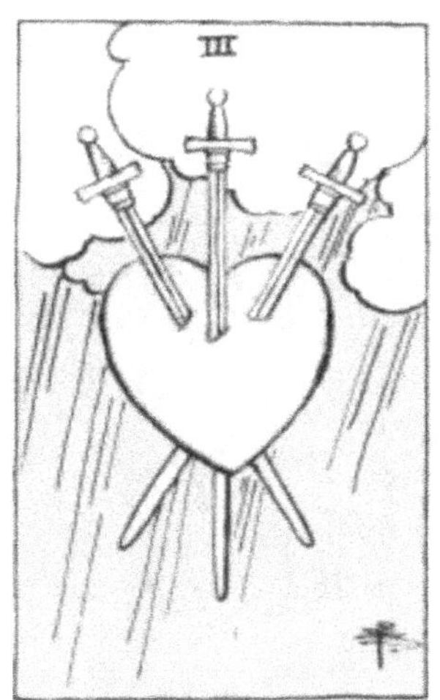

BATTLE FOR THE COAST

Prenny bit her tongue as Commander Vuntil very politely told her off for interfering in his business.

"Your presence here only adds to our risk. I will have to take men from the fight to guard you."

"I do not need guarding." Prenny frowned at him, fighting down the anger. "I led the fight against smugglers, both in town and when they came for revenge. I held the rearguard against the Rau'ch to give my people time to escape the invaders. I can show you the scar from the arrow I took if you wish. Then I walked halfway across the forest to seal the treaty with the De'e'tcha. I came back to see my people returned to their homes."

"My dear girl—"

"You will address me as Lady Prenny. I am Countess of the

North Shore, and you are here at my request. Did the king not brief you at all?"

"General Huston sent me to retake the coast for the king."

"And I am his representative having given my oath to serve him and my people with my whole will. You will not force me to break my oath."

"I am commander."

"Would you be having this conversation with Lord Torrance or Lady Marriette or my mother, Lady Joan? I think not. Do not let my age fool you. I am as determined as any of them to serve the people. This conversation is over. You will listen to the information I have to give you and my input on how to retake my people's home or I will dismiss you as commander."

"You wouldn't dare—"

"Try me at your own risk."

"Commander, sir. If I may have a word." Sergeant Smithson nodded his head to the side.

"We aren't done, Lady Prenny." The commander made an insult of her name.

Their whispered argument carried on for quite a while, the commander turning alternately pale, then red.

The commander walked back, then knelt in front of her.

"Lady Prenny, forgive my temper and my rudeness. It was inexcusable."

"Very well, Commander. We will not speak of this again." Prenny put out her hand to help him up, but he took it and kissed her signet ring, now back in place.

He stood and bowed. "We will meet to discuss strategy in one hour. I look forward to your input." The commander saluted and left, asking where there was a room in good enough shape to hold a meeting without wearing full winter gear.

"Thank you." Sergeant Smithson saluted her. "You didn't need to be so gracious."

"I don't want to command, but I must have input." Prenny looked at him. "What did you say to him?"

"Among other things, I pointed out that you had been trained by the last person to fight a battle in Belandria."

"I was a kid at the time."

"Lady Joan was not, and she raised you. If I may be so bold, she did a fine job of it."

"Thank you, Sergeant."

An hour later, the sergeant escorted her into the room with Commander Vuntil and his officers. They all stood and bowed to her.

"Lady Prenny, if you would give us your information, we will plan from there." The commander spoke as if having her there was all his idea.

"Thank you, Commander." Prenny took a deep breath. "Early in the winter, a force of northmen called the Rau'ch invaded the three active villages. They used a captured Belandrian ship to gain access to the docks. The same ship visited all three villages.

"At this time, each village has a complement of twenty to thirty younger warriors under an experienced officer. In Tansent's Arm and Coshport, successful raids destroyed their supplies. The raid on Sham's Harbour failed according to my information.

"I am told it will be no easy task to remove the Rau'ch from the villages. They've had the winter to familiarize themselves with the terrain and fortify positions. That is your area of expertise. I have two other important pieces of information which must inform your plans.

"The first is the Rau'ch have settled an abandoned village north of Tansent's Arm, a day's travel by coach. From the number of longhouses, I would estimate between three and four hundred people. Not all are warriors, but it will be a very different fight from retaking an essentially empty village."

The men muttered, arguing quietly until the Commander rapped on the table.

"The other item?"

"The other bit of news was picked up during the raid on Tansent's Arm. A man speaking Imperial and sounding very much like an Imperial agent was giving orders to the Rau'ch. It is my opinion that this attack is meant to pull a substantial portion of Belandria's forces north while someone plans an attack on another front. I have no information to support this, but my instinct is the southern border."

The men looked at her in stunned silence.

"What are we supposed to do?" One of the men asked. "We

can't leave these Rau'ch in our north, but if we're needed in the south..."

"My suggestion is this." Prenny clenched her fist. "We must move quickly. Preservation of the villages comes second to the removal of the threat to the north. If the enemy holes up in the village, we will burn them out."

"There were rumours that you'd burnt a village to drive off smugglers."

"It is true. We rebuilt once; we can again."

"And what would your people think of such a cavalier attitude toward their property?"

"If I asked it, they would wield the torch themselves."

"Very well, you heard the Lady. Ideas?"

They spent the afternoon making and rejecting plans, Prenny dove into the discussion using her familiarity with the villages to help.

"Very well gentlemen, we have our plan. Teve, you make contact with the fleet and fill them in. We may be giving them the harder job. It depends on the orders those holding the villages have. It begins tomorrow. Make sure your men are rested. Rotate the scouts and double the roster. We want to stop word getting to the Rau'ch before we arrive."

They stood and saluted.

"Lady Prenny, I will invite you to join me at my command post. It won't be as warm as this place, but I believe I will need you at hand."

"It will be my pleasure." Prenny nodded her head. "I will need a quantity of arrows and armour if any can be found to fit me."

"I will inform Sergeant Smithson to find what you need."

The commander saluted and walked off, relaying orders to his aide.

Sergeant Smithson found her in the room sitting on the table.

"The men are calling you 'our lady' and are determined not to disappoint you."

"I will endeavour not to disappoint them either."

"The arrows I've already collected for you. Since you'll be at the command post, I've set aside two dozen war arrows for you. They will shoot close enough to your hunting arrows."

"I would like a chance to try them out."

"We can do that." The sergeant grinned as if he'd expected the request. "The armour will require some trial and error. If you will come with me."

She spent the next two hours having two men fit her with armour which was a jumble of styles but would serve.

"The squires will be pleased that you are using some of each of their armour. They will wear army issue."

"Give them my thanks." Prenny moved her arms. "Let's go and try those arrows. I will wear the armour to get used to it."

"Lady Prenny, you are going to make me rich."

"You are gambling on my choices?"

"Soldiers will gamble on anything. If you want, I'll give you a cut of my winnings."

"I will hold you to that." They walked to the courtyard where targets had been set up. "Some of the men were practicing in the cold."

"This is spring, Sergeant. It is warm." Prenny grinned at him. Men stood casually around the courtyard. A soldier ran up with her bow and a quiver of arrows.

"These are practice arrows. They are the same length and weight as the war arrows."

"Very good." Prenny strung her bow, then unstrung it and tightened the string by twisting it. This time when she strung it, she nodded. The arrows were indeed a bit heavier than her hunting arrows. "Let's see how they shoot."

She aimed the first at the bullseye, but it dropped a hand's span low. Some muttering came from around the courtyard. Prenny grinned. The next arrow struck the bullseye as did the two following.

"Let's see how they do at a distance." She pointed to the target at the far corner from her. "Have them turn it to face me." Two soldiers ran out and swivelled the target. When they were clear, she put six arrows into the bullseye in rapid succession.

"I believe these will do nicely." Prenny unstrung her bow, and a soldier took it from her. Another took the quiver while others ran to retrieve the arrows she'd fired.

***

They marched out in the morning leaving all unnecessary gear behind. The quartermaster's crew would pack it and bring it along.

"I hear you've been enjoying yourself." Yennet rode up beside Prenny.

"I wondered later why you weren't around. Could it be you were testing me?" Prenny kneed her horse closer to Yennet. One of the privileges of being in command is she got to ride rather than walk through the wet snow.

"Let's just say I was sure you could handle the commander, and I wasn't wrong."

"Garr'son and the De'e'tcha are with the scouts?"

"As you suggested. It will give them something important to do but keep them out the main action."

"I don't want to lose any of them."

"My lady, I must confess I was upset to be detached from the queen's service to be your maid. I changed my mind during that first trip. Now, even if the queen asked me to return, I would refuse in order to stay by your side."

"That makes me very happy indeed," Prenny said. She pointed up the hill they were walking past. "Motion at the top of the hill."

"They are ours, but well spotted." Squire Hesley waved, and the men on the hill waved back. "We are clear. No one has spotted us."

"Good." Prenny looked at him. "Wouldn't you rather be riding with the commander?"

"I won the toss to be the one to squire you today." Hesley grinned at her. "I know a good armourer in the capital. Next time you visit, we'll get you a grand set of armour."

"I hope not to need to wear it often."

"But you keep it for those times you do."

"Very well, when I visit the capital next."

He rode with a very satisfied smile until they reached the road to Sham's Harbour.

A frozen hand poked out of the snow, and Prenny had to swallow hard.

"Hesley. There will be bodies under the snow, both Rau'ch and villager. When we are done with our work today, I want a detail to find them so we can give them proper burial when it is time."

"I will pass on your order." He dropped back and spoke with the sergeant leading the column behind them. "They will mark them as they see them." He looked a little green. "I've never had the chance to get used to bodies."

"Don't." Prenny spoke more sharply than she intended. "Don't get used to them. Each body is a life cut off, even if we are the one to do it. We do what we must, then grieve later."

"Have you seen a lot of battle?"

"More than I'd have chosen." Prenny sighed. "Three-quarters of battle is reacting faster than the enemy. The other quarter is not stopping until the work is done."

"I will remember that."

"Lady Prenny, the scouts inform me we are at the final turn before we come in sight of the enemy." The commander rode back to her. "If you will join me at the turn, we will watch as events unfold."

"Thank you, Commander." Prenny rode forward with him. "Does it ever get easier holding back from the fight? My gut wants to be there supporting our men."

"I think that is a sign of a good commander." He pulled up where they could see the village down the hill. "Now it begins." The column marched past them, holding their spears at the ready, shields on their left arms.

In the village, grotesque corpses hung on poles by the warehouse.

"Archers are in position." A messenger saluted.

"Signal them to fire on their own judgement." The messenger ran to the front and waved flags in a complicated pattern. A trumpet blew, shattering the silence. The Rau'ch boiled out of the houses holding shields and axes or spears. One of the men yelled in a harsh language. The enemy formed up, shield to shield.

"There are more than our estimate," Commander Vuntil muttered. "No matter, the strategy is good."

The Rau'ch charged at the front line of the column. The trumpet blew again, and the column shifted into a double line. It grew wider as men arrived behind until it blocked the way out of the village entirely. Arrows flew from the hillside, and some of the Rua'ch stumbled but none fell.

"Range is too long," Prenny said. "Order them to hold where they are for the moment. Coming down the hill will give them no easy retreat." A messenger ran and waved his flags.

A wolf ship came around the headland, and even knowing it was coming, Prenny's heart beat faster. The Rau'ch commander yelled, and they doubled their efforts. The line bowed; soldiers moved to support the centre. Prenny couldn't see how many had fallen on either side.

The line broke, and the Rau'ch surged through. Some turned to engage the Belandrians while most charged up the road toward the command post. Prenny strung her bow and checked that her arrows were within reach.

Archers trotted past the command post and opened fire into the charging enemy. Behind them, the Rau'ch fought a desperate holding action. The wolf ship landed on the dock, and Belandrian soldiers poured off the boat and marched through the village to support the soldiers in action.

Spearmen stepped in front of the archers and formed a shield wall. Another formed behind them as the archers retreated.

Now much closer to the battle, Prenny could see the brutality of the fight. Vastly outnumbered, the Rau'ch fought to the last man.

"Let's search the village," Commander Vuntil said. "Be careful. Check each house by the numbers."

They walked past the bloody snow. Healers crouched over men, speaking in low voices. Soldiers checked each house, room by room, marking the door to show they were empty.

The light changed, and Prenny looked up as a Rau'ch launched himself from the roof of a house. She'd fired an arrow before thinking of it while Hesley shouted. The Rau'ch crunched into the ground, her arrow sticking out the back of his neck.

"They told me you were good with that bow," Commander Vuntil said. "Beware the roofs." His bellow echoed off the hills.

"All clear." One of the men from the wolf ship saluted. "With your permission, we will start up toward the next village. The fleet will land a ship to hold the village until the action is complete."

"Good work," Commander Vuntil said. "We'll meet you there in two days."

The next two days were repeats of the first battle with the exception that in Tansent's Arm the fleet set soldiers ashore in the cove the smugglers used.

"That's the easy part done." Prenny stood in the main room of the inn, hardly believing she was back.

"We were fortunate to maintain the surprise over the course of the week." Commander Vuntil stretched. "Are you sure about the course of action you've chosen for the last village?"

"I have to try. This is different than driving out warriors. I don't want to be the one causing the death of innocents."

"Very well. The fleet will do as you command. Choose the people you want for the parley."

They rode north.

"Scouts report signals from the fleet. Wolf ships spotted to the north."

"They know we're coming."

"I still want to try talking to them, but let's be prepared for the worst." Prenny sighed.

"Double the scouting parties," Commander Vuntil ordered. "March at the ready.

They passed the coach. It had been torn apart and burned.

The next morning, the vanguard of their force came in sight of the village. Prenny and the commanders rode near the rear of the column.

"Motion to the right." She pointed. "It should be one of ours." Hesley shaded his eyes. "No response. Possible enemy sighted on the hill to our right."

"Understood." The rearguard moved up closer and took position between the column and the hill.

Prenny strung her bow and settled a quiver on her saddle. Her neck ached from looking up the hill. She stretched out the kink and caught a glint of something in the forest.

"To the left, form up!" she screamed as the Rau'ch poured out of the forest. They were less than a bowshot from the column, charging for the horses. Prenny snatched an arrow from her quiver, aimed and fired while her scream still echoed. A roar came from the hill as the enemy charged down it.

The column reversed and formed as sergeants yelled orders.

The Rau'ch carried shields making her targets the glinting eyes of the charging enemy. She jumped up to stand on her saddle and kept shooting. Somehow every time she reached for an arrow there was one there. When the Rau'ch lifted their shields, she aimed for the foot.

There wasn't time to stop them. Then they started falling as arrows struck them from the flank and then behind them.

A warrior in the front rank had three of her arrows stuck in his shield. Her arrows had glanced off the armour on his legs. Hesley rode out between her and the charging warrior low in the saddle, sword extended. The warrior's spear caught the horse on the leg, and it tumbled, throwing Hesley to the ground. Miraculously, he held onto his sword, but Prenny could see he was hurt.

The warrior pulled an axe off his belt, keeping his shield between himself and Prenny. Hesley swung at the man's feet. He danced back, catching the sword on the bottom of the shield. Prenny shot at the Rau'ch's eyes, but the arrow struck the forehead on his helmet. He staggered back a step. Prenny reached for an arrow and one slapped into her hand. She put the arrow through the man's eye.

Another arrow and another target. Another warrior staggered back, a dent in the front of his helmet. A spear stabbed him, as a wall of shields and spears formed up in front of her.

"I'd come down now." Commander Vuntil stood beside her, a fist filled with arrows. "Don't give them a target." Prenny crouched on the saddle, then slid off the horse. She staggered and he caught her.

"You'd make one heck of a general." He helped her sit on the ground. "A few seconds difference and they would have had us."

Prenny didn't pay much attention to the rest of the battle. Instead, she fought nausea and the shakes rattling her body.

"Breathe deeply." Yennet crouched beside her. "You make me wish I was an archer."

"I could teach you," Prenny gasped.

"I'd like that, my lady." She brushed Prenny's hair back. "Maybe in the summer when my fingers won't freeze." Pulling out a kerchief, she wrapped Prenny's fingers. "You've rubbed them raw."

"I guess I won't be knitting for a while."

"The battle is done." Commander Vuntil crouched beside Prenny. Are you ready to ride? This is not a good place right now."

"Hesley?"

"Leg's broke, but he's alive thanks to your shooting."

"I grew up hunting squirrel with the bow," Prenny said. "It stuck with me.”

Commander Vuntil hoisted her to her feet, then helped her onto her horse.

Prenny pointed to the warrior who’d almost killed Hesley. “Bring him along. I think we need to make a point.” She kneed her horse into motion, Yennet on one side and the commander on the other. They came into sight of the village. Slaves were lined up across the road holding sticks and farm implements.

“Hold up.” Prenny held up her hand. “Form a line and await orders. Commander, you’re with me.” Two soldiers rode in front, shields at the ready.

“I need Garr’son.”

A few minutes later he came up beside her. “My lady.”

“Please translate.” Prenny waved at the soldier carrying the warrior. They rolled him onto the road.

“You have a choice. Come out and talk or die.” Garr’son yelled her words. The slaves didn’t move, but someone shifted behind them.

“I am waiting.” Ships rounded the headland, and the fleet hove to off the shore from the village. She pointed at them. “Help will not be coming. Not today, not tomorrow, not ever. Your fate is in your own hands. Step out and speak with me or die.” She sighed. “To be honest, I’ve had enough of killing today, but it is your choice.”

When no answer came from below, Prenny clenched her fist.

“Spears and shields ready. Archers on the flanks.”

“Wait.” A woman ran out with her hands up. She yelled something, and the slaves dropped their weapons.

“Bring every man, woman and child out into the open.” Prenny held up her hand. “I swear no harm will come to you if you commit no treachery.”

Women and children stepped from behind buildings and crowded the open space between them. There were a few men too young or too old to be warriors. Prenny felt sick. Almost the entire male population of the village lay dead behind them.

“I am Lady Prenny, Countess of the North Shore, and this land is my responsibility. I give you the choice of leaving this place forever or becoming my people and living under my rule.”

A few people knelt slowly, then all of them.

"My first command is to cut the collars from the slaves. All people in Belandria are free."

The woman who had spoken took out a knife and began cutting the collars from the slaves.

"Garr'son, take some men and go through every building, make sure no one is hiding. Be careful. Explain what you're doing. I don't want one person's action to doom the village."

The check of the village revealed no one hiding other than a few children too terrified to go outside.

"Lady Prenny, a signal from the fleet. Wolf ships approach. They are flying a parley flag."

"Let one of them land. They are to leave all weapons on the ship. I will guarantee their safety."

A wolf ship tied up on the pier. Shield walls formed a path for the northmen to walk past on the way to Prenny. The men saluted, then one stepped forward.

"I am Kerhin, Thane of Westhelm." He spoke Imperial with a strong accent.

"Lady Prenny, Countess of the North, representative of the King of Belandria."

"I ask mercy for my people." He looked over the woman and children shivering in the cold.

"Garr'son, they can go inside and get warm."

"Very well, my lady."

"What weregild will you ask for their return to Westhelm?"

"They must decide for themselves if return is what they want. I would guess all but the oldest grew up in this place."

"This is true." He looked around. "I see no warriors."

"They threw themselves against our spears and died."

The thane sighed. "Perhaps we have become too proud of our warrior tradition."

"I do not wish to see a repeat of this war." Prenny waved her hand around her. "Many have died, and for what? To forward the ambition of an Imperial noble in the south."

Kerhin started, then laughed bitterly.

"We were told you were weak, a slip of a girl. I should have listened to the words of those who told how you burned your own village to punish their transgressions. You are a valkyrie come to stand against us for our pride.”

“I would have peace over war,” Prenny said, “but it depends on you. We agree to the signing of a treaty here and now, or we bar every one of your ships from our water. If you attack again, we will find Westhelm and burn it down around your ears.”

“Let us have peace.” Kerhin put out his hand. Prenny took it, and they shook.

“Send your negotiators and we’ll hammer out a treaty. I must get the blessing of my king on our endeavour, but I am confident he will agree.”

“What are your terms?”

“The return of all captives taken from the villages. Until the treaty is signed, people who will live with us act as a surety for your word.”

“I will remain here myself. My son needs time to learn to lead the Helm. My men will also stay. We will leave arms and armour behind.”

“They may stay in this village. It will be some time before my people welcome yours.”

“Very well.” Kerhin gave orders to his men. They saluted, then some returned to the wolf ship. “They will carry word to my other ships to return home and carry word of our pledge.”

“Since we have decided not to kill each other today, let’s retire to the tent and talk more comfortably.”

“Very well.” Kerhin bowed.

***

“Commander Vuntil, please carry my report to the king. I have commended you for the work you have done.”

“Are you sure one ship of the fleet and fifty men are enough?”

“If they break their word, not the whole command will hold them back, but I believe Kerhin is being truthful. They have a great deal to lose by breaking faith.”

“As you will. The ships will depart tomorrow and sail to the south. Most of the men will sail with them. I will ride with the rest. It will be much quicker than marching. With your permission, we will leave the wounded to recover at the old mansion.”

"Certainly. If there is anything they need, tell them to ask."

"My thanks, Lady Prenny." Commander Vuntil's lips twitched. "The men have taken to calling you their Valkyrie. You are doomed to become a legend."

"Express my thanks to each and every one of them, Commander."

"I will." Commander Vuntil saluted. "It's been a pleasure serving with you."

Prenny watched them ride off from the window of the Inn. Garr'son had stayed with the northmen in the village they'd named Valkhelm. Most of the garrison stayed there as well.

"My lady?" Leohl spoke behind her. "Your meal is ready."

CHAPTER 22

QUEEN IN HIDING

After a week of meeting Mathial in the garden nightly, Phenos sent a messenger to apologize that he'd been detained. Fury watched the stars with Nikay and Mathial, the messenger's presence hanging on the edge of her awareness.

Mathial was disappointed not to have her guide to the heavens. Fury didn't want to explain that this was the next part in Phenos' plan. She'd listened to enough stories from the maids and guards to recognize the tactics.

The queen was grumpy through the next day, arbitrarily changing her mind about what she wanted and complaining about Nikay's attempts to get her through the day.

"Tonight, we leave." Nikay leaned against the door. He looked tired. "Tomorrow will be too late."

"Would it really be so bad to stay?" Mathial trembled where she sat on the bed, blankets pulled up to her chin.

"If we stay, we lose our chance, and you will end up wearing a collar like this," he pointed to his neck, "only yours will be gold."

Mathial slashed her hand and Nikay went to his knees, his face white.

"Mistress, you will kill him."

"I will never be a slave." Mathial shook like a tree in a storm.

We must destroy the collar. Fury spoke within her.

You said it could kill him.

He will die anyway if you don't.

Fury ran over to Nikay and knelt beside him. She took the black gem between her fingers. *All right.* Fire passed from her fingers into the gem. It cracked, and Nikay screamed then collapsed on the floor.

He wasn't breathing. What had he done when she'd stopped breathing? She forced his mouth open and sealed her lips against his, blowing air into his lungs. Mathial beat on her shoulders, but Fury kept breathing for him until he gasped and thrashed on the floor. She held him tight until he quieted.

"Thanks." His voice rasped painfully. "I knew you would be able to do it."

"You knew this was going to happen?" Fury shook him, tears streaming down her face now that she knew he would live.

"Mathial wouldn't leave the castle until her memories awoke."

Fury helped Nikay sit, then turned to look at the queen. She quivered, but now Fury could feel the heat of her rage.

"They murdered my parents while I watched. I was six. We'd just finished a special meal to celebrate. The men in masks broke in and cut them down. Then *he* came in and told me I needed to be obedient to him from now on. When I refused and spat at him, he had them whip me, then ordered me again. I said, 'Yes, Master.' Then he touched my forehead, and I forgot everything except obeying."

She dropped to her knees beside Nikay and took his hands. "Forgive me."

"There is nothing to forgive, Mathial." Nikay smiled at her. "The pain of that memory can't be any less than what I felt."

"You are no longer my slave." Mathial leaned forward and kissed

Nikay on the lips. "Will you be my friend?"

"Gladly."

Mathial turned and took Fury's hand. "You too, Fury." She kissed Fury on the cheek and caressed her face.

"I too will gladly be your friend."

"Tomorrow we escape, then we will destroy him."

"If I stop breathing, you know what to do." Fury reached up to her collar before her courage failed and let the Fury within her crush the gem. The pain was like nothing she'd ever experienced.

She felt someone breathing air into her lungs. *Nikay.* She smiled and opened her eyes to see Mathial's face over hers.

"Nikay wasn't recovered enough." Mathial kissed Fury's forehead. "Now we are bonded as equals."

She helped Fury and then Nikay to the bed before lying down between them, holding their hands tightly.

"I'm still scared," Mathial whispered, squeezing her hand tight on Fury's.

"That is good," Fury said. "I am too, but we must do this. So together, we'll get past our fear."

***

Fury sat in a corner as they spent the day in Mathial's room. The queen claimed she had a headache and would rest. A listener came by for a short time.

After the evening meal, Mathial ordered the slaves to dress her. She'd walk through the halls before going to bed. When they'd left, Mathial slipped her jewellery into her wrap while Fury put the dress on over the clothes she wore. She looked around the room, was there anything else they needed to take? *Nothing.*

The halls were almost deserted as they walked.

"I heard you were feeling poorly." Phenos came over to them. Fury's heart raced. Would he notice the collars?

Peace. The Fury within her slowed her heart.

"A headache." Mathial smiled up at him. "Thank you for your concern."

"Rest well tonight, and perhaps tomorrow we'll look at the stars."

"I would like that."

Phenos nodded and stalked away.

"Since we're out, let's go visit the stars," Mathial announced and swept down the hall.

The hall over the garden was deserted. Fury sensed someone close by. In the passage. One man.

"Look at the garden in the moonlight." Fury stopped and stared over the rail. Mathial stopped beside her.

"It is beautiful."

Fury put her hand over Mathial's and pressed it down on the rail. The queen nodded. Fury ducked down and slipped over to beside the door.

The man within pushed it open. He already had a tube to his mouth. Fury gripped his throat, cutting off his air, and kicked his feet from beneath him. His voice box crunched in her fist and he was dead.

"Come," Fury hissed. "He was kind enough to open the door for us."

Nikay led Mathial to the door, and they stepped over the assassin's body. He picked up the lantern from the floor. Fury dragged the man out of the passage and closed the door.

"Let's go."

With the light and knowing where they were going, it didn't take long to get to the door to the outside.

"We are going to be wandering in a strange city at night," Nikay said.

"No choice." Fury stilled the pounding in her chest. "We will get darker clothes at the first opportunity. The alley is clear."

"I want to breathe free air." Mathial wrapped her arms around her chest.

"Let's go then." Nikay turned the lantern down to the barest flame and opened the door.

They slipped out into the night, and Nikay closed the door behind them. Fury helped Mathial change into less obvious clothes. She bundled the jewellery and gold cloth in a spare pair of pants, tying the legs shut, then Mathial insisted on carrying them over her neck, tucked inside the dress.

Fury took the lead. She'd done night training at home with Sam shadowing her and others placed as challenges to her safety.

"Don't sneak along the street. We walk like we have a right to be there. If we try to hide in the shadows, we'll only draw attention." Fury took Mathial's hand, and Nikay took the other.

They strolled out of the alley into the street. Mathial looked around at everything.

"Mathial, relax," Nikay said. "We're out. No one knows we're gone, and they will assume from the assassin's body that someone has abducted you."

She leaned her head on his shoulder.

"If I die tonight, I will be happy."

"I don't plan to let you die." Fury shook Mathial's hand, but she grinned.

There were a few people out on the street, but they walked with their heads down and paid no attention to Fury and her friends.

"Let's get off the main street." Nikay pulled them down a smaller street. It wove between high buildings. They didn't look like homes, perhaps businesses of some kind as Fury didn't sense anyone inside them.

The night wore on and Mathial began to stumble between them. Fury was tired too. They needed a place to hide and make plans for tomorrow.

"Let's pick an alley and get some rest." Nikay pointed at a narrow passage between two of the buildings."

"Sounds good." They walked into the alley. Nikay turned the lantern up a little. Doors let out from either side into the space. Fury could reach out and brush fingers along both walls. At the end of it, they found a tiny yard.

"Someone is sleeping there." Fury pointed to a shuttered window. "Let's go back a bit."

They huddled in between doorways, Nikay and Fury on either side of Mathial.

Fury woke when people approached and blocked them in. She'd wait to see what they wanted before taking action. Light taps on Nikay and Mathial shoulders woke them.

"Play asleep," she whispered.

"Look what we have here, lost little lambs." One of three men stopped. The other two a pace behind, blocking the alley. "We should get a good price for these."

"Let us go and take this." Mathial dumped the gold onto the cobbles. The men stared open-mouthed at the riches.

Fury launched herself bounding up the walls to land on the shoulders of the two blocking the way. She broke their necks on the way down. The last man had a knife out and had spun to face her. Nikay kicked the back of his knee.

Fury lunged forward, taking the knife hand with her left and crushing his throat with her right.

"Good move dumping out the gold." Fury grinned at Mathial. "It certainly distracted them."

"I expect they intended to visit the person at the end of the alley," Nikay said. "We should change our clothes and get out of here." He helped Fury strip the bodies and used the man's knife to cut the pant legs to length. A piece of rope one man had carried made for belts. The cloth was surprisingly good quality but made to look nondescript. They ended with tunics over leggings, odd but better than the grey of slaves. They split up the jewellery between their pockets while Mathial wore the queen's medallion under her clothes. Nikay cut the leather collars from his and Fury's necks and put them in a pocket.

Mathial made a face at putting on dead men's clothing but said nothing. She let Nikay take the lead out of the alley. They wandered through the day with no intention but to get away from the palace.

"We need a safer place to stay and make plans." Nikay sighed and stretched.

"And less conspicuous outfits." Mathial looked around. "People keep staring at us."

"You're right." Fury's nerves jangled with all the people around. She asked Fury to pull back the sense of others.

"You're new." A young girl assessed them. "Let's find somewhere more private, and you can tell me what you need."

Nikay shrugged, and they followed the girl through a maze of street and alleys.

"All right, no one is following you. I'm surprised, given the get up you're wearing. You look like you mugged members of the Guild."

"They attacked us first." Mathial put her hand on her heart. "I've never been so scared."

"You're telling me you took on three members of the Guild and not a scratch on you?" The girl frowned and began to back away.

The place they stood was almost as narrow as the alley that morning. Fury bounced from one wall to the other to land like a cat behind the girl. She opened her hands.

"If you want to leave, you may." Fury stepped back against the wall. "But we really could use your help."

"Fine, but no lying." The girl's frown didn't disappear. "You obviously aren't any normal kids."

"We can pay." Mathial held out an earring, a fine gold hoop.

The girl made the earing vanish. "Come with me." She led them through more alleys to a door and knocked on it.

A man opened it and scowled at them.

"Come on, Trader, they're kids. What am I going to do with three kids?"

"I need help." Trader held up a cupped hand. From the man's face, Fury guessed the earring sat in it.

"Get in here." He stepped back and they crowded into his shop. Pottery sat on shelves. "Sit down; don't move." He pointed to the floor. "Trader, talk fast."

"I spotted them walking down the street, oblivious to everything." Trader leaned forward. "Look at what they're wearing. That's Guild gea, and not underlings either. Word will have reached the Guild, and the search will be on by now."

"All the more reason to toss you out on the street." The man folded his arms.

"Theniar, these aren't regular kids. I've already got one person tangled with the Guild. I won't stand back and let others get taken."

"I thought you were busy replacing the money your uncle stole." Theniar frowned. "People have noticed you aren't as nice as you were before."

Trader looked down and clenched her hands on her shirt. "I know, but I don't know how to stop." Tears rolled down her cheeks. "I don't like myself much, so I have to do this. If it means giving up the training, then I will do that."

"Very well," the man said.

"Thank you." Trader bowed to the floor.

"First thing is to get rid of those clothes, far away, somewhere the Guild will find them and chase in the wrong direction." Theniar handed Trader a bunch of coins. "Buy replacements, not all in the same place. Bring them here, and I will tell you what we'll do next."

"Give me your clothes." Trader stood and pointed at Fury and the others.

They emptied their pockets, Trader and Theniar's eyes growing so wide Fury wondered if they'd fall out of their heads. Then Mathial shed the Guild clothing and stood in her shift, the queen's medallion hanging on her chest.

Theniar went to his knees, head down.

"My queen."

Trader stared at him like he'd lost his mind.

"You met my mother," Mathial said.

"Once, I brought a special order to the palace. She was like a goddess but welcomed me. She wore that medallion. I looked it up when I got home. No one but royalty may wear it and live."

"You're the *queen*?" Trader's voice squeaked. She backed away from them. "And your bodyguards, of course." She fell into a huddle on the floor. "Forgive me, forgive me. I didn't know." Her voice quavered and broke.

Mathial kneeled beside the girl and brushed her hand over Trader's hair. "How were you to know when we were hiding it from you? You have helped us, and you have our thanks."

Trader lifted her head and peered at Mathial "Really?"

"Truly." Mathial took Trader's hand and lifted her up, then hugged her tight. "We shall be friends." Trader froze, then hugged Mathial back.

"Whatever I can do," Trader said in the tones of one making a vow, "I will do it. I would die for you if you asked."

"So now we are four." Mathial looked over at Theniar, "Five."

"I am Mathial, and as you have guessed, queen over the Confederacy."

"Princess Arthuria Siana of Belandria, called Fury." Fury bowed, almost laughing at Mathial's wide eyes.

"Nikay leBraun, heir of Lord leBraun and the Lady Marriette,

Chancellor of Belandria.”

“I knew you were noble, but…” Mathial bowed to them. “Did I do that right?”

“You did.” Nikay grinned at her.

“Fate brought us together,” Mathial gave Trader a last squeeze, “and now you have joined us too. I plan to take my country back from the people who are running it now.”

“Tall order.” Theniar put a hand to his head. “But you have my support, such as it is.”

“I will get the clothes.” Trader stuffed the Guild clothes into a sack Theniar gave her. “Wait for me to return.” She slipped out the door.

“I have blankets in the back.” Theniar stood. “So much nobility wearing so little clothing is unsettling.”

He vanished down the hall. Fury look at the three of them. Mathial in her shift, Nikay and her in breeches. She looked as much a boy as he. For a moment, she envied Mathial who already began to have a woman’s shape, then she laughed at herself.

Nikay was poking through the jewellery on the floor, being obvious about not looking at Mathial. He was sweet, always had been, following her on her madcap outings. Bittersweet feelings swelled in her. He’d never looked away when they’d changed clothes on the road. Fury didn’t know what it meant, but whatever happened, she’d always be his friend.

***

Nikay relaxed when Mathial wrapped herself in the blanket. He didn’t understand his reaction. It didn’t bother him when Fury wasn’t dressed. They were as close as he could imagine being to someone. He was glad they were friends.

Trader returned and handed out clothing.

“Sorry, it won’t be as nice as what you had.”

“It is fine.” Mathial threw the blanket off, and Nikay’s face heated. Fury stood and helped her into a dress. It somehow made Mathial look older. He scrambled into rough pants and a shirt. A pouch hung from his waist. Fury wore a similar outfit, looking tough and, like Mathial, older.

“I bumped into a friend.” Trader shuffled her feet. “I asked her to help.”

“If you trust her, then it is fine with me.” Mathial smiled then held out the skirt of her dress. “This is so much nicer than what I usually wear.”

“I can’t imagine.” Trader bowed her head.

“I get wrapped up in this,” Mathial nudged the roll of gold fabric, “and half the time, I can hardly move.”

Someone knocked at the door. Theniar opened it and let them in.

“What do you want, Trader?” The woman stopped and stared at Fury. “Your Highness?” She came closer and looked into Fury’s eyes.

“I remember you,” Fury said. “You came to the palace a few times.”

“Cameto came here looking for you.” She turned to Nikay. “And you must be Nikay.”

He nodded.

“I am Leandra,” the woman introduced herself.

“Welcome.” Mathial stepped forward. “I am Mathial.”

“Good to meet you, Mathial.” Leandra’s eyes dropped to the floor and widened. “You have enough gold to buy a country here.”

“Good, then it will help me get my country back.” Mathial grinned.

“Mathial is the queen of the Confederacy. She’s been kept captive in her own palace by a Lusian noble.”

“I see.” Leandra put a hand on Trader’s shoulder. “You honour me with your trust.” She walked around the three of them. “You mentioned disguises. The best are simple and redirect the eye away from what you don’t want people to see.”

“Like lying.” Mathial looked at Nikay and smiled.

“Exactly.” Leandra stood back with her hands on her hips. “Fury, would it bother you to be a boy for a while?”

“I’ve always wanted to try being a boy.” Fury blushed.

“Cut your hair, and that outfit will work.”

Nikay handed Leandra the knife. She worked for a few minutes and when she’d done, he hardly recognized Fury.

“We’ll call you Art.”

Fury nodded and moved her head. “It is strange without the

long hair."

Leandra reshaped Nikay's hair as well. "You can be Tor."

She looked at Mathial's hair. "If we take out the gold, you will be fine." She ran her hand over Mathial's hair, then showed her the beads and thread. "We'll add them to your war chest."

"It will be all but impossible to sell any of the jewellery." Theniar sighed and leaned against a wall. "They are all one-of-a-kind pieces and instantly identifiable."

"What if we use them as a guarantee?" Leandra tilted her head thoughtfully. "We will need a lot more people. I thought to hire the Nekkest."

"They are traditionally royal bodyguards," Mathial said, "but they vanished after my parents were murdered."

"Well then, it so happens that we know where to hire the Nekkest, right Trader?"

Trader laughed. "This will be the biggest deal of my life."

CHAPTER 23

OBSTINATE OBSTACLE

Aimee stared up at the walls of Meicen. They were as tall as the ones around Lusia. The gates were closed tight. The helmets of guards peeped over the crenellations above the gate.

They'd arrived to find the city shut up tight. No one would even talk to them. The Shung camped around the walls of the city. They didn't hold back traffic to and from the place. The gates didn't open for anyone. The farmers and traders were happy enough to sell to the Shung, probably relieved the horde didn't simply claim the goods for themselves. All of them were sent away with the message that Shu was bringing peace to the Empire.

Messengers came and went daily from the other cohorts. Two continued their way west toward the ocean, a third patrolled the northern boundary of what Shu claimed, watching for legion activity.

Aimee had learned the legion prisoners were sent home. Those who refused to swear peace with the Shung lost their right hands. She'd cried for a day, then decided they'd brought it on themselves.

While they waited, Aimee rode through the camp talking to people. Everywhere she went, an honour guard travelled with her. They were led by a man named Ba. He never smiled, but she'd caught him sneaking sweets to the children. She was comfortable with him.

Today they rode toward the west gate of the city where Wen commanded the Shung. The first she knew of an attack was arrows hitting her escort. One man fell from his horse. The others rode between her and the danger, holding up shields to protect her.

Aimee's stomach ached, and she had to fight to breathe. Her hand dropped to the knife at her waist. Strong arms yanked her from the saddle, and a hand covered her mouth. When she drew her dagger to fight back, a fist struck her head.

***

She woke in a stone cell, hands tied and a thumping in her head. Aside from that, she didn't think she was injured.

"You're awake." The door opened and a man in expensive clothes stepped in. "If you promise to behave, we will loosen your bounds and bring you food and drink."

Aimee stared at him. He looked soft, the bulging clothes showed his body was uncareful for, but his eyes were cold and made her shiver. *What good will it be to sit tied down?*

"I will behave."

"Swear it." The man frowned at her.

"I have said it." Aimee met his gaze until he threw his hands in the air and left.

Aimee watched the sunlight travel across the floor. The man had told her a great deal about himself. Papa always told her people expected others to have their worst faults. The man would lie and break his word to suit his purpose.

When the light reached her, she closed her eyes and soaked in the warmth.

"Have you reconsidered?" The man stood in the door again.

"I have said I will behave. I swear it on the Balance."

"You don't look like a waggoneer."

"I don't look like a lot of things." Aimee shrugged. Another man came in and cut her bonds. He was as hard as the first was soft.

"Don't give us trouble and you won't be hurt." He showed her a cut on his arm. "This earned you a clout on the head."

"I should have cut you deeper." Aimee glared at him.

The man laughed and lifted her to her feet.

"You promised..." the soft one frowned.

"She won't go back on her word." The hard man interrupted him. "Give it a rest."

They walked along a stone hall to a heavy door. The hard man banged on it and it opened. The evening sun made Aimee's eyes squint and her head hurt.

She followed them across a courtyard to a room full of men and women in uniform. They were eating, but they stopped and stood when the hard man entered.

"As you were." The hard man pointed to Aimee. "She is our guest. Treat her with respect. She's given her bond." He pushed her over to a table. A woman slid over and let Aimee sit.

"Nice cloak."

"I'd forgotten I had it on." Aimee shrugged and reached for a plate. "It is part of me."

"We watched you from the walls," a man across the table said.

"Then you know I'm harmless." Aimee tucked into the food, plain but good quality.

"The barbarians worship you, so you make a good hostage."

"Shut up, Lemse, you talk too much." The woman poured a cup of water and put it by Aimee's plate.

"If your friends give us what we want, you'll be fine."

"Now who's talking too much?"

Aimee let the argument float over her. Cathedral bells rang dolefully.

"I'd like to visit the church." She pushed her empty plate aside.

"Captain said she'd given bond." The woman looked at Lemse.

"Don't see what harm it would do." Lemse stood. "I'll take you. It's just next door."

He walked her out a door and along a street and up a flight of stairs to double doors which stood wide open. They didn't look like they ever been shut. Dust had built up around them making them seem to rise out of the stone.

Inside Aimee shuddered.

"You have the plague."

"How do you know?"

"The sound of their prayers." Aimee walked into the church.

"It only affects the children," Lemse said.

"It affects everyone. The children will die first. They have the least strength to fight despair." She knelt beside a mother holding a toddler. "Tell me about your son, all the things you love about him, the dreams you hold in your heart for him."

"Who are you?"

"I am the Golden One." Aimee brushed her hand over the boy's forehead. The Cup was gone. All she could bring was peace. The mother's story flowed over her, then she talked to another and another. Time passed. The bells rang but she didn't notice.

The first mother screamed, and Aimee fought back the tears.

"He opened his eyes! His fever is down. Dovas, do you hear your mama?" Others spoke to their children. They were waking. Aimee didn't understand why or how, but she wouldn't stop.

"What are you doing here?" The soft man scowled at Aimee. pushing a mother out of his way.

"Praying." Aimee didn't look up at him. "Leave me be."

"You will come with me so I can keep an eye on you."

Aimee stood and met the man's gaze. "I will stay here. You know where to find me."

He grabbed her hand to drag her out, and a growl ran through the crowd.

"Let her go!" a mother shouted.

"She's an angel. She healed my daughter."

"Let her be," the hard man stood behind the soft man, "unless you want to be caught in the midst of a riot. The crowd on the street you were cursing? They are here to see this girl. Dragging her out by force would not be wise."

The soft one let go and snarled.

"I'm holding you responsible." He stomped out of the church, pushing people away.

"I am sorry." The hard man looked down at her. "My son lies dying as we speak. If you could spare a prayer for him..." He closed his eyes. "Never mind, why would you pray for your enemy's child?"

"What's his name?" Aimee put a hand on his arm.

"Kintel."

"Go tell Kintel all the reasons you love him, all the reasons why he should live. He's dying of despair. Fill the darkness with love, and he may come back to you."

The hard man ran out of the church. Aimee continued her way around the church. Word had spread, and parents were talking to their children, laughing and crying.

A wail came from the other side of the sanctuary, and Aimee ran over. A woman held a young girl maybe five-years-old. The girl was grey and motionless.

"Why?" The woman screamed at Aimee. "Why did she have to die? You healed the others." She pushed the child into Aimee's arms.

"Why does anyone die?" Aimee said. "I've never understood. Some live long and joyful years, and others wither too soon. Her tears fell on the girl's face. "What is her name?"

"Channah, but we called her chatter because she never stopped talking..." the woman's words poured out until she took her daughter back from Aimee. "I'm going to miss you, darling." She walked away from Aimee.

In the midst of recovery, other children died, and Aimee heard the grief from their parents until her feet couldn't hold her upright. She sat on the steps at the front of the church, tears pouring endlessly from her eyes. Yet she still took the children and heard the stories.

"Let us help." A voice spoke from beside her. She scrubbed her eyes to see a man in the black clothes of the priesthood. Others like him moved through the crowd. "You showed us the way." He took her hand and warmth flowed into her.

"I think I'm going to sleep awhile," Aimee muttered and curled up on the step.

***

Hands gently picked her up, and Aimee looked blearily up at the hard man's face.

"How is your son?" she asked.

"He lives."

"I am glad." Aimee struggled to stand on her own, but the man wouldn't put her down. "Fine, carry me into the sunlight."

"We're going up on the wall. There will be plenty of sunlight." He walked through the crowds. People reached to touch her and made signs of blessing. The people watched as they climbed the stairs back and forth to the top of the wall. The sun streamed from the east.

"All right, we've given them until the sun was up," the soft man said. "Stand her on the edge."

"Stay steady," the hard man whispered to Aimee. "I've got you." He lifted her onto her feet in the space between crenellations.

Aimee lifted her arms and closed her eyes. The light flowed into her, lifting the burden of grief from her heart.

"Here's your golden girl," the soft man shouted from the wall. "If you want her back, leave all the gold you have at the gate and leave."

"We will not abandon the Golden One." Shu's voice floated up to her, and she smiled.

"Remember it was your choice!" the soft man yelled. He pointed at Aimee. "Throw her from the wall."

"No." The hard man didn't slacken his grip on her. "She spent the night with the people curing the plague and grieving the dead. What did you do in your fancy house?"

Soldiers stepped between the hard man and the soft.

"This is mutiny!" the soft one screamed.

"No," the hard man said. "It is rebellion."

The soft man shoved forward. One of the soldiers punched the man in the gut, then pushed him toward the wall. He fell with a gurgling scream.

The crowd in the street below roared.

The hard man lifted Aimee high and shouted.

"The Golden One is safe. We will open the gates and speak with her people."

"Good choice." The soldier who'd pushed the soft man off the wall straightened. "May I have my daughter back?"

"Papa!"

The hard man put Aimee down, and she ran to Rodrigo and hugged him tightly.

"Thank you for loaning her to us for the night." The hard man knelt. "I take responsibility for her abduction. My life is in your hands."

"Don't hurt him, Papa. He has a son named Kintel."

"I noticed you never faltered holding Aimee on the wall." Rodrigo put a hand on the hard man's shoulder. "Go give your son a hug." He offered his arm to Aimee. "Shall we go meet Shu at the gate? He was worried about you."

"Shu worried?" Aimee raised an eyebrow.

"He was going to tear the city down and sow salt where it once stood. I convinced him to let me come in and check on you. As soon as I heard the crowds, I knew you'd be fine, but I followed you up on the wall to be sure."

They walked through the city to the gate which already stood wide open. Aimee stopped in the gate and turned back to the people who'd followed her.

"Keep your gates and your hearts open." She held up her hand for a few heartbeats, then turned and walked to Shu and hugged him tightly. "Thank you."

"You are the Golden One." Shu squeezed her until she could hardly breathe. "I need to realize you belong to the world, not just the Shung."

Ba stepped up and knelt to her, the others beside him.

"We failed you."

"I was meant to go inside the walls." Aimee put her hand on his shoulder. "You didn't fail." She looked around at the gathered Shung. "They're going to be talking for a while. Can I get something to eat?"

CHAPTER 24

FURY UNLEASHED

Leandra sat in a tea shop. The tea was fair and the food ghastly, but she had a reason for being there.

The men from the Guild walked in and stared at Leandra. She waved at them.

"We keep seeing you around." The men sat at her table. "It is concerning."

"It is time we had a chat." Leandra pushed the half-eaten plate aside. "I do not work for you. I had my reasons to play in your arena. Those reasons are ended."

"We are not good people to annoy," one man said. The other put a hand on his arm. "Did you have anything to do with three collectors dying the other day?"

"If I was to start killing the Guild people off, I would have started with you." Leandra sat back. "I am a dangerous person, and you have annoyed me enough. You will stop."

"You are going to do what? Destroy us?" The man laughed. "Others have tried and failed."

"I know every place your Guild does business. I know where you meet to get your orders, where you store your goods. You've seen me in the arena."

"The arena is very different from the streets."

"Yes, it is." Leandra drew a rune on the table. Men throughout the tearoom cursed and dropped knives and other weapons on the table "In the arena, I was holding back so no one would get hurt. I don't care if you get hurt."

The men paled.

"Do you want to see more? Should I burn down the warehouse by the river?" She lifted a hand.

"No!" the men spoke in unison.

"Good, we have an understanding." Leandra drew a rune in the air. "You recognize it? It is the rune to bind an oath. I will swear to leave you be as you leave me and mine be. There will be no second chances. If you act against any of my people, I will rid this city of every last one of you."

She put two gold coins on the table.

"You will swear on these coins."

The men looked at each other then each put a hand on a coin. "We swear for ourselves and all who are part of the Guild."

"And I swear on the Balance." The rune glowed brightly, and Leandra left while the men were still blinking.

***

Trader walked into Zafre's courtyard.

"Hello, Trader." He came out and nodded to her.

"I'm here to tell you I won't be training with you." Trader took a shuddering breath. "There is something more important I must do."

"A friend of yours was worried about you. It seems she no longer needs to be concerned."

"No, she doesn't."

"May I ask what this important thing is?"

"The queen hugged me and called me her friend." Trader smiled as the warmth of that memory lifted her mood.

"Important indeed." Zafre nodded again. "Now that you will not be a student, you may visit me as a friend."

"Really?" Trader ran and hugged him.

"Of course." Zafre patted her head. "It would brighten an old man's days."

"Then I will." Trader hugged him again, then ran away. Her feet didn't feel like they touched the ground.

Back in the Hall, she went into the mess hall and sat beside the oldest of the Nekkest.

"If I wanted to hire some Nekkest, how would I do it?"

"What does a girl need of the Nekkest?"

"I can't tell you yet."

"If I am your agent, I am bound by oath to keep your secrets."

"All right, you're my agent." Trader put a gold bead from Mathial's hair on the table.

He picked it up and looked at her.

"Let's go for a walk, boss."

In the end, Trader had to ask Mathial to show Wunkit the medallion. He knelt and pledged his service to the queen.

Now the Nekkest met in the hall, everyone who lived in the hall and many who were out on contract. There was hardly room to breathe.

Trader stood on a table. A murmur went through the room.

"Why should we listen to a child?"

"Because I ask it." Wunkit hammered his fist on the table. The muttering subsided.

"I want to hire all of you on behalf of someone!" Trader shouted. "I promise it is honourable work."

"And what can a child pay us for this honourable work?"

Trader tilted the gold jewellery onto the table.

"There is more. It is a surety for payment. Wunkit will hold it, and if we can't pay the value in gold, then you keep this and the rest."

"Why didn't you bring it all?"

"Because I didn't want to spend the day picking it up again." Trader crossed her arms as the Nekkest laughed.

"You aren't joking." The speaker stood up. "Who are you acting for and what is this work?"

"Please call them in, Wunkit." Trader pointed to the door. He wove his way through the crowd and opened the door.

The muttering started again when Mathial, Fury and Nikay walked in. Fury jumped onto the table and lifted Mathial and Nikay up beside her.

"You are bound by the laws of the Nekkest to never speak to outsiders of what happens in this room."

"We know the law and will keep it."

"Show them, Mathial," Trader said.

Mathial lifted the medallion out and laid it on the front of her dress.

"I am Mathial, queen of the Confederacy. I am hiring you to take my throne back from those who would use it for their own ends."

Starting with Wunkit and the one who asked the questions, the room knelt.

"Does this mean we have a contract?"

"It does." The questioner stood. "I am Axili, and I will serve you to the death."

One by one the Nekkest stood and gave their oath.

***

Nikay looked around the room. Only the core of their group was present.

"It is all very well to hire the Nekkest to serve the queen," Axili leaned forward, "but what is your plan?"

"The council meets monthly," Mathial said. "I will attend and claim the Queen's Seat. It has been empty too long. There will be those who will not be pleased. They have at least some control of the army. The Nekkest will be my guarantee of safety."

"Even we can't fight the entire army." Axili shook his head, tapping his fingers on the table.

"Much of the army has marched north under General Mabian," Wunkit said. "They offered a good contract."

"Even what is left will be a problem. We will probably have to fight our way into council."

"I will deal with the guards in the Council Chamber." Fury spoke from where she leaned against the wall.

"Alone?" Axili raised his eyebrows.

"I am not alone." Fury frowned.

"I will go with her." Leandra lifted a hand.

"Magic is forbidden in the Council Chamber."

"I will be there to make sure all present remember the law."

"Cameto and Raphael will come too." Nikay closed his eyes where he leaned beside Fury.

"He's not even six." Axili threw his hands up.

"We will fail without his presence," Nikay said. "We didn't ask you to tell us what can and can't be done but to make what must be done possible."

"Very well." Axili sat back. "We need a disturbance to draw soldiers away from the chamber. They will block the council in to keep them safe. Smuggle those who need to support the queen in before council begins, then no one will be able to leave before you can reason with them."

"Send your fastest person to General Mabian. The message is 'Queen Mathial orders him not to start hostilities.' They will carry this." Mathial put a necklace on the table. "He gave it to me for my birthday. It will tell him my message is true."

"How you do know he will obey you? He is your uncle, but he's under Phenos' thumb."

"The message will make it clear the hostage is free, as my uncle intended."

Axili picked up the necklace. "I will see to the necessary arrangements." He bowed and left.

"He is one of our best." Wunkit sighed and rubbed his eyes.

"Honest questions are welcome." Mathial stood. "The next council meeting is in a few days. Everything must be ready."

"It will be, my queen." Wunkit bowed and followed Axili.

Fury and Nikay sat and put their arms around Mathial.

"You did great." Nikay kissed her cheek. "You will be a strong queen."

"Now, about how to get you into the council chamber." Leandra waved a hand, and Nikay sat back to see her better. "We still have your slave greys and the collars. I can make something for Mathial which will look like one. No one pays much attention to slaves. Cameto has learned the Council Chamber is cleaned the morning of the meeting."

"Won't they notice us not coming out?"

"Cameto will be guarding the door while you clean. He will let Raphael and me in when the coast is clear. That way I can deal with any problems that might arise."

"And Trader?"

"She is doing what she does best. There should be quite a crowd outside the council building."

"I don't want a riot."

"That's what the Nekkest are for. They will protect the people and reveal your presence in the chamber. You will have the popular support. And Hojiam is there if someone uses magic."

***

Nikay kept his head down like the other slaves. Mathial moved stiffly, but no one noticed. This group of men and women were as indifferent as any he'd met. He suspected the dark blue instead of black gem on their collars had something to do with it.

They followed orders and cleaned every finger's breadth of the room. Nikay discovered a section of the panelling that looked familiar. He pressed it as he scrubbed, and a door opened with a click. Closing it again, Nikay worked his way around the room. It was the only panel he found.

Finally, the door opened and Cameto ordered everyone out. Nikay ducked down to hide behind a chair. He couldn't see Mathial or Fury, but they knew what to do. When Cameto closed the door, they stood up behind the largest chair. He guessed it was the Queen's Seat. Nikay waved them over to the secret door. The space inside was larger than he'd expected, almost a room.

Fury pulled the gold fabric from around her waist and wrapped Mathial who put the medallion on the outside.

"People come," Fury whispered and pulled them to the wall opposite the secret door.

"I tell you, there were slaves who didn't come out of the council chamber."

"I didn't see anything out of order." Cameto's bass responded. "Do you see anyone in here?"

"No," the first voice spoke grudgingly. "You're new."

"Just got my promotion." Cameto sounded proud.

"Right, then, as you were." The door outside closed, and Nikay breathed a sigh of relief. Fury held him against the wall and pointed to the ordinary door which let into the room opposite the secret one. Nikay kicked himself for not noticing.

The door opened and three men walked through.

"Maybe something will happen this time and we'll get some action."

"Shut up, you're getting paid—"

Fury hit them from behind. She dragged the bodies back through the door into the passage and closed the door.

"Thank you," Mathial whispered. "I didn't want to wait with bodies in the room."

Fury handed Nikay a sword and kept one for herself.

"I hope I can remember what Father taught me."

"Don't think. Just let your body act." Fury put a hand on his shoulder. He nodded.

The outside door opened again and then closed.

Fury pointed to the door, so Nikay opened it and waved to Leandra.

"A secret door," Raphael said as he walked in. "Why don't we have any secret doors?"

"It would be hard to have a secret door in our wagon."

"Yeah, I guess so."

"Axili told me that Lupji, Pounjou and Teekja left with the necklace immediately after our meeting. They will make it in time. They are desert walkers."

Mathial nodded her head, but as they waited, she began trembling. Nikay stood behind her and wrapped his arms around her and held her tight.

"You will be fine. You are strong."

She reached back to caress his face. "What am I going to do when you go home?"

"Fury and I will always be your friends."

Fury gave him an odd look, but Nikay put it out of his mind. He kind of liked holding Mathial this way.

For a third time the door opened, and people filed in chattering loudly until it sounded like the roar of the ocean on the far sound of the room.

They'd have to get halfway around the room to the large chair. He hadn't thought there would be so many people.

The roar quietened and was replaced by a droning voice that could have been chosen to put people to sleep.

A crash interrupted the voice.

"Councillors, there is trouble outside," Cameto's voice boomed. "For your protection, the doors will be barred." The door slammed, and something banged into place.

"Now, while they are distracted." Nikay opened the secret door and stepped out, followed by Fury and then Mathial.

For all the confusion, it didn't take long for them to be noticed. Then Phenos shouted.

"They are traitors, stop them!" He put his hand out as if trying to control Nikay and Fury. Nikay tore his collar off and threw it aside.

"I have been held prisoner long enough," Mathial announced in a loud voice.

"She's a fraud. Everyone knows the queen is mad." Phenos pushed one of his guards. "Kill them, kill them all."

The guard ran at them, followed by a dozen others. They all looked like legionnaires. In the rest of the room, chaos ruled. Most of the councillors scrambled out of the way of guards who fought to reach Mathial, whether to kill or protect her Nikay had no way of telling.

"Stay with Mathial." Fury crouched between them and the approaching legionnaires. "I will always love you, Nikay." She sprang into action before he could ask what she was talking about.

***

Fury looked at the approaching soldiers. She couldn't deal with them alone. *Fury,* she called the being within.

There will be no going back. We will be one.

I don't care as long as he's safe.

Fire poured into Fury's veins as her muscles changed.

"Stay with Mathial," she told Nikay. "I will always love you." There would be no other chance to tell him.

She leaped at the oncoming enemy, smashing two and tossing them aside. The others stepped back with their swords raised. One ran to the side. Fury jumped at him and kicked him across the room, but two more moved to pass her as she stepped out of their way. Bouncing off the railing, Fury landed on their backs and snapped their necks. Swords bit into her back. She howled and spun, ripping the swords out of her. Punches landed on armour, but still she pushed the men back.

Fury had dropped the sword before she started. Stupid. Attacking before the soldiers regrouped, she got a sword into her hand, but more cuts. They wouldn't get to Nikay. She'd fight until she died, and even after that, to save him.

***

Nikay thought he was used to Fury's ferocity, but she blurred into action. A guard jumped out of the chaos, pointing his sword at Mathial. Nikay lunged forward, and his sword cut the man's throat. A woman stumbled out and slashed at him with a dagger. His return cut separated her hand from her body. He kicked her back into the mess of bodies. Mathial huddled against the wall but slid along it toward the chair.

Fury's howls reverberated in the chamber, and now people were trying to get out past Cameto who pushed the crowd back and used the flat of his sword to keep them clear of the door. Shouting and crashing came from the other side of the door.

Nikay barely dodged a sword strike. The man didn't have armour. Nikay ran his sword into the great artery in the man's leg. Something stabbed his side, and he whirled to slash the woman's throat. He left the dagger where it was.

Three men pushed their way out of the crowd between him and Fury. They grinned nastily before Fury landed on them, snapping one's neck and beheading another. Nikay lunged and ran his sword through the third man's armpit. He lost his sword, so he picked up another and cut a woman attacking with a sword open.

The legionnaires were down to two, but Fury bled from wounds all over her body. Mathial stood ahead of Nikay. He stumbled to her side and held his sword up, but his arm felt like lead.

Fury screeched and threw herself onto the legionnaires' swords. They fell dead under her, but she didn't move, the points of the swords coming through her back. A big man charged out and grabbed Nikay by the throat. He couldn't get his sword to work. Then the man grunted and fell back. Mathial held a sword dripping blood in her hand. Nikay pushed himself along the wall to protect her, but his legs wouldn't cooperate, and he fell to the floor. Even on the floor, he tried to push himself along but lacked the strength.

Mathial stepped out of his sight, and he dropped his head in despair. They'd failed.

***

Mathial held the bloody sword and sidled toward the chair. No one came out of the crowd now. They pushed away from her. Her friends had died trying to help her. She wouldn't stop until she too was dead.

Rage burned in her, fighting with the terror trying to turn her legs to water. Phenos stepped in front of her with a sneer.

"You could have married me and stayed queen."

"I'd rather die."

"I thought you'd say that." He slapped the sword out of her hand and wrapped his hands around her neck. "You can't know how long I've wanted to do this."

Black spots danced in her eyes and something burned at her chest. Scratching at his hands didn't help. Her hand brushed the medallion and fire ran up her arm. She yanked on it, snapping the chain it hung on and pushed it against Phenos.

He screamed and fell back clawing at the medallion that burned against his chest. Black spread across his chest then he convulsed violently before lying still.

Now you're a murderer. A voice whispered in her ear. All this just so a little girl could play at being queen.

"No." Mathial pushed the thoughts away. "My people need me. They've been corrupted." She crouched down and picked up the medallion from Phenos' corpse. She couldn't wear it with the chain broken, so she held it tight in her hand, staggering the last few steps to fall into the chair. Light burst from the medallion through her fingers. The chaos in the room died as the people stared at her, then one by one they went to their knees.

Raphael stepped out of the secret room, followed by his mother. Mathial's tears were playing tricks on her because she saw a huge black jaguar walking beside the boy.

"You've done enough bad things." Raphael pointed at something she couldn't see. Then a growl echoed in the room, and the black shape jumped forward to catch something she couldn't quite see and shook it like a cat with a mouse. The great cat padded over to where Fury lay. He became more solid with each step.

"You get one wish, child." He nudged her with his nose.

"I want him to live. Let him be happy with her." Fury's voice was weak.

"You don't wish to live?" The jaguar nudged her again.

"I want him to live more." She dropped her head.

"Very well." The jaguar turned and breathed on Nikay. His wounds closed and his colour returned. He lifted his head and looked at Mathial.

Then she understood Fury's wish, and her tears flowed harder. Nikay's blurred shape came toward her, then his arms wrapped around her and his tears dampened her wrap. She wiped her eyes and hugged him back.

"I am curious about you, little one." The jaguar nudged Fury again "Though you yet fight for life, you gave it to your friend." He breathed on her. The swords dissolved, and her wounds vanished. Fury sat up.

"Why?"

"I felt like it." The jaguar chuckled, and it shook the room. Then he turned into smoke and drifted away.

Fury stood and walked over to sit on Mathial's other side. Nikay stared at her in wonder.

"Why?"

"I felt like it." Fury wrapped her arms around both of them. Mathial heaved a deep sigh; maybe this would work after all.

The banging at the door had stopped.

"Open the door, Cameto." Mathial shifted so she could put an arm around each of her friends.

He lifted the bar and dropped it to the side. The door opened, and Axili stood with sword in hand.

"My queen," he saluted. "We have secured the council building and the city is quiet, but the people want to see you."

"Then they shall see us." Mathial stood and tugged on Fury and Nikay. "You don't think I'm going to go talk to them alone, do you?"

CHAPTER 25

THE CENTRE OF EMPIRE

Tomak watched from the wall as the endless lines of horsemen filled the space in front of Lusia's main north gate.

People had brought wild stories with them. The leader of the horde was a madman who collected the right hands of his enemies. He was a beneficent leader who scattered gold wherever he went. A girl travelled with him who had power over life and death.

"Look how they ride." Striphona pointed down at the lines. "They are avoiding trampling the fields. What kind of invader takes that much care over farmers' fields?"

"The kind who plans to stay." Deathsdotter leaned on the wall on Striphona's other side. Maybe it was his imagination, but she looked taller now.

"Is this what everything has been working toward?" Tomak

asked.

"This is a tangle of fates," Deathsdotter said. "The players are here, but what will happen I cannot see."

"What are the options?" Striphona asked her.

"Everybody lives, everybody dies, or something in between." She was rolling her eyes, Tomak could hear it in her voice.

"Helpful." Striphona turned away from the horsemen. "They won't be doing anything soon. Let's go."

He led the way along the wall, Tomak and Deathsdotter on either side and Tomak's crew in loose formation around them. They walked down the stairs to where the crowd waited in the yard on the inside of the gate.

"They can't break Lusia's wall," Striphona called to the crowd. "Go, get on with your lives. Today's meal is more important than tomorrow's doom."

"Inspiring." Deathsdotter scowled at Striphona. "Wrong, but inspiring."

"What would you tell them?" Striphona looked at her.

"Never mind." She walked away and Striphona matched her stride. Heurfotter following a few paces back. Tomak stood and stared at them. How old was his sister? He counted on his fingers. Sixteen, seventeen. He'd always treated her as younger because of her illness. She was Deathsdotter. He was imagining things.

"If I didn't know better, I'd say they were falling for each other," Harik said.

"Shut up." Tomak pushed his second in command away.

"You too, huh?"

Tomak put it out of his mind.

A messenger from the horde came to the gate the next day.

"If Lusia opens her gates, Shu will be merciful."

He didn't wait for a reply.

"What does that mean? Shu will be merciful?"

"I imagine Shu is the name of the leader." Deathsdotter waved her hand. "What is more important is how you will respond."

"If I thought he'd be good for my people, I'd open the gates and deal with whatever he did to me."

"But?"

"I can't be sure. Even if he's merciful today, will he remain so? Would he punish all of Lusia because my nobles tried to kill him?"

"How do you know they would try to kill him?" Tomak sipped at his water.

"Killing each other and their emperor is their pastime, do you really think they wouldn't try?"

"Good point.

"Single combat," Deathsdotter said. "Whoever lives decides the fate of Lusia."

Tomak looked at his sister.

"This is what's been keeping you up at night, isn't it?"

She looked down.

"I'm not very good with a sword." Striphona held up his hands. "I wouldn't last a heartbeat."

"I will go." Tomak stood up. "It's my fate, isn't it? To die at this Shu's hand?"

"It's more complicated than that." Deathsdotter wiped at her face. "You aren't certain to die or certain to live. There is someone else who will hold your life or death in their hand. Remember to trust."

"Don't cry for me, Sister. I doubt I have much reason to live, but I will do my best."

"Try not to kill Shu." Deathsdotter didn't look at him. "He's important."

"So I'm to fight a duel to the death with the man, somehow win but not kill him?"

"I don't know." Deathsdotter jumped up and stomped her foot. "Everywhere I look, I see people dying. You, me, Striphona, Shu. Everybody, and she won't tell me what to do!" She ran out of the room, Heurfotter glanced reproachfully at Tomak before following.

"Why don't you go talk to her?" Tomak told Striphona. "I'm going to get ready. There's plenty of light left to get this over with."

He picked up his axe and shield, his armour was already on.

"You're in charge, Harik, until I get back."

Tomak left before Harik could reply. He didn't expect to come back. Lydia flashed across his mind, her face bruised and bloody as the traitor dragged her away. Could she have survived? He hoped so, but his heart had given up.

"Let me out the postern, then bar it behind me," Tomak growled at the man guarding the gate.

Outside the gate, the horde looked even bigger. Tomak walked toward them, shield in his left hand, axe in his right. When riders separated from the mass, he put shield and axe on the ground and lifted his empty hands.

They roared up to him then stopped as one. Impressive riders, though he expected no less.

"What do you want?"

"Emperor Striphona wishes to save bloodshed on both sides. He's sent me out to challenge Shu to single combat. The survivor decides the fate of Lusia."

One of the men laughed, and Tomak peered up at him. He looked like the kind of person who'd rule this host of people.

"Tomak?" One of the women who flanked Shu stared at him through one dark eye.

"You know this man, Hoárr?" Shu looked over at her. The woman on the other side might have been made of stone.

"He is my husband." The one called Hoárr said. A reference to the northmen's one-eyed god. Tomak peered at her more closely. She wore leather, not armour like the other woman, as she slipped from her horse. Tomak saw she was expecting. His heart cracked as he recognized Lydia. She clearly belonged to this Shu.

Remember to trust. He heard it as if Deathsdotter spoke in his ear.

"Very well." Shu leaned jumped from his horse and pointed at Tomak. "You may choose. Let this man live, and I will sack Lusia and take the emperor's crown. Let him die, and I will spare the city."

"Lydia." Tomak's mouth was dry. He wanted his last words to her to be kind, loving. The Lydia he knew would never betray him, not purposefully, and she wouldn't sacrifice a city for him.

"Have you decided on a name for our son?"

"I think I would like a daughter." Lydia stood like a statue.

"A daughter would be wonderful." Tomak ached to take her in his arms, but that would be too cruel.

Then she ran to him and hugged him, covering his face with kisses and tears.

"I thought you were dead," she cried in his ear. "I saw you die."

"Freya bought my life." Tomak held her tight. The baby in her kicked him, and he laughed through his tears. "I never thought to see you again. She wouldn't let me chase after you."

"She brought you here to me." Lydia clutched him tight, then spun to look at Shu.

"It isn't like you to give such a cruel choice, but I have chosen. I will save the city, but you will kill both of us. If you try to leave me alive. I will kill myself and curse you with my last breath."

"Shu." The other woman turned to him. "Think about what you are doing. You knew she wasn't yours and never would be."

Lydia's arm tightened around him, and Tomak breathed in her scent.

"Shu, I am content. My life is complete."

Shu roared wordlessly, and Tomak expected him to charge. Instead, he sagged and hung his head.

"Hoárr, forgive me, I am a fool." He fell to his knees and wept.

Lydia moved to step forward.

"Go, he's your friend, comfort him." Tomak pushed her toward Shu.

Lydia ran to him and wrapped her arms around him. Tomak couldn't hear the words. He didn't need to.

Shu finally stood and straightened his shoulders as he led Lydia back to Tomak.

"You are a good man. You never doubted her." Shu bowed to Tomak. "Please invite Emperor Striphona to talk with his brother Shu. I will guarantee his safety. He can bring as many guards as he likes." He looked at Lydia. "Go with him."

"Thank you, Shu." Lydia touched his cheek. "And you too, Vakate." The woman bowed on her horse.

"Come, my sister will be thrilled to see you." Tomak led Lydia toward the city.

"Aren't you going to pick up your axe and shield?"

"Don't need them." He took her hand. "What about Rika as a name for our daughter?"

"I like it." Lydia let go of his hand and wrapped her arm around his waist. "I'm not going to let go of you for a very long time."

"I can live with that."

***

Tomak stood with Lydia to the side of Shu and Striphona. Harik had the men in good order. Deathsdotter kept looking at Lydia as if she feared she would vanish again.

Vakate stood with Shu, and a Rehego with a hook for a hand stood on the other side of him. Behind him, a Rehego woman and a girl with a gold cloak and gold hair sat on horses. Shu had no warriors.

"Your country looks prosperous," Shu said to Striphona. "You must be a good emperor."

"I try. I have good advisors."

"As do I." Shu took Vakate's hand. "People who have the courage to disagree with me."

"That's important." Striphona nodded his head. "I have brought the south of the Empire out of chaos. Farmers plant their crops with no fear of soldiers trampling them. Traders move up and down the roads."

"I have tried to do the same with the north." Shu pointed behind him. "I had to be firm with the legions, but they have learned their lesson."

"Meircen is approximately the border between north and south," Striphona said. "I will trust the north to you if you will trust the south to me."

"I think I can do that." Shu put out his hand and Striphona shook it. "Should I get my scribes to write out a treaty?"

"I have said it," Shu flipped his hand, "but if you wish pieces of paper, I will sign them when I have time."

The golden girl giggled, and Shu looked over his shoulder at her.

"I trust your word." Striphona said, "but I can't promise my scribes won't send a wagonload of paper to you. Take as long as you want to deal with them."

"Good to see peace winning out over war." A voice spoke behind Tomak, and he turned to see who it was. An old man in black stood with two other younger men behind him. "I told your people I was friends with Lydia, and they let me through."

"Holy Father." Lydia turned red.

"You look well, Lydia." The Holy Father smiled and patted her hand. "I should have expected something of the sort from the Holy Mother."

Everyone except Rodrigo and Aimee stared at Lydia. Tomak's heart pounded.

"I married the Holy Mother?"

"Well, she clearly needed a husband, and you are a good man." The Holy Father put his hand in Lydia's. "Live a long and happy life. God knows what he is doing."

Tomak hugged Lydia close to him.

"Striphona, I'm glad to see you've got things under control."

"We would like to have your guidance."

"My pleasure."

The Holy Father walked up to Shu.

"Welcome, Shu, live and be blessed. Now, I must be going." The Holy Father held his hand up in benediction, then walked away, followed by the two men.

CHAPTER 26

VISIT HOME

Nikay leaned against the wall and watched Mathial talk to the Nekkest delegation. The elders from Home had sent Elder Jupcis to check out the new queen.

"While it is traditional for the Nekkest to be the royal bodyguard, hiring the entire nation is unprecedented."

"With the unrest, I felt it wise to keep a force I knew was loyal." Mathial sat straight but not stiffly. He was proud of her. "There were those who have tried to subvert the army. General Mabian has had to completely reform the command structure."

"I imagine the council is unhappy about losing all their power."

"I have no intention of taking away the council's power, only balancing it. They were growing more concerned about their own wealth than the well-being of the people. Since I am forbidden from owning any business or earning money, I can be an advocate for fairness." She leaned forward. "I am young and open to hearing counsel from others, but I will not be patronized or relegated to a ceremonial position."

Jupcis smiled. "It seems that the frantic reports of megalomania were more than a little exaggerated. If you are willing, I will stay as an advisor from the viewpoint of the Nekkest. Perhaps the time to be simple mercenaries to the highest bidder has ended."

"You would be most welcome." Mathial put her hand out. "The council will take some convincing, but I'm sure I can arrange for you to attend meetings, if not hold a chair. There are a few vacancies."

Jupcis peered across the table. "Your bodyguards...there are rumours."

"Nikay and Fury are not my bodyguards; they are friends. I don't know what the rumour at the moment is, but Fury defeated a dozen legion soldiers by herself. Nikay held off guards from certain nobles who tried to kill me."

"And Nekhaize?"

"He was there. Raphael told me Nekhaize was his friend. Axili explained who he was. I am honoured he appeared."

"Nekhaize is a large part of why the Nekkest are beginning to change our ways. That Hojiam who came through with Shi'iposu and the boy has returned to Home. They are a most interesting person."

"I heard a delegation has gone to the Oasis."

"We felt it was time to repair the rift in our family." Jupcis sighed, then chuckled. "It appears life is about repairing the mistakes of our ancestors."

"Not everything our ancestors did was a mistake." Mathial stood. "We build on their shoulders. Let me walk you out."

Nikay stepped into place beside Fury and followed them through the palace.

"Mistress," a young woman greeted Mathial, "a dressmaker from the city would like to meet with you."

"Thank you, Lisbeth, please schedule a time and let me know."

"As you wish." Lisbeth smiled and bustled off.

"You have no slaves."

"I freed them all." Mathial frowned. "I will have no slaves in my presence. The council is close to passing a law forbidding the slave trade. Our neighbours to the north do very well without it."

"The Nekkest have never kept slaves." Jupcis patted Mathial's arm. "I approve."

They stopped at the door. Nekkest guards opened the door, saluting Mathial.

"General Mabian came by, said he'd see you at lunch," one said.

"Thank you, Kanjo, how's your daughter today?"

"Running around like a wildcat, seems she just had a childhood fever."

"I'm glad to hear that."

Mathial walked to the library where they entered a closed room. She opened the book on the table and, with Nikay at her side, worked her way through the story.

"Reading is getting easier." Mathial closed the book and sat back. "The stories are fascinating."

"I'm proud of you." Nikay squeezed her shoulder.

"I never liked reading, but I admit it is a useful skill." Fury had leaned back in her chair and closed her eyes. "And it gives you two time together."

"You aren't giving up on that are you?" Nikay's face heated, and Mathial blushed.

"Just from a political point of view, it is brilliant." Fury grinned at them. "Well, it's almost lunchtime, and your uncle is visiting." She jumped to her feet. Mathial shook her head and stood.

"Let's not keep him waiting."

They ate lunch in a small dining room with windows overlooking the city. Mathial had dragged Nikay and Fury through every room in the palace exploring over the last couple of months. She'd changed their bedroom three times before settling on the suite her parents had lived in.

"Good to see you, Mathial." General Mabian stood when they entered. "Lord Nikay, Lady Fury."

"You're the only one who calls us that." Nikay bowed.

"It is important to remind ourselves of the depth of gratitude we owe you."

The servants came in with trays, so Nikay seated Mathial, then took the chair on her right. Fury sat on the other side.

"As much as I delight in visiting my niece," General Mabian pulled out a letter, "I have received an official invitation for you to visit King Harald in Belandria."

Mathial took the letter and unfolded it. Nikay read it as she worked her way through it.

"Are you sure it is wise to leave the country?" Mathial folded the letter and pushed it away.

"There is never going to be a perfectly safe time, but the Confederacy is stable, and it is only for a month. I will be able to keep things from falling apart until you get back."

"I don't know." Mathial frowned.

"You can't deny who your friends are forever." General Mabian handed a kerchief to Mathial. "They need to go home."

"You're right, I'm being selfish." Mathial dabbed at her eyes.

"There is a solution." Fury stood and took Nikay and Mathial's hands and joined them.

General Mabian's eyes widened, then lit up.

"It would be a very good match."

Mathial looked at Nikay. "Would it be so bad?"

His heart race from the warmth of her hand. He'd held it so often, why was it now different?

"I am yours." His throat was so dry he couldn't finish the sentence.

Mathial burst into tears and fell into his arms. He didn't try to understand; he just held her while Fury smiled at them.

"What about you?" Nikay asked softly. "We've been friends forever."

"And we always will be." Fury patted his shoulder. "That's why I want this. You'll both be happy."

"I will write back to say you will be travelling to Belandria."

Mathial sat up and wiped her eyes. "I will take Leandra, Cameto, Raphael and Trader. You're staying here to run the country, so I'll ask Lord Pamre to come. He's as stuffy as they come but smart. Lady Dulca too, I want to keep an eye on her."

"She wants to be important, so give her a grand-sounding title and she'll be yours forever." Nikay squeezed her hand.

"I could make her Minister of Trade, at least until Trader is old enough for people to take seriously."

"I will ask Axili to put an honour guard together for you."

"I'll have Nikay and Fury."

"It might not go over well to have the Lord and Lady as bodyguards."

"Right." Mathial looked at their joined hands. "I'd like to leave within the week."

CHAPTER 27

PRISONERS RETURN

Prenny finished looking over the accounts for the month. Life had returned to normal much faster than she'd expected. The fishing boats were out, and the catch was good. If she could only find a way to get fresh fish to the capital, they'd double their income.

On the other hand, the De'e'tcha had declared the winter hiding places Treaty villages. They'd become centres of trade. The furs and other goods were astonishing. They were full of De'e'tcha. Some of Prenny's villagers had stayed on too.

"I'm going for a walk to stretch my legs." Prenny closed the book.

Yennet looked up from her mending. "Enjoy your walk. Pick up some thread for me at the merchant's."

"I will."

She went to the merchant's first, so she didn't forget, then headed down to the pier to see Petan. He'd wanted to talk to her about a new fish house for drying their catch.

The men were lined up on the dock pointing out to sea. She joined them and shivered.

"Run and get Kerhin."

One of the men dashed away, but Prenny didn't take her eyes off the approaching wolf ships, three of them.

"They're flying a white flag, my lady." Petan stood beside her.

"That's a relief." Prenny's stomach returned to normal.

Kerhin strode onto the dock.

"Flying the white flag, they're friendly."

"Let's give them a proper welcome." Prenny clapped her hands. "Can we move the boats to give them more room to tie up? Someone let the Inn know we'll have guests."

She watched as they approached. Yennet appeared and put a cloak around Prenny's shoulders.

"You still never dress for the weather."

"I have to give you something to do."

The ships came close enough for Prenny to see people on board. Two hove to, and the last came to dock.

"Permission to land." A young man stood on the bow of the ship, unbothered by the waves.

"Granted," Prenny called.

They pulled closer, then the young man jumped from the ship to the dock and made fast the line he held. Men on the ship threw more line, and the ship was soon tied securely.

"You must be Lady Prenny." The young man went to his knee. "I bring the prisoners back to you, as you requested."

"My thanks." Prenny grinned. "Bring your ships in. We have food being prepared.

"I'd best let Leohl know there will be a lot more guests."

The young man bounded to his feet, gave a shrill whistle, and waved.

"Dolthin, it is good to see you." Kerhin stepped forward.

"You look good, Father. Maybe I should take a turn as hostage."

"Don't tempt me."

The ships landed and people climbed onto the dock. Prenny didn't see as many as she'd hoped.

"Three ships seems excessive for the number of passengers."

"I wanted them to be comfortable on the voyage. I also took the liberty of bringing some trade goods."

"Leave them for the moment. Our merchant will be interested in what you have. She is also our agent for trade with the capital."

"Wonderful." Dolthin stood back and looked Prenny up and down. "You don't look like a valkyrie."

"Don't get her angry." Kerhin slapped Dolthin on the shoulder. "She and her men destroyed the entire Rau'ch presence on the coast, then stole our village back from us. When I met her, the body of Chieftain Valloc lay at her feet."

"My apologies if I offend." Dolthin bowed.

"No worries. If you get too obnoxious, I have cells I can lock you in." Prenny suppressed her giggle at his dumbfounded look. She imagined he usually had women falling at his feet.

The whole village turned out for the feast, setting tables in front of the inn. Dolthin had people in stitches, but Prenny was all too aware of the returning prisoners who stood to the side, silent and wary.

"What can I do to help them?" she asked Yennet.

"Sadly, I don't believe there is anything you can do. They must come to terms with their memories and fears themselves."

"Your pardon, my lady." A man she didn't recognize came over from the prisoners. "We're happy to be free, but most of us don't think we can live here. We used to love the sea. Now I can't stop watching it in fear."

"I understand. Wherever you want to go, I will help you."

"We don't want to leave you, my lady, only not have to look at the sea."

"There are the treaty villages with the De'e'tcha," Yennet said.

"That might work." The man looked doubtful.

"The old manor." Prenny clapped her hands. "You can have the manor and all the land around it. I was talking with the army about restoring it for their use, but this is much better. We'll arrange for people to help you build houses. You can use stone from the manor. They did that with my mother's estate."

"Lady Prenny." A woman in army uniform stood at attention. "The king has called you to return to Belopolis ."

"I can come in a week or so."

"Pardon, my lady, but my orders are to bring you immediately."

"May I at least pack a bag?" Prenny's stomach tied in a knot.

"Be quick."

"Yennet!" Prenny yelled across the crowd. "Travelling bag, now!" The maid waved in acknowledgement.

"What's going on?" Leohl came over and stood, hands on her hips.

"I have been called to the capital." Prenny pushed her worry aside for the moment. "I need you to help organize people to build homes for the returnees. Whoever wants one. I'll pay for it somehow."

"Don't worry about that now." Leohl glowered at the woman.

"Are you arresting our Lady?"

"My orders are to escort her to the king, not to arrest her." The woman sighed. "I can say no more than that."

Yennet ran out and handed Prenny a bag.

"We go, now," the woman said. Prenny followed her to the coach and climbed in.

There were coaches waiting at intervals. Prenny sank further into a funk. For there to be this much effort, she had to be in deep, deep trouble.

She hoped whoever took over from her would treat her people right. There was still much to do.

They arrived at the palace in the middle of the night. Lieutenant Baker escorted her to the door. Her name was the only thing she'd said to Prenny the entire trip.

Sam waited at the doors.

"You made good time." He nodded at Prenny's escort who saluted and left.

"This way." Sam strode down the halls forcing Prenny to jog to keep up. She couldn't remember being in this part of the palace. They arrived at a door and Sam knocked, then pushed the door open.

"Thank goodness you made it." Catrin ran over to hug Prenny.

Prenny saw the thin figure on the bed and suddenly all her worries vanished. This was much worse than anything she'd thought.

"Mother!" She ran to the bed and knelt, taking her mother's hand.

"Prenny." Lady Joan didn't speak above a whisper. "I wanted to see you one last time. I asked the king."

Suddenly the rush made sense.

"I thought..." Prenny shook her head sending tears flying. "Never mind what I thought. What can I do for you?"

"I heard you were busy having adventures this winter. Tell me about them, all of them."

***

Prenny woke with aching knees, still kneeling by the bed. One of Catrin's quilts was wrapped around her shoulders.

"We came to the city to see a healer, but she got worse and we couldn't go home. Then she talked about wanting to see you. The king said he'd get you here no matter what."

"I thought I was being arrested for my actions this winter."

"Were they so bad?"

"I yelled at the king's commander, then practically took over his command, then made a truce with a foreign power without asking the king's permission. That doesn't even touch the treaty with the De'e'tcha which I'm sure went over well at council."

"I'll let His Majesty talk to you about all that, but I will tell you that you are a hero to the people. The stories are crazy. Like the one where you single-handedly stopped an enemy charge with your bow."

"That isn't quite true." Prenny ducked her head.

"And the one where you got a village of the enemy to surrender by yelling at them, then made them part of Belandria?"

"That one's true."

"Sorry, I slept through your talk with Joan."

"I'm glad you made it." King Harald walked into the room.

Prenny went to her knee. "Your Majesty." She choked up and couldn't continue.

He lifted her up and embraced her.

"I'm sorry for your grief." He held her gently. "I remember when my mother died. If there is anything I can do for you, ask."

"How much trouble am I in?" Prenny buried her face in his shoulder.

"You've been in the centre of a great deal of trouble, but as for being in trouble. No. I'm sorry I didn't explain, but when they called me home, they told me mother was dying, and I was frantic the entire ride. I was one of the worst experiences of my life."

"I think you were wise." Prenny sighed. "Thank you. Do you treat all your nobles like this?"

"Your mother asked something similar." King Harald held her out at arm's length. "My answer is the same. 'Only the ones who are worth it.'"

Prenny sobbed, all her fears and grief combining in a knotted tangle in her heart.

The king held her until the storm passed.

"When you are ready, ask Sam to bring you to the parlour to make your report."

"Yes, Your Majesty." Prenny reluctantly stepped out of his arms. "I never knew my father, but in my dreams, he held me like that."

The king pulled her close, kissed her forehead and left.

Two days later, Lady Joan breathed her last. Prenny wept until she felt empty, Catrin stayed by her side sharing her grief.

"I must go see the king." Prenny lifted her head. "Mother would not want me to grieve forever."

"She was so proud of you. We both were." Catrin sighed and wiped her eyes. "There I go again."

"What are you going to do now?" Prenny stopped and turned to Catrin.

"I was doing most of Joan's work the last year. I expect I will continue."

"You are always welcome in my home." Prenny hugged her. "Always."

"Thank you, my dear." Catrin gave her a push. "Go see the king. You have responsibilities."

Sam led Prenny to a door she'd been through a few times with her   mother.
"The king has been informed and will attend shortly." He let her into the room.

"Welcome, Prenny." The queen looked up and smiled at her. "I would offer you tea, but Harald likes to serve his guests himself. Make yourself comfortable."

"How is Fury, I mean Princess Arthuria?"

"She prefers Fury." The queen wiped at her eyes. "You wouldn't have heard, but she and Nikay were abducted during the winter. They are coming home any day now."

"Good heavens." Prenny put her hand to her mouth. "The south? I worried the attack in the north was to draw strength away from the south."

"You were right." King Harald walked into the room. "But fortunately, it didn't develop into an invasion. General Huston and the Confederacy general had a delightful time by all accounts."

Prenny stood. "Your Majesty."

"You will call me Harald in this room. You are part of a very select group."

"And I am Sarandia." The queen nodded firmly.

"Harald," Prenny paused waiting for lightning to strike her. "I am ready to make my report."

"Have a seat." Harald waved her into a chair. "Would you like some tea or are you old enough for wine now?"

"I think I could use the wine." Prenny sat on the edge of her chair.

"Relax," Harald handed her a glass, "pretend I'm your father if it helps."

Prenny sipped at the wine. She'd tasted the odd bit here and there; this wasn't bad. She took another sip, then started telling her story.

Harald alternated between laughter, tears and anger. At the end of it, he saluted Prenny with his glass.

"That will put an end to the worries about the Northern Duchy." Harald rubbed his hands together. "Most of the people on the council haven't done that much in a lifetime.

"Northern Duchy?" Prenny looked up at the king.

"You are the heir." Harald looked at her with an odd expression. "Joan planned to retire anyway, even if she hadn't gotten sick."

The shakes started in her gut and moved outward. She put the glass down on the table beside her lest she spill it.

Harald lifted her and wrapped her in a hug while Sarandia

rubbed her back. When the shaking subsided, she flopped in the chair and picked up her wine.

"I'm happy being Countess of the North Shore." Prenny spun the glass in her fingers.

"By all means, keep the title." Harald knelt and put a hand on her arm. "But I need you running the north. You've proven you can do it."

"I won't leave the coast." Prenny lifted her chin.

"Just like her mother," Sarandia said.

"All the more reason." Harald sent a glance at Sarandia. "You can live wherever you want."

"I'll need to build a road south of the forest to connect the two halves of the Duchy. Catrin is willing to continue administrating the west, but I can't put all that burden on her for long. She's grieving too."

"She will get a pension from the crown." Sarandia sighed. "It won't bring Joan back, but she'll be comfortable."

"We also need to get that treaty with Westhelm written and signed." Prenny wrapped her arms around herself. "There's so much to do."

"Just do the thing that's in front of you." Harald pushed himself to his feet. "And don't be afraid to get help."

"Your friends from Westhelm showed up two days after you did." Sarandia rolled her eyes. "That Dolthin has been running his escort ragged."

"He's like that," Prenny laughed.

"They refused to negotiate with anyone other than Lady Prenny, Countess of the North Shore. Yennet came as well as a fisherman named Petan. Yennet is visiting with the other queen's women. She said she'd come as soon as you called but didn't want to intrude."

"I haven't given her a break. I'll let her relax for a while." Prenny sipped the wine. "But why did Petan come?"

"Apparently he was delegated to explain to the king just how important their Lady Prenny is. I have someone touring him about the city and the port."

"Pardon, Your Majesties, but the delegation from the Confederacy is here. A messenger has been sent to Lord Torrance and Lady Marriette." Sam put his hand to his head. "It's the oddest delegation I've ever seen. Most of them are kids."

"The great hall is too public. Show them here first."

"Very well."

Harald paced the room. "I haven't seen Fury for almost a year. I can't think."

Sarandia cried in her chair.

"Harald." Prenny put her arms around him. "It will be all right. She's your daughter. I will leave you to your reunion."

"No." Harald and Sarandia said together. "You're practically her sister. She'll want to see you."

"Your Majesties," Sam opened the door again. "Queen Mathial didn't want to overwhelm you, so only she, Nikay and Fury are here." He stepped aside, and three children walked into the room. Queen Mathial was a striking beauty with her dark complexion and deep brown eyes. Prenny didn't recognize Fury at first. She'd cut her hair short and didn't so much walk as prowl into the room.

Nikay saw her and nodded but didn't move from Queen Mathial's side.

"Mother, Father, may I present our dearest friend, Queen Mathial of the Confederacy." Fury pulled Mathial forward, and Nikay took her other hand, interlacing their fingers.

"It's all right. They don't bite." Nikay smiled at Mathial. She walked over to the King and Queen of Belandria and went to her knee still holding on to Nikay.

"Our deepest apologies for the pain our country has caused you. The perpetrators have been punished, but that doesn't give you back lost time with your daughter."

"Please stand," King Harald said. "We understand that is also due to your efforts that our countries are at peace and we have our children back."

A strange expression crossed Mathial's face, but then the door flew open and Lady Marriette ran into the room. Lord Torrance followed at a slower pace.

"Nikay." She went to him, then stopped short of hugging him. Queen Mathial let go of his hand and nodded to him. He threw himself at his mother and father. Fury reached for her parents at the same time.

Prenny stepped away, uncomfortable at being present with so many emotions. Her grief for her mother surfaced, and she fought back sobs.

"I didn't think Fury had an older sister." Mathial looked up at Prenny.

"I am Lady Prenny, an old friend of Fury's. I think the king and queen feared meeting their daughter again after all this time."

"Will they be all right?"

"Oh yes, they just need to talk, a lot." Prenny held out her arm. "Shall we go for a walk?"

Mathial looked over at the reunited families. "Yes, let's." She took Prenny's arm.

"I think I will tag along," Sam said. "Don't mind me."

"So, tell me about yourself." Mathial's arm shook on Prenny's.

"I was born a bandit's brat in the forest…"

***

King Harald sat on the throne in the great hall. Nikay and Fury flanked Queen Mathial. He'd panicked the day before when he saw she wasn't in the room. The maid said she'd gone with Prenny and Sam was with them, and he'd been able to relax a little.

They'd moved from babbling about their adventures to talking about Fury's plan.

Nikay had thought he'd die, but his parents had taken him seriously, talking about the good and bad of the idea until late at night. From the look on Fury's face, she'd had a similar talk with her parents.

"Welcome." King Harald's voice echoed in the room after the delegation had been announced. "We are pleased to announce not only Her Majesty Queen Mathial's visit but that we will be negotiating a treaty for peace and trade. They have very skilled negotiators."

They must have been introduced to Trader. Nikay kept his face straight. The hard part was coming up.

"As an introduction to that treaty, we have a couple of announcements." King Harald took a deep breath. "First, to solidify the new relationship, we have agreed to the betrothal of Nikay leBraun and Queen Mathial."

Mathial reached over and took his hand and gave him a shy smile. He squeezed and smiled back. They had a few years to get used to the idea. His parents had insisted on a wedding at sixteen and no earlier. He and Mathial had agreed happily.

"Lady Marriette is our ambassador to the Confederacy and will be accompanied by Lord Torrance."

King Harald closed his eyes for a moment. "Lastly, Princess Arthuria, known fondly by all as Fury, will return to the Confederacy. She has built bonds in that country she is reluctant to sever. She has our blessing and goodwill."

That must have been quite the conversation. Fury's face held no emotion. She only got like that when she felt overwhelmed. The king continued to talk, but Nikay let it flow past him. The warmth of Mathial's hand in his took all his attention.

***

Harald sat with Sarandia in the parlour. They hadn't wanted to let Fury go, but she would be stifled in this palace. He wasn't ready to announce that she was seriously considering abdicating her position as heir. He'd convinced her to defer her decision until she was fifteen and of age to take her oath.

Sarandia held his hand tightly, not saying anything. The twins curled up on chairs. They hadn't understood why their sister was going away again but were accustomed to her absence.

"We will visit every year," Harald said.

"That would be nice." Sarandia leaned her head against him. "I always knew we'd have to let our children make their own way, but not so soon. She's barely twelve."

"Did you see young Nikay and his queen? There is already something growing between them." Harald sighed.

"Did you hear he slept outside of the room Fury and Mathial shared?"

"After what they went through, do you blame him?"

"Not in the least. They didn't say as much, but I expect they shared a bed in the palace in the Confederacy." Sarandia took a long breath. "We have to trust them, as hard as that is."

"Torrance and Marriette are braver than I am. They've already turned down the queen's offer of rooms in her palace."

"They are wise."

"Pardon, Your Majesties," Sam said as he opened the door, "but there is someone here to see you."

"Send them in," Harald said. "We need distraction."

"Very well." Sam stepped aside, and a young woman holding a baby walked into the room. She had a patch over one eye. A man followed her, then stood with his hand on her shoulder. He obviously adored her.

"May I present Lydia, known as Hoárr in the east, Holy Mother-to-be, and her husband, Tomak of Getthelm." Sam stepped back and closed the door while Harald's mouth still hung open.

"Mother, Father." Lydia rocked her baby. "I will call you that in this room."

"Of course, dear." Sarandia had already gone to Lydia. "She's a beautiful baby."

"Her name is Rika." Lydia's voice was soft.

"I guess, in this room, that makes me Grandfather." Harald dangled his crown over the babe. She reached for it and gripped it tight.

"We have been sent as envoys from the emperors of the North and the South. They wish you to know that peace has come and trade will resume." Tomak's voice was a rich tenor.

"How long will you be staying?" Sarandia didn't take her eyes from Rika.

"Shu and Striphona have asked us to establish an embassy here to facilitate trade."

"Sit down and tell us your story." Harald went to the sideboard. "Would you like tea or wine?"

EPILOGUE

THE DAY BEFORE

Nikay woke up and stretched. After four years, he still hadn't got used to sleeping in his own room again. He'd never thought that betrothal to Mathial would mean he'd see less of her. Now that he was Lord Nikay, he couldn't live in the same room with Mathial and Fury, no matter how much he missed their warmth at night.

No, that isn't right, not warmth, their presence.

"My lord, breakfast is served in the green room." His servant, Ditzan, opened the curtains. "I've laid out your clothes as requested."

"Thank you." Nikay dressed quickly and went to join his friends for breakfast.

"Good morning." Mathial greeted him with a kiss on the cheek. Fury nodded.

"You're looking good this morning." Nikay admired her dress. The red and gold set off her dark skin and the cut made the most of her curves. He had to admit his mother's wisdom as much as it annoyed him. The sight of his betrothed set off feelings in his gut he didn't want to deal with while sleeping in the same room, never mind the same bed.

"I looked at the guest list and took Fury's advice and invited everybody." Mathial spooned jam onto her toast. "We'll have a small gathering just for family before the wedding."

"That sounds good." Nikay poured himself tea. "I've been looking at the ceremony, and with a couple of additions it will satisfy everyone."

"What additions?" Mathial's hand paused on the way to her mouth.

"The signing of a register and an exchange of rings. I'm told the archbishop in Belandria wants to officiate, but since we're getting married in the Confederacy, it should be celebrated by whomever you choose"

"Won't he be angry?"

"You aren't getting married to make the archbishop happy." Fury nibbled on a piece of fruit. "He'll be fine."

"Very well." Mathial took her bite of toast. "I've been talking to the elder from Home about the service. Could you run your ideas past him? If he's all right with it, then I'm happy."

They finished their meal, then headed to the courtyard Fury had taken over for her training.

Ten Nekkest warriors in full armour saluted her with their blunted spears. Fury put her armour on over her clothes. She wore the loose shirt and pants she always did, only the colour setting it apart from what they'd worn as slaves.

Fury didn't have the curves Mathial did, and the armour hid what she did have. She still kept her hair short too. Mathial took Nikay's hand as they watched.

"Ready." Fury lifted the two arm's-length batons she'd been using for the last year. They were easier to carry than a full staff.

The warriors charged, and just as he did every morning, Nikay winced in anticipation of the attack. He was happy to keep up with one attacker, never mind ten. Fury flipped over two of the attackers, tapping them on the helmets. They froze where they stood. She rolled on the stone and came up in a low crouch. The warriors regrouped and fanned out in a semi-circle. Fury dove toward her right moving inside the reach of the warrior's spear. One more down.

She feinted and tumbled through the sparring match, never stopping her motion until one of the spears caught her on the back. There were three warriors left not frozen.

"Good," Fury saluted them. "Once more."

"Why does she push herself so hard?" Mathial shuddered. "I'm always afraid she'll get hurt. I can't forget the sight of her lying mostly dead in the Council Chamber."

"Neither can she," Nikay said. "This is how she deals with it."

"She's tried to teach me, but I'm terrified."

"Fury has been teaching me since I was four," Nikay laughed, "and she still terrifies me, but she has absolute control over what she's doing. Watch how she taps the warriors, enough to let them know she's struck them but not enough to cause injury."

"But why does she need to fight against so many?"

"I think because if she doesn't lose, she can't learn to get better." Nikay squeezed her hand. "And speaking of getting better."

"Time for reading." Mathial sighed. "The only good part about it is that you're the one teaching me."

They left Fury to her deadly dance and headed to the library.

***

"The guests have started to arrive." Trader waved her list at Nikay. "King Harald and Queen Sarandia are staying with your parents at the embassy. Lydia, Tomak and Rika have rooms in the palace. Leandra, Cameto and Raphael have rooms with me. Xiuefa and Malahoun insisted on staying at the Hall, but it's bursting at the seams with all the Nekkest here for the wedding." She ran her finger down the page. "A Lord Haphin is representing Emperor Striphona; he keeps trying to sign trade deals." She rolled her eyes. "I don't like him. He doesn't take me seriously."

"He'll learn." Nikay grinned, "You're half the reason the Confederacy is doing so well."

"Oh, and a few people have sent regrets along with gifts. Some of them are different. It isn't like you and Mathial need anything, so people send weird things. Lady Prenny and Dolthin are watching Belandria while the king is down here. They sent figurines carved from what look like giant teeth. Shu sent a pair of horses he insists will be able to survive the heat. Rodrigo and his family came with them. They're staying at an inn close to my place. Their older daughter is extraordinary, like she's made of gold. Half the city is in love with her."

"That's great, Trader." Nikay's head spun, but he trusted her to track everything. "Have you got any ideas about what I asked you?"

"Sorry, I couldn't think of anything." Trader rolled up the list and put it in her bag. "What do you give someone who can have anything they want just for the asking?"

"It's been keeping me awake." Nikay rubbed his eyes. "I want it to be special, something Mathial will treasure."

"You could give her a rock from the side of the road, and she'd treasure it." Trader slapped his shoulder. "She adores you." She waved and dashed off.

He swore she'd only gotten faster over the last four years. He didn't know anyone in the city who worked as hard as she did, and she was only fourteen. Too bad she didn't have any suggestions about a gift for Mathial. Maybe his mother would have some advice.

Beatifa opened the door of the manor house his parents used for the embassy.

"Hi, they're with the king and queen." His sister let him in. "Halto is running around here somewhere with Raphael."

"Raphael will keep him out of trouble."

"If you were going to give a gift to Queen Mathial, what would you give her?"

"How would I know?" Beatifa scowled at him. "Mother and Father are giving wine from their estates."

"She doesn't drink wine, at least not yet." Nikay waved his hands.

"Maybe her guests will."

"True."

Beatifa knocked on the parlour door, then pushed Nikay into the room.

"Nikay, good to see you." King Harald shook his hand. "You're getting tall."

"Thank you, Your Majesty."

"We're going to be equals in a few days." King Harald grinned. "Then you'll have to call me Harald."

"Right." Nikay couldn't imagine it. "What kind of things did people give you for your wedding?"

"We got all kinds of useless things."

"Now, it wasn't all useless." Sarandia wagged her finger at him. "That set of wine glasses have come in very handy."

"What was your favourite?"

"That's hard to say after all this time."

"You still have that pouch on your side table," Sarandia said.

"Right, that. The stable hand who looked after my horse made a pouch for me to carry treats for the horse. He must have spent hours on it."

"Still looking for the perfect gift?" His mother came over and hugged him. "Give her something only you can give her."

"That doesn't help much." Nikay frowned.

"It will when the time comes."

***

Fury walked through the city. Mathial and Nikay were working on her reading and writing, and Fury wanted to give them that special time together. It had taken her years to get them to enjoy their time without her.

"Hey, you're that kid who supposedly took on ten legionnaires." A man, bigger than Cameto, looked down at her. "You don't look that tough."

"Looks are deceiving." Fury's hackles went up.

"Maybe you'd give me a chance to try my hand against you."

"Come by the Nekkest training grounds, and we'll find you a practice sword. Wear your armour."

"Practice sword?" The man sneered. "I have a good blade here." He slapped his scabbard.

"Only a fool spars with sharpened steel." Fury clenched her teeth. "No one uses steel in the training grounds."

"If you're afraid to fight with steel…" The man leered at her.

"Not afraid, just not stupid." Fury walked away before she lost her temper.

The man came by the training ground with Lord Haphin, who set Fury's teeth on edge for a different reason. He reminded her of Phenos.

"My man says you won't spar with him."

"No, I won't." Fury crossed her arms. "I don't like his attitude, and I won't have it on my training grounds."

"Your training grounds?" Lord Haphin raised his brows. "You're awfully young and pretty to be running training."

"I am in charge of the queen's security." Fury bit her words off to keep from cursing him. "I don't have time to humour people who want to prove something." She glared at him until he stalked off, giant idiot in tow.

***

"...she insulted my man and through him, me." Lord Haphin whined to Mathial. Nikay kept his hands deliberately relaxed. He didn't look over to see Fury's face, but the heat of her anger reached him. *Doesn't this idiot know how close to disaster he walked?*"

"Princess Arthuria is not my servant, but my dearest friend." Mathial had her hands clenched in her lap. "She doesn't exist for your entertainment. You will cease harassing her over this matter."

Lord Haphin smiled ingratiatingly at Nikay. "Come, man to man. You must—"

"My queen has spoken. Do not look to me to contradict her." Nikay kept his words civil for the sake of the others in the room.

"I am a personal friend of the Emperor Striphona. He will not be pleased at this insult to the Empire."

Lord Haphin turned and stalked out of the room. Fury growled, but Mathial took a shuddering breath.

"What an odious man."

"I don't like it," Fury said. "He's making far too much of a fuss about something which isn't worth his time."

"Publicly insulting the queen will not endear him to Striphona. I wonder if the emperor sent him just to get him out of the way." Nikay stared at the door, his gut churning. "If you will excuse me, there is someone I would like to talk to."

"The queen and I will retire to our rooms," Fury said. "Let us know when you return, and we will join you for tea."

Queen Mathial stood and the guard formed about her as Fury followed her out of the room.

Nikay went to his room and changed out of his palace clothes, then found Axili. "I need a few warriors to shadow me through the city."

"That Lord Haphin idiot?"

Nikay nodded.

"They will be there if you need them." General Axili frowned. "I will set a watch on the man as well."

"Thank you." Nikay headed out, not looking for his guard but much happier knowing they were there.

Trader lived down the hill, not far from the Hall. One of her staff pointed to the back when Nikay knocked on the door. He walked around the building to find Trader, Rodrigo and a crowd of young men trying not to look like they were vying for Aimee's attention. All her focus was on the two horses in front of them.

"I've never seen horses like this." She petted one and its skin rippled, and its right front foot pawed the ground. "Very nervous temperament. I'd love to ride her, but not in the city."

"They're from across the Lower Sea," Rodrigo said, "exceptionally fine specimens, but they will take some training." He sounded like he looked forward to the challenge. "Since Queen Mathial has never ridden before, these are not the horses to begin her on."

"I have a friend who deals in horses for wagons. Maybe she has something the queen can start on." Trader looked into the distance. "She might even offer lessons to the queen."

"I will leave that in your capable hands." Rodrigo grinned at her. "My talents are wasted here."

"Don't think that flattery is going to make me soft," Trader laughed.

"They are working on a deal." Aimee stood beside Nikay. "It's a game for them. I think it is for a wagonload of fruit or some such thing."

"Flattery?" Rodrigo was saying. "Nothing but the truth."

"I would like to talk to Rodrigo when he's finished trying to soften Trader.”

Aimee giggled, then pulled Nikay over to her father.

“Nikay would like to talk to you.”

“I would like to consult with you about a gift for my bride, but perhaps we could talk where it would be more private?”

“Certainly.” Rodrigo nodded at Aimee. “Could you put the beasts back in their stalls?”

“Of course.”

Rodrigo led Nikay into the house to a room where Milene sat working at something in the corner.

“Now, you didn’t come all the way down the hill just to ask me about a gift.” Rodrigo lounged in a chair and waved Nikay over to another one.

“No, though your advice on a gift would be most welcome.”

“What does Queen Mathial want from you more than anything else?” Milene spoke from the corner?

“I have no idea. I would give her anything she asked. She knows that.”

“What is important is what she wants but is afraid to ask.” Rodrigo grinned. “That’s what makes it fun.”

“To you, everything is about fun.” Milene smiled at them.

“Gift aside, there is something, or rather someone, I’d like to ask you about.”

“That wouldn’t be a certain Imperial noble whose been bending everyone’s ear about what barbaric people live here?”

“I assume you’re talking about Lord Haphin.” Nikay frowned. “There’s something off about him. He’s risking alienating the people he wants to trade with over a perceived insult to a guard.”

“I’ll poke my nose into it. I happen to know where he likes to drink.” Rodrigo winked at him.

“Only because Trader is part owner of the place and told you,” Milene said.

Rodrigo just winked at Nikay again.

***

Nikay put the matter of Lord Haphin out of his mind. He had more important things to worry about, like the fact that he still had no idea what to give Mathial. No one had been much help.

A timid knock on his door interrupted him.

He opened it to find Mathial staring at the floor.

"Can I come in?" Mathial asked. "Fury wants to take the man apart, but I can't let her do that." She put her hand on Nikay's shoulder. "Do you think I was right about what I said?"

Nikay led her over to a chair and sat her down, then knelt in front of her holding her hands.

"Mathial, you are the queen. You made it clear Fury was a friend. I think you were perfect."

"But that man asked you."

"He did and, by doing so, insulted you. You would have been well within your rights to have him tossed out of the country. Trust me, no one in that room thought you any less than regal."

"Tomorrow is the last day before the wedding." Mathial didn't raise her head. "Are you sure you want to get married? I made you my slave. I almost killed you." Tears dripped from her face onto his hands. "It's been so different since then."

"We are growing up." Nikay rubbed her tears away with his thumb. "That means changing. What we could do as kids, we can't do as adults, but that has only made every moment I spend with you that much more precious."

"Really?" Mathial lifted her head, and he lost himself in her deep brown eyes.

"Really." Nikay smiled at her.

"If you could have anything in the world from me, what would it be?"

"I'd want you beside me to help me be the best queen I can be for my people. I don't know how to be a queen. I never knew my mother or any of my ancestors. What if I'm doing everything wrong?"

"You aren't." Nikay squeezed her hands. "Everything you do is out of love for your people."

He stood and lifted her to her feet. They were exactly the same height. He hugged her tight, then kissed her gently.

"I'd better let you go while I still can." Nikay cradled her face in his hands. "One more day, then our lives change again."

"I'm scared." Mathial quivered in his hands.

"So am I, but I think we're supposed to be." He kissed her once, then escorted her out of his room.

He turned around when a tapping came from his window. Rodrigo stood on the balcony.

"You have a problem." Rodrigo grinned as if a problem was the best thing in the world. "Axili and I have a plan, but we'll need your help, and that of your brave young queen."

"Tell me what you need."

***

Mathial ordered a last-minute reception to officially greet King Harald and Queen Sarandia. The staff set up the ballroom, which hadn't been used since Mathial's mother died. Nikay had them arrange it exactly as he wanted, then went to bring Mathial and Fury to the room.

"You remember the plan?" Nikay held Mathial's hand.

"Of course, I do." She frowned at him.

"Sorry, I'm just nervous," Nikay admitted.

Mathial smiled and squeezed his hand.

"Let's go." Fury grinned ferociously.

Axili let them into the room and flashed a hand sign. Part one had been taken care of. It would be up to Mathial and Fury to deal with the rest.

People mingled in the room. Nikay sat Mathial on her seat, then walked through the crowd. Many people handed him scrolls of paper which he slipped into his pouch.

"What were all those people handing you?" Mathial asked when he'd returned to her side.

"I will tell you tonight." Nikay couldn't help grinning.

"You're up to something." Fury tilted her head. "I can smell it."

"I am, but it doesn't have anything to do with this event."

Lord Haphin swaggered into the room with the giant by his side. He looked up at Mathial on the throne and humphed. He walked over to the wall and stood, arms crossed, scowling at the people.

"Friends, thank you for attending on such short notice." Nikay stepped forward. "My bride wished to welcome the parents of her good friend properly to her country." He made a sign to Axili at the door who opened it and ushered in the King and Queen of Belandria.

Lord Haphin stepped away from the wall and pointed toward

the royal couple.

"Lord Haphin," Mathial's voice rang clearly in the room. "We have arrested your men, most of whom have already confessed their part in the plot." She scowled at the man. "We wished to have proper evidence before we acted. You will be escorted from our land and put on a ship to return to the Empire where my brother Striphona may deal with you as he sees fit."

Guards stepped forward to take Lord Haphin into custody, and the giant reached under his tunic.

Nikay didn't see Fury move. One second, she stood behind Mathial in her accustomed place, the next, she'd hit the giant, broken his arm and was holding him to the floor with her hand on his throat.

"Your plan to eliminate Fury failed." Mathial didn't sound like someone had just tried to commit murder. "You misunderstood her reason for not training with sharp weapons. It isn't to protect her, but the people she is sparring with."

Lord Haphin paled and tried to move away from Fury.

"Take them away. Splint the broken arm, then dress them in prisoner's clothes and bind them with chains. They will return to the emperor in shame." Mathial flipped her hand, and the guards dragged the men out.

"Our apologies," Mathial turned to King Harald and his queen, "that we needed to put you in harm's way to deal with this plot."

"We knew with Fury in the room there was no danger." King Harald bowed to her. "Your warning that the man would try to assassinate us saddened but didn't surprise us. Being royalty is not a safe position, which is why we are so happy to know that Fury is guarding your back." He smiled at his daughter. "We have convinced her to remain as our heir until Alfric is of age to take his oath, but we cannot deny her desire to make your country her home."

"We welcome you to visit whenever you wish." Mathial beamed joyfully at the king.

"You also are always welcome in our home." Queen Sarandia curtseyed gracefully.

Fury hugged her parents and the crowd applauded.

***

"Now, you were going to tell me about those mysterious bits of paper." Mathial put her hands on her hips. Nikay laughed and pulled a leather book from his pouch.

"These are letters from everyone I could think of who would have known your mother and even your grandmother. They talk about what great queens they were, what they were like, little things like conversations they had. The letters also talk about how proud they are of their present queen." He handed the book to Mathial who opened it with shaking hands.

"You did all this for me?" She scrubbed tears from her face before they fell on the book.

"I thought of it when you said you didn't know what your mother was like. There had to be people who knew her, who could tell you the stories. I wanted to connect you to your history."

Mathial handed the book to Fury, then hugged and kissed Nikay, lighting a fire inside him.

"I'd better go." Nikay reluctantly stepped away.

"Stay." Mathial held his hand. "One last time, let's sleep in the same room."

"I will stay until you fall asleep." Nikay sighed, "As much as I'd like to stay longer. Tomorrow night..." He grinned.

"Tomorrow I will move into my room," Fury said. "I will miss the closeness we have, but I will be happier for the new relationship you two will share."

Nikay closed his eyes while Mathial changed. To his surprise, he wasn't at all tempted to peek. Fury turned down the lamps, and they lay on the bed, Mathial in the middle under the blanket with Nikay on one side of her and Fury on the other. Mathial's breathing evened out, and Nikay chuckled.

"She always was the first to sleep."

"And I was the last," Fury said. "I would cry myself to sleep, then wake strong for the next day." She reached over and took Nikay's hand. "I've loved you since we were children. It is because I love you that I wanted this for you."

"When did you know?"

"You started comforting Mathial almost immediately. She became stronger because you gave her your strength. I didn't need you, no matter how much I loved you, but she needs you, and you need her."

"I love you too, Fury. For as long as I can remember, I wanted nothing more than to be part of your life. But Mathial, she lights a fire in me. I want to be with her to find out what she will make of me."

"You know, that day in the Council Chamber, you fought as hard as I did, and without Fury inside you to help. I couldn't live if you didn't get to share that fire with Mathial."

"There may be someone who comes along who lights that fire for you."

"Maybe." Fury rolled onto her side, and her eyes glinted in the dark. "But even if they don't, I'll be all right. I don't think I'm like other people." She lay back down. "If I cry tomorrow, they will be tears of joy."

"I'd better go." Nikay sighed, "You wouldn't believe how much I've missed this."

"We missed you too," Fury said. "I didn't understand at first, but then I watched how you grew closer because your time together was precious. Don't ever lose that."

"I won't." Nikay brushed his lip across Mathial's cheek, then squeezed Fury's hand. "Good night."

He slipped out of the bed and headed down the hall to his suite. The clothes for the morning were already laid out. Nikay undressed and crawled into bed. He expected his nerves would return in the morning, but for now, he lay on his back and smiled until he fell to sleep.

OTHER BOOKS BY ALEX

Series:

Calliope Books
Calliope and the Sea Serpent
Calliope and the Royal Engineers
The Third Prince and the Enemy's Daughter

Spruce Bay Books
Wendigo Whispers
Cry of the White Moose
Disputed Rock

The Belandria Tarot
The Devil Reversed
The Regent's Reign
The Empire Unbalanced
The World Widens
The Fury Unleashed

Blue in Kamloops
Tranquille Dark

Celticfrog Publishing Anthology
Mythical Girls

Stand alone books:

Generation Gap
The Gods Above
Tales of Light and Dark
Like Mushrooms (poetry and photography)
The Heronmaster
Blood and Sparkles, and other stories
Princess of Boring
By the Book
Sarcasm is My Superpower
Playing on Yggdrasil
The Unenchanted Princess

Read short stories and excerpts from his novels at alexmcgilvery.com